Loose Dogs

Kirsten Mortensen

This book is a work of fiction. Names, characters, places, and events are either products of the author's imagination or are used fictitiously. Any resemblance to actual events, locales, or persons, living or dead, is entirely coincidental.

ISBN: 0615788629

ISBN-13: 9780615788623

Manufactured in the United States of America

For pit bulls and the people who love them.

ACKNOWLEDGMENTS

I'd like to extend an enormous and heartfelt thank you to all who helped me get this book to the place it is today. To Brighton Animal Control, for your generosity in helping me research the book. To the talented Aussie author Julie Harris for encouraging me to continue when my last book hit some speed bumps. To Joe Mader, for urging me to revise *Loose Dogs* yet again. Joe, I hated to hear it, but it's a far better book thanks to you. And to the many people who lent their time and their eyes to the manuscript, helping me to weed out those pesky typos and continuity errors. Emily, John, Ron—you guys are the greatest, and Ken. . . well. You know ;-).

Part I

1

It finally felt like spring, and wouldn't you know it, I got a call about an Eskimo dog.

Hah.

Anyway, I assumed I was looking for an Eskimo dog, based on the description. "Like a fluffy white fox."

Admittedly, that was second-hand information. The call had come from a lady in the high school main office, but it wasn't the lady who'd seen the dog. Some kids had reported it: a dog, loose, running back and forth along the edge of the school grounds.

Scared, maybe.

Or maybe not.

Maybe he was happy to be running around free.

I looped through the neighborhoods bordering the school property. The snow had pretty much melted, finally, and what was left of it was ridged along the streets, sunken, crystallized, filthy. I had to crane my neck to see over the ridges, and I drove slowly, windows rolled down, peering back and forth, looking, and listening too—sometimes you find out where a loose dog is when you hear the squeal of car brakes.

A normal day, in other words—me just doing my job. My town's official Ms. Dogcatcher Lady, trying to return a loose dog to where he belonged.

It isn't easy. Loose dogs don't follow rules. They aren't predictable. They don't keep to the sidewalks or respect property boundaries. They don't come when called.

Loose dogs are elusive things.

◊ ◊ ◊ ◊ ◊

I circled back to the school again, parked the truck and went inside to find the person who'd called me. "Angie." In the main office. She caught sight of me right away and came to the visitor window.

"Sorry," I said. "No sign of the dog."

She sighed and made a sad face. "Poor thing."

In my work duds I look kind of like a cop, which is fine by me. It keeps things unambiguous. I wear a badge, and a white shirt, and navy slacks with sharp seams. Cell phone hanging from my belt. Hair tied back. But for all that, it's the dog person Angie saw when she looked at me. So I nodded, feeling my face pull as sad as hers. And then excused myself, saying "most of the time, they find their way back home"—not true, fewer than half of the dogs we pick up get reclaimed. But I didn't take this job to spend time thinking about that.

I went back out to the parking lot and opened the door of my truck.

Then I heard the shriek.

Make that a chorus of shrieks, and the peculiar high-pitched laughter teenage girls can let loose sometimes, and something told me the ruckus was about the dog. I grabbed my catchpole out of the truck and ran around the side of the school and sure enough, there was a gaggle of girls, seniors I suppose straggling back from lunch, and they were bending over and laughing and falling on themselves, and beyond them: the dog, running flat out across the athletic field.

One of the girls saw me and shrieked again, "there! there!" Pointing. I kept my expression neutral and nodded "thanks" and started running after the dog.

I could run, at that point, because he—I didn't know yet if the dog was a he or a she, but I'd started thinking of him as a he—he didn't know yet that I was there, so my running toward him didn't matter. I was also thinking as I ran that he belonged to somebody who lived nearby, or he wouldn't have shown back up at the school. Territory thing. Which meant that if I missed him this time, I might still get another chance. So that was good. Assuming he was smart about dodging cars.

2

Or lucky.

At the edge of the school property the dog froze, then started to double back and saw me. But I'd anticipated that. I'd already stopped. I turned my body sideways to him—showing him I wasn't a threat—watching him out of the corner of my eye.

He sniffed the ground. Good sign.

I approached, but not direct on—approach straight on and he'd likely take off again—my body still turned sideways, avoiding direct eye contact, making a kind of elliptical spiral to camouflage that I was closing in.

He dropped into a down position.

Tired of running.

Ready to trade away his freedom.

I stopped and crouched, still avoiding eye contact while I fumbled for my pouch of liver treats. He was looking away from me, his head turned, and I left the catchpole on the ground as I stood slowly back up, circled a bit closer, and tossed a treat. I was talking to him now, "good boy, sweet boy." Happy voice, but not loud. Relaxed. Like the way we women coo to our dogs while we're curled up together on the living room couch.

The strays I catch are almost always pets, of course, although when they're off their home turf they don't always act it. Still, tell them "sit" or "down" and half the time they'll do it. Then you can just walk up and leash them.

But this time, I didn't even need to go that far. He came to me and then crawled into my lap, taking another treat from my hand.

Sweet boy.

I stroked him to make sure he was relaxed about being handled and clipped the leash to his collar as he took another treat. Then I slipped an arm under him. His belly fur was gray and straggly and dripping with gravelly mud, and he stiffened when I lifted him and turned his head away from me but he didn't struggle so I knew we were going to be okay.

Collar, but no tags.

Back at the truck, I scanned him with the handheld I keep

in the glove box. No microchip, either. But he was a sweetheart, so even if his people didn't claim him, somebody would want him.

That's what I was thinking after I dropped him off at the animal hospital—first stop for most of the strays I pick up.

There might be a happy ending. For this dog, at least.

◊ ◊ ◊ ◊ ◊

It was late by then so I swung by the office to drop off the truck and then I headed home.

I live in the westerly half of the only double in my neighborhood. The sole rental on a fairy tale street of sturdy old homes and 100-year-old trees.

Got to my place about 5:30, parked my Civic in the driveway and went in through the front door so I could grab my mail. And there it was, sticking up out of the top of the mailbox: a package.

Well, not really a package. It was one of those bubble wrap-lined manila envelopes, but with a lump in the middle, something-other-than-a-letter inside, and then I saw the handwriting.

It was from Gil.

I stared.

And then I knew what was inside.

I just knew.

I tore open the envelope and cripes, the bundle was all duct tape. Freaking duct tape. How like a guy.

So I had to take it inside and get some scissors.

I cut through the duct tape, and inside it was another little bundle of bubble wrap, and through the layer of plastic bubbles I could see the ring.

Impossible.

Yet there it was.

The Ring.

You think you know what you're doing. You're pretty sure you do. But it's always possible you're wrong. It's always possible that someone you expect to do one thing will do something else entirely, and when it comes to love, the gamble, of course, is that you might lose. You might lose him forever.

I'm not afraid to gamble. But the stakes this time were so high . . .

I sat down at my kitchen table and tore a hole in the bubble wrap, and my heart was beating hard, like all the fear I'd stored up—all that fear that I might be wrong about him and lose him—it all punched through the wall now and hit me, all at once.

He actually bought the ring.

When?

It didn't matter.

All that mattered is that he'd bought the ring.

That silly, oversized, not-a-diamond ring.

And now I was holding it in my hand.

Everything from here on in would be easy.

2

I didn't really want to talk to Charlene—I didn't want to talk to anybody right then, let alone someone who might notice that I sounded unsettled. But she was visiting a friend in Des Moines, and I was supposed to pick her up from the airport when she got in, and she still hadn't told me what time her flight was even though I'd reminded her about fifty thousand times. I don't mind picking her up, that's fine, but it would be nice if I knew what time I had to be there. Ya know?

I should mention that Char claims to be a psychic. So maybe she forgets, sometimes, that the rest of us come by our information the old-fashioned way.

I took a deep breath and I dialed her cell.

"So Char," I said, but before I could ask her about her flight, she launched into some story about her Des Moines friend's job search, and then when that story was over she said, "and how are things going with you?"

And I said, "fine," and—just as I predicted—she came back immediately with, "What's going on, Paige? You sound funny."

I should have waited a little longer before calling her.

"Nothing's going on," I said.

"Right. You know you can't get away with that," she said. "You've heard from Gil, haven't you."

So then I was caught. "Yeah," I said. "I heard from Gil."

"And?"

"Remember what I told you the last time he was in town—about the ring?"

"The one you saw that time in the junk shop? Back in Ithaca?"

"Yeah, that one."

"Sure, I remember!" she said. "He said he'd bought it for you.

But you didn't believe him."

"Yep," I said, although that isn't exactly what had happened. What had happened is that after a year and a half of him on one side of the country and me on the other, I'd had enough. Oh, I'd been careful how I handled it! Just a hint here or there, subtle as can be—just enough to make him think he should be worried, that maybe-just-maybe there might be another guy in the picture. And then, when he caught on and started acting a bit jealous I said in the joking-est flirtiest way possible that it wasn't like Gil and I were *engaged* or anything. And then he'd said "well you know I bought a ring"—and I admit, that caught me a bit off guard.

Okay. A LOT off guard.

The ring?

THAT ring?

But I recovered well, I hid my surprise, kept it light: "You don't mean the ring I tried on in that junk shop in Ithaca?" I laughed. "I don't believe you for a minute, Gil Rudman!" And he said "yes, that ring," and I said "where is it, then?" and he said "back in Seattle" and I said "suuuure, it is."

And I kissed him and changed the subject. But on the inside— oh! On the inside! I was exultant.

The ring!

And of course I also came to a natural conclusion, namely, that dropping a hint, now and again, that the guy might have a rival is exactly what our stalled relationship needed to give it a bit of fresh juice . . .

"So what about the ring?" Char broke into my thoughts.

"I got home today and there was a package—and it was the ring. He mailed it to me."

I could hear a tinge of glee creep into my voice.

"No *way*." Char said.

"*Way*." I broke into a grin, now, feeling not only exultant but even a little triumphant. Because Char had advised against my plan—against pretending that there might be someone else. "You love him," she'd said to me. "You need to be up front about it and tell him. You start playing games and you'll mess it up."

Because she's a romantic, too, in addition to being a psychic, or maybe being a psychic and being a romantic are the same thing, or too closely related to tell them apart. Anyway, she believes minds can touch each other across space and that people meet each other because they're fated to fall in love. And both psychics and romantics believe that, right?

Most romantics. I mean, I'm a romantic, too, but for me the romance is the embellishment, the curlicues and flourishes that make things that would otherwise be harsh, maybe even brutal, relatively pleasant. Romance is nature's way of making it bearable. It's the Prozac Nature has slipped into our drink.

Romance doesn't govern things however, and if you think so you're deluding yourself.

Nature governs things.

Which means romance isn't enough. You have to be shrewd. You have no other choice.

"The guy can't live without me," I said, "and I knew it."

Char laughed. I couldn't tell if it bothered her or not, that she'd been wrong—that my plan had worked. But so what? The important thing is that it *had* worked.

"He was taking me for granted, taking us for granted," I said. "Now, he's not. Now he's figured out that he needs to close the deal if he wants to keep me."

"I'm glad it worked out." She was being gracious. But what choice did she have? "So you're together, officially? I mean— engaged?"

Engaged. The second I heard her speak the word I realized how strange it was. Engaged? What did it matter, today, when people marry and unmarry as thoughtlessly as they swap toilet paper brands or favorite television shows? The only thing that mattered was the behavior.

Does he come home at night?

Yes?

Then what does it matter, what name you give it?

So I laughed. "We're as engaged as anybody," I said, slowing down on the word "engaged" so that I could feel how it sank down into the back of my mouth and crunched between my back molars.

"Mmmmm." She was humoring me and we both knew it. "So you're wearing it," she said. "The ring."

Ugh. Her asking bothered me for some reason and I wished I hadn't put it on—hadn't given in, yet, to the ritual of it. And so I lied, quickly—good thing her purported psychic powers weren't engaged. "Wearing it? Um, no," and I squeezed the phone to my ear with my shoulder so I could twist the ring off my finger.

The ring popped free.

"I mean—I put it on, but only for a minute," I said. "Aw, dammit. Now I've dropped it."

I crouched and there it was, way back under the table in the horrible groady crease where the linoleum meets the wall.

"Paige?"

"I'm here, I found it. It's okay."

"Found it?"

"The ring. It fell under the table." I stood back up. "Anyway, it doesn't matter if I wear it or not. It's not—what matters is—"

"The behavior. I know. So what's next, then?"

"He'll turn up." I felt very confident, now that he'd sent back the ring. "Within the next month. Tops. And he'll stick around, this time, I'll make sure of it."

I heard her sigh, and I felt a little irritated because now I felt defensive and why should I be? But I defended myself anyway. "This is how people learn."

"Just be careful, Paige," she said, and then—"You sound happy, anyway, and that's what matters."

I picked up the pen next to the Post-Its on my counter. "Actually, Char," I said, "I didn't call to discuss my love life. I need to know time your flight's coming in."

"Oh!" she said. "That. I'm not sure. I'm trying to switch it—I want to get on a later one."

I set the pen down again. "Great," I said. "Just make sure you let me know, okay?"

"Will do," she said. "I'll text you." And "I'm glad you've got him back, again, Paige," she said before she hung up.

I dropped the phone on the table and looked at the ring again. Then I went upstairs and untangled a gold fill chain I found in the intaglio box where I keep my jewelry. Slipped the chain through the ring, fastened it around my neck and tucked it under my shirt.

It fell down into my cleavage.

It was bulky and when I stood up I felt it cool for a second against my skin.

I took a breath to clear my head.

It was impossible to know when, exactly, Gil might roll into town. So there was no way of knowing how much time I had to prepare.

I had to move fast if I was going to be ready for him.

3

There are two animal control officers in my town. I'm the full-timer. Doug Bailey is part-time. He works on Tuesdays, all day, and Saturday mornings, and is on call three evenings a week, Mondays, Wednesdays, and Fridays. It works out great for him. He has four kids and his wife is a stay-at-home mom, so the job lets him bring in some extra money. And his other job, property manager for a bunch of apartment complexes in Webster (up on Lake Ontario, east of Rochester) is flexible enough that if he does have to back me up, he can usually swing it.

I like Doug okay although it would be nice if he had his own desk. He's into granola bars. I mean, he apparently survives on them. So when I get into work after his shift, usually the first thing I have to do is shovel the rolled oats off the desk.

At least that morning there were no ants.

I pulled my bagel out of the bag and unwrapped it.

The phone rang.

"Paige Newbury speaking," I started to say but I don't think she heard. She was already talking, I think, before I answered: "—don't know how she got out, we keep the garage door locked, I don't know how it happened, and now I just don't know what to do next—"

My first thought was *maybe this is the Eskimo dog's person.*

But I was wrong.

"Ma'am, ma'am, slow down. You have a missing pet?"

"We knew it could happen, of course, so we were being extra careful—"

"Ma'am, you need to slow down, please, and start at the be—"

"I just can't believe this happened!" She was really working herself into a state now.

"Ma'am." Voice raised, but only slightly. Have to be careful not

11

to cross the line. "If you don't slow down and tell me what's going on, I can't help you, okay? Do you have a missing pet?"

"Well, you don't need to get snippy!"

Oops. Guess I'd crossed it. "Ma'am, I realize you're upset, but unless you tell me what's happened, I can't help you."

"Nobody can help me," she said sharply.

I looked longingly at my uneaten bagel. "Look, I need to ask you some questions, okay?"

I took her silence to be acquiescence.

"Okay. First, are you missing a pet?"

"No, of course not."

Oh, brother. "Okay, I'm sorry, I don't seem to be following you. Didn't you just say something about a garage door being left open?"

"It wasn't left open."

"Well, you said something about a garage—"

"She got it open. Somehow. But it wasn't left open."

"Fine. Okay. She got it open. Who is 'she'?"

"Lady."

"And Lady is—who?"

"Our dog. Black, with a white star on her chest. Well, my husband, he calls it a star, it's really more of a blotch."

Educated guess: a lab cross. I jotted LabX? on the notepad on my desk. "I see," said as I wrote. "Okay, then. And how long has Lady been missing?"

"She's not missing, as I was trying to explain to you earlier—"

"Ma'am, that's great. I'm pleased she's not missing." I set down my pen. "So why don't you explain why you have called me, then?"

"I think she's going to have puppies."

I rolled my eyes. "Ah. Well, in that case, you need to phone your vet, not Animal Control—and you might also think about having Lady spayed, so this doesn't happen again."

"What are you saying, that you can't help me?"

I gritted my teeth, pulled the pad back toward me and jotted down the date. Obviously, this was not going to go away, which meant I'd better take complete notes after all. "Help you how, ma'am?" And then, because I couldn't resist, "Has Lady bitten someone?"

"Oh, no! Of course not!"

"Attacked someone else's pet?"

"No!"

"And she's in your home now?"

"Look, I pay taxes, you know—"

Uh oh.

"—and the way I look at it, that means you are working for me! So I expect something a bit more helpful than this—"

"Ma'am, unfortunately, I can't make a pregnant dog un-pregnant."

"I know that!"

"So what is it that you want me to do?"

"Well, I can't keep them!"

"That," I pointed out, "is precisely why Lady ought to be spayed."

"So I thought you could come and, you know, take her, until after the puppies are born—"

I gritted my teeth and forced my voice to remain calm. "Ma'am, I'm sorry, but it doesn't work like that—"

"I pay my taxes!"

Taxes, again. "Okay. Let me take some information. What is your name?"

"My name? Are you going to take the puppies?"

"As I'm trying to explain to you, it's not the Town's job to take care of peoples' puppies." I waited and when she didn't say anything I went on. "These puppies—they are your responsibility at this point. You are the one who is responsible for Lady, so you are responsible for her puppies. You need to have her seen by a vet, if you haven't already, and then put an ad on Craigslist so you can find the puppies good homes. It may take some time, and it's going to cost you some money to get them all wormed and their shots and everything. But hopefully after Lady has her puppies you'll think about—"

The line went dead.

And her Caller ID had been blocked. So I finished my notes with *anonymous caller* and the time that the call had ended, and dropped the paper into a folder in the desk.

Nothing but trouble when dogs get out.
I looked at my now-slightly-stale bagel.
I had to get out of there.
I headed out to the truck.

◊ ◊ ◊ ◊ ◊

I spend most of my work day in that truck.

People are sometimes surprised by that. But my job, if you think about it, is to help maintain some sort of community order, and I can't really do that from behind a desk. So instead I like to get out, keep an eye on things. And people appreciate it. I get flagged down a lot. Someone wants to complain about a neighbor's pet, or ask a question about a wild animal they've seen. I get a lot of that, especially if there's a story in the paper about a coyote or a fox—next thing you know, everyone has seen one. My working theory is that newspaper articles about coyotes somehow trigger instantaneous coyote clones. One day, we've got a dozen or so in the entire county. The next day— thousands.

I get a lot of questions about the laws, too. Leash laws, barking laws.

And dog poop laws. Phew. That's a big one when the snow starts to melt. People in my town are supposed to clean up after their dogs, but a lot of them don't bother. In the warm months, dog poop tends to break down and get washed away when it rains. But during the winter, forget it. The stuff is cryogenically preserved. Then come March and Presto, you have two or three months' worth of fabulous parting gifts greasing the sidewalks. And man, do people gripe about it.

Not that I blame them. On the contrary. And my being out there in my truck helps, in fact, because when people think I might come by, they're more conscientious about picking up. I try to hit the neighborhoods around the parks in particular—because that's where people walking dogs tend to congregate—I try to be seen there first thing in the morning and again at the end of my shift, since most people walk their dogs right before and right after work.

Something else about being in my truck. I know it's an illusion, because in reality all I really do is drive in circles around my town. But when I'm driving, I feel like I'm getting somewhere. I feel like I'm accomplishing something. And honestly, it's a lucky thing when you have a job where you get the feeling of accomplishing something, even if you're not.

Unfortunately that day everything was quiet.

It was the weather. The temp had dropped again overnight and the wind was up, so everybody was inside.

I needed something to distract me and the whole town was dead.

And so of course my mind starts wandering.

Gil.

No. Let's not start with Gil.

Let's start with his cousin.

4

His first cousin, Mike.

They didn't look anything alike, though. Mike was this skinny smart-ass from my hometown who'd become a kind of mascot to the really popular kids. Partly because he was a smart-ass but mostly because he had no dad living at home and his mom let him and his friends drink beer at their house. She was one of those "I'd rather have him doing it here where I know what he's up to" people, who apparently overlooks the fact that all the other kids who are there drinking beer also have parents, and those parents have no idea what their offspring are up to. Which is, of course, getting bombed.

Some of them, anyway. I wasn't so much interested in drinking beer, for me it was something else—Mike's parties, you see, were so enormous that they exerted their own gravitational force, irresistible to any teenager within a 20 mile radius. It helped that there was nothing else around to interfere with the signal. There aren't many wild places left in New York State but I grew up in one of them, one of a small cluster of counties that are too out-of-the-way to grow a city, not quite rugged enough to become a tourist attraction like, say, the Adirondacks, but on the other hand are too rugged to really farm. Not that people don't try. It was all pretty much farmland at one point, in fact, but except on the river flats, the soil is so thin and rocky, and then the Depression came, and much of what had been farmland was abandoned. And so the forest came back, and by the time I was a teenager it was pressing against the edges of the remaining farms, and against the bits of land that had been claimed as housing lots, and on the back roads the crews have to come through every few years with chainsaws and backhoes to re-carve the roadside banks and ditches and keep the forest back.

And the deer and turkeys and raccoons, and the big predators, even—the bear and coyotes and bobcats—were our neighbors. They intermingled with us. There was nothing alien or exotic about them. Keeping animals—our horses and dogs and cats and goats and cows—seemed natural, too. I don't think I knew anyone who didn't have some sort of domestic animal when I was growing up. It was natural, at least it seemed to me. It's why I decided I wanted to be a veterinarian. First, because I was brought up like all the girls my age—all the smart girls anyway—to put career first. Career equals power, and power is good. But you're also supposed to find something to do that you love, and for me it was animals.

More than love. It was a part of what I was. Animals were a thing I understood.

Living there was isolating too, though, unless your house was in town. The forest belonged to the animals and it also separated the people from one another. I don't think it matters once you can drive but when you're a teenager you notice it, and you also feel keenly your dependence on the adults because they're the ones who have to drive any time you want to see your friends—it presses in on you. Even on me, as focused as I was from such a young age on my career plans and my schoolwork—I still felt it, the pull to be around other kids.

People who have grown up in a city or even the suburbs don't know what it means to turn 16 when you live in the country. Finally you can go out on your own to hunt for your peers, you can get yourself to places where your peers are congregating.

Like Mike's parties.

And that's where I first saw Gil. He lived in another little town pretty much identical to mine but being 15 miles away he may as well have been from Rangoon or Murmansk or something.

He wasn't what you'd call good-looking the first time I saw him. We were both 15. I had breasts by then, or a reasonable facsimile, and hips, and because it was a party I was experimenting—I was wearing sparkly lip gloss and a look I'd snagged out of *Seventeen* magazine. Gil, on the other hand . . . I don't even know why I noticed him. Maybe I felt sorry for him. He looked about 10, with scruffy jeans and a stupid short frizzy haircut, and he kept his head turned up at a funny angle because he was smaller than the jocky guys hanging around Mike, who as I said gave a pass to Mike but not Gil—they either ignored Gil or had their fun at his expense. Spitting in his beer, probably pissing in his beer, stuff like that, that teenage boys get off on.

So. Fast forward to encounter #2 a year later, and the guy has . . . sprouted. Okay. I mean, he has . . . he has acquired this simply gorgeous body. All big and loose and lanky, topping out over six feet—jocky guys are leaving him alone now of course—and those amazing shoulders, and a way of standing that he's somehow grown into, too, one hip cocked, his jeans almost slipping off his hips so you can see the edge of his briefs' elastic peeking out at the waist—oh, I should mention this was a summer kegger so when my girlfriends and I tumble out of Char's parents' car and walk up, the guys, who had started hours ago, are shirtless. Relaxed and shirtless and flushed from the heat and the beer. And Gil's hair, I should also mention, is now grown out. It's not frizzy any more, it's now long and caught back in a ponytail—he's pure gorgeous nouveau hippy.

That was Gil Rudman.

I didn't have a boyfriend. I didn't want a boyfriend. I wanted a career, and I knew better than to let anything distract me from that. I had a year-round job at a vet clinic, which went to full time hours over the summer, and from when I was 12 I also volunteered at the local animal shelter—my job was to socialize the animals up for adoption—mostly the dogs. And get the dogs started on some basic obedience.

Turns out I had a knack for it. I understood dogs. I understood how to move around them, how to get their attention, how to get them to do what I wanted them to do.

So at a time when the other girls were becoming interested in boys my attention was elsewhere.

I'd separated myself from boys, from the idea even of having a boyfriend.

Until Gil.

And it wasn't just how smoking sexy hot he was. It was that I'd caught his eye, as well. Don't ask me how I knew, but I did. I could tell the same way I could tell when the little Sheltie I'd been working on that afternoon at the shelter was no longer aware of the other dogs in their kennels, and was now only aware of me. I remember it so clearly! Standing there chatting with Char and some other people and he ambled by and stopped, kind of hanging on the edge of the group of us, and I knew it. He didn't even have to look at me, it was as if the plane of his body suddenly shifted and arced and I was suddenly caught in the concave cup of his attention.

The bottom of my stomach dropped out.

I reminded myself to breathe.

And just like that I flipped from being happily, decidedly single to knowing that it was Gil, that he was the one.

That I had to have him.

And the second I knew that, my instincts kicked in. I could feel it, feel how my body shifted. Oh, it was subtle! I doubt any of the others, standing there, noticed the change. But I could feel it. The change in the angle of my chin (slightly exposing the throat), the way my eyes flicked to his face (acknowledging him as the high status individual within our group), the way I began immediately to smile more, laugh more.

But I also controlled it, became deliberate with it. He shifted closer to me, and I responded by turning my shoulder slightly, signaling—*don't get too close. You're not invited to get too close. Not yet.* I knew that it couldn't be too easy. I knew, instinctively, that I had to make him wait. And so a minute later when Char saw another friend of hers I followed her, let her lead me away from where Gil was standing.

I could feel the connection between us attenuate as I walked off.

But it didn't break.

The rest of the party, I knew where he was without having to look. I could feel it.

And he knew where I was. He was watching me.

I waited.

And then, out of the corner of my eye, I saw him by himself, crossing the yard, headed toward the keg to draw himself another cup of beer.

I was with Char, still. She was telling her friends about a new business idea—she'd read in some magazine about a woman who started a cookie bouquet business and thought she could make her fortune doing it too. Selling them door to door.

I was skeptical. When the local per capita income is 25 percent below the national average, it's hard to make a fortune selling cookie bouquets. But I'd kept my mouth shut. What did I know? I was only 17. Maybe her dreams would come true.

Her friends seemed to think so—in fact they were asking for jobs.

"Count me in," Silvia said.

I leaned over and said into Char's ear, "Check her references. I'll be right back."

She was too engrossed in debating cookie flavor ideas to pay attention.

I re-scanned the yard.

As usual at these parties, when the kids unloaded the keg they rolled it over the lawn to the spot where they tapped it, so for the first couple of hours the pours are four-fifths foam, meaning it takes forever to get a glass of beer. Open the tap. Let a little beer run down the inside edge of your tipped plastic cup. Blow as much of the resulting four inches of foam as you can off the top of the half inch of beer.

Repeat eight times.

Then drink.

I suppose it slows down the drinking, which isn't necessarily a bad thing. Hah.

So I didn't need to hurry, which was good because I needed to look like it was complete happenstance, to find myself next to that guy again.

His back was turned so he didn't see me at first. Then he caught sight of me out of the corner of his eye and said "oh. Hi." And, oh, my, close up—the smell of him, how does anyone smell like earth and man and soap at the same time? And then, before I had a chance to answer he said, "you know, I've been thinking how it's one thing to paint Cubist people or buildings or something, but the whole Cubism thing falls apart if you try to paint a flower or a tree. Seeing that organic shapes are inherently whole and how can an artist with any integrity break them up?"

I know. Cubism? In 1992? But remember, we're 17. We thought The Doors were cool, too—stop laughing. We were 17! So it doesn't matter that Jim Morrison was dead and totally over, many times over, by then, when you're 17 and you've just heard Break On Through for the first time, c'mon, of course you'll think you've just glimpsed the holy foyer. Break on through indeed. I just might. Only let me do it, please, pressed up against this boy's fine young strapping bod . . .

"You must be an artist," I said, and he nodded and grinned.

5

Char missed her flight.

I didn't find out right away. In fact, I didn't find out until after I'd driven to the airport once, and parked, and went inside, and waited for her for like 45 minutes until it became pretty obvious that she wasn't on the flight she'd said she'd be on.

I got her text ten minutes after I got back home.

So I was a bit annoyed when I pulled up to the curb in the Arrivals lane, again, six hours later.

She, on the other hand, did not look the least bit annoyed. She looked great. When we were growing up, by the way, she had this wide wide mouth that always reminded me a bit of a frog's. Then she hit her teens and filled out and then she was 21 and a drop-dead beauty. She's a bit on the heavy side even but it doesn't matter. She's one of those women who carries an extra 15 pounds and not only doesn't she mind, she positively celebrates it, while I on the other hand torment myself over every ounce. And she's got that long curly hair. That day she was wearing it in a ponytail on the top of her head, her "I-Dream-of-Jeannie-Do," so that strands dripped down sexily around her face. So you get the picture. After a five-hour plane flight, I would have looked like a piece of bread someone had dropped on the floor and stepped on.

"Thanks for letting me know you missed your flight," I said when she slid into my car.

She's traveled with a carry-on only, a big canvas backpack with peace signs stamped all over it. She pushed it down onto the floor by her feet and pulled the car door closed. "Didn't you get my text?" she said.

"Yeah, I got your text. But next time, try sending it, ya know, before I leave for the airport the first time, okay?"

"What's the matter?" she said. "Are you still upset about Gil?"

"No," I said. "I'm fine about Gil. I'm upset about you."

"Did you decide what you're going to do? I see you're wearing the ring."

I glanced down. The chain had come out from under my shirt. I tucked it back in.

"Yeah," I said. "I'm wearing it."

"So, I suppose you've got a plan."

Char knew me pretty well.

We reached the expressway and I eased out into traffic.

"Paige?"

"Well," I said. "I've got some . . . ideas."

I could feel her looking at the side of my head. "You going to explain what you mean by 'ideas'?"

I merged from 390 south onto 590 north. "It's not a big deal," I said. "I just need to keep the pressure on, is all."

She didn't say anything but I could guess what she was thinking.

"I know what I'm doing, Char," I argued with the response I'd imagined she'd made. "And it's working. Which is obvious, right? Months and months I wait patiently. Then I finally decide to make him worry a little bit and—" I snapped my fingers. "He digs out a ring he must've bought before he left for Seattle in the first place and then he *mails* it to me. You've got to admit . . ."

I trailed off and glanced over. Char was leaned over, re-arranging her backpack to make more room for her feet. "I suppose it makes sense," she said, straightening back up. "He was taking you for granted. Now he's not."

I nodded. "Exactly. Which is why, when he turns back up, he's going to find out that he has more to worry about than he realized."

I couldn't resist checking her reaction. And sure enough, her eyes were kind of wide. "Paige," she said. "*What* are you cooking up?"

"Hey," I said. "I could be dating, you know."

She gave a light little laugh. "Oh, Paige!"

"What?"

"You had me for a second there!"

I scowled. "I'm serious!"

"You're going to *date* somebody?"

"It's not like I don't have offers!"

She laughed again. "But you never *do* anything! You live like a *hermit*. Hey, do hermits even exist anymore?"

I felt my scowl deepen. "And who's the one who's constantly telling me I *ought* to get out once in a while?"

"Well yeah. But—"

"Whatever, Char. "I'm going to get a boyfriend. Sort of."

It sounded pretty raw, putting it in those terms—but it was out there now. I'd said it.

"Paige," Char was saying, "You can't just get a boyfriend just like that," she said, snapping her fingers on the "that."

Gah. I love my cousin. But she was annoying me, now. "Char. You're the one who always says that anything is possible."

The strand of hair had come untucked again and from the corner of my eye I saw her push it back from her face. Then she fiddled with the air vent in the dash. "Well," she said finally. "And even if you somehow manage to land a boyfriend in time, aren't you afraid it might backfire?"

"You could be a bit more supportive."

"I *am* being supportive!"

"No," I said, "you're not. Lookit . . ."

I paused. We'd hit a little clump of traffic and the stupid driver in front of me was going too slow.

I checked my mirrors. No dice. Stupid drivers in the left hand lane wouldn't let me pull out around the stupid driver in front of me going too slow.

"Paige," Char said, "I know you're frustrated, but if he really loves you—"

I cut her off. "Of course he loves me," I said. "We've got chemistry. You know that. It's just that . . ."

"Isn't love enough, Paige? I mean, should you just trust it?"

Like I said, Char's a romantic. And cripes, if I didn't believe in love I'd have given up on Gil long ago. But I don't think love is enough. I think it needs a little help, sometimes. "I know the guy so well, Char. If he gets the idea that no matter what he does, I'll always be here for him because I know he's the one—"

"But Paige."

"I need to show him that maybe I don't think that."

"Think what?"

"That he's The One."

Char giggled.

"That's funny?"

She made herself stop with the giggling. "Oooh! I'm sorry!"

"Why is that funny?"

"You don't want him to think he's The One, when you *do* think he's The One?"

I didn't answer. What could I say?

"Well . . . just be careful, Paige."

"Careful of what?"

"That it doesn't backfire on you."

I frowned. Of course it won't backfire.

But it bothered me that she'd said the words.

What if she'd just jinxed it?

She fiddled with the vent again. "I suppose you know what you're doing," she said. "And anyway, good luck finding someone to play the boyfriend part."

Ha.

What Char didn't know is that I didn't need luck, because I had such a marvelously well-qualified candidate.

His name was Larry Crawford. A lawyer I'd met through work.

He'd used me as an expert witness on a case he was prosecuting a couple years back.

And although I didn't know Larry all that well, I'd picked up enough to know it would work. Because first of all, he is on the make, always. As he explained one of the many times he was putting a move on me, he's into a completely honest thing, all up front, you scratch my back I'll scratch yours. I mean, this is a guy who, when he was in law school, took out classified ads in the local daily personals canvassing for "unfulfilled" wives. Or so he told me once, before saying later he was just joking. Yeah, I know. Sleazy. But like I say, it was all up front—and if there are wives out there who want a little sizzle on the side with no strings attached I guess that's their business.

In other words, if I did this thing with Larry, I could tell him exactly what I was up to. And he'd play along with it.

Of course there was a chance he'd figure that by playing along he might get into my pants. But that wouldn't work, of course, so it would be the perfect arrangement.

6

Gil didn't kiss me that first night. It took about a month.

But that was okay by me. It was by design, in fact. I knew it would be better if it took a little while for things between us to gel. There needed to be a build-up.

Which isn't to say that I wasn't busy. On the contrary, I re-ordered my priorities a bit. I cut back a bit on my volunteering. And I started going to all of Mike's parties, even though, to be honest, they started to wear on me after a while—they were awful affairs, really, coarse and way too beery and jangling with too-loud music played until too late at night. But I tolerated it, because I had a new goal, now, and the first step was to get another glimpse of this person. This personage, this prince who had emerged from the scrubby backwoods of Cortland country as improbably as a Venus sweeping up, on her shell, from a garbage dump, except that I'd seen it with my own eyes, so I knew it had really happened.

What a lot of time teenage girls waste on boys! But I wasn't stupid about it—I wasn't as bad as a lot of the other girls I knew. And every second I spent was an investment.

I'd start by planning how to dress. The goal was a touch of sexy—just a touch, I took care not to cross over into slut—combined with a bit of artsy playfulness, and of course a big dose of "girl's got brains." So I stayed away from Grunge (unless you count my shortalls, but I'd do things like pair them with a Union Jack tee) and Hip Hop for the most part—I needed stuff that looked smarter and close-fitting, so I went more preppy. One party I went all black, I remember. I didn't own a pair of black jeans, so I dyed my favorite pair of drainpipes . . . That was also the summer I grew my hair out so I could get a Rachel-of-Friends mid-length cut.

Once at the party, I played it cool. I let him come to me. And then finally one humid August evening it happened.

I'd spent four hours moving in and out of his orbit, feeling that connection between us stretch out, spring back, stretch out, spring back . . .

And it happened: a soft, slow kiss and the words "mmmm, you're nice," murmured into the hair on top of my head.

This, while standing next to Char's parents' car, which Char needed to have back by 11:00 or face, no doubt, certain torture and death, and since I was technically on an overnight at her house I had no choice but to leave, too.

He asked for my phone number.

And a minute later we drove off, me cranking my head around to watch Gil slouch sexily back toward the bonfire.

So then what came next?

Simple.

Awful.

He didn't show up at any more of Mike's parties.

I went from being sure things were under control to totally doubting myself.

I finally asked Mike about him, as casual as can be. "Hey, I haven't noticed your cousin around lately. Gil."

Mike shook his head.

"Aw, that Gil," he said. "He's gone out West."

I'd never heard anything like that before. Out West? Like a pioneer?

"Out West?" I said.

"Yeah, why you ask?" Mike was crouched over a portable CD player, picking out some music. He glanced at me. "You tryin' to get something goin' with him?"

Gil's said something about me to him— the thought flashed into my mind and my heart began ramming my ribs. But I didn't lose my cool. Instead I shook my head. "Oh no!" I said. "I just noticed he wasn't around and wondered . . . that's all."

Whatever you do, don't make him think you're after him.

Mike hit the play button, and stood up.

"Gil," he said, "is his own man."

I was 17. I wasn't even sure what that meant.

His own man?

But I knew what it meant for me—that Gil had gotten away.

And summer was winding down.

And the next thing you know I was packing my things to leave for Ithaca, for Cornell, the terror of finally leaving home merged perversely with the heartsickness of knowing I might never see Gil again, and even if I did who knew what might go down in the interim.

To a boy—no, worse, a man!—like that, running around loose. Oh, so available.

And no way to know if I'd made impression on him—the sort of impression, I mean, that would stick.

Argh.

7

I met Larry for lunch at Highland Park Diner in the city, one of those 50s railroad car diners where you pay an extra couple of bucks per entrée for the privilege of sitting inside a narrow deco-esque aluminum tube, not that it looks much different, on the inside, from any other retro diner, other than being quite a bit more cramped.

He was on his cell phone when I got there. Grinning ear to ear. He hung up as I sat down, still grinning, and told me he'd been razzing a buddy about some bet he'd won on a college basketball tournament.

I'm not really into sports, but I listened politely and gathered that he'd been to Vegas recently and had done pretty well for himself. And that winning more money than his buddies had been as much, if not more fun than watching the games. That's Larry for you, who in addition to sleeping with unfulfilled wives also gets off on besting other guys, and—guilty pleasure here—I have to admit there is something attractive about him when he thinks he's about to give someone a good drubbing. I guess that's true of any man. The way they get all revved up and play their games like kings.

It helps that he's good-looking. Good-looking enough that now that he also has money, he doesn't need to take out personal ads any more. Plus he's in amazing shape. He has a personal trainer who comes to his house three times a week for a workout in the state-of-the-art gym in his basement. Yeah, I've heard all about it. I let him buy me dinner a few times when I was working on that case for him. I told you—I had plenty of practice keeping the guy at arm's length.

The server came over to take our order. She was plenty curvy, so he left off his basketball betting story to chat her up—asked her what her name was, she answered "Pat"—and then he watched her rear end as she walked away afterward.

Probably thinking about how much he'd like to pat Pat.

When she was gone I finally had a chance to get a word in edgewise.

"So, Larry," I started, then caught myself. I'd almost said "I might need an extra boyfriend once or twice during the next few weeks." But you have to be careful how you choose your words around Larry, since he'll take just about anything, such as "will you pretend to be my boyfriend," to mean "let's have sex."

Maybe I should have rehearsed a bit more.

So I switched tactics on the fly. Decided to put everything out in the open. This was Larry, right? It's not like it would shock him.

"Larry," I said, picking my words carefully. "Here's the deal. I phoned you because—well you know my fiancé, we ran into some issues—"

Despite my intention to maintain control, I noticed my face felt slightly warm. I knew why, too. Back when I was working with Larry on that case I'd made sure he knew how crazy I was about Gil. It helped keep the man at bay. Now I was admitting, albeit in retrospect, that the fortress walls weren't as thick as I'd led Larry to believe . . .

But I ignored the little upward twitch of Larry's eyebrows and went on. "Nothing serious," I added quickly. "But he's coming back to town, and it's important to me that I—I was hoping you might agree to pretend . . ."

I paused. Okay. I admit it. This seemed like a better idea before I actually said it out loud. Now it felt embarrassing and awkward and worse yet I suddenly felt a tremor of a doubt. But I should have expected it, right? *Managing* Gil—which is all it was—that was one thing and frankly . . . well, I knew Gil awfully well. But this was different. I'd never involved someone else before. It felt more like . . . plotting.

New territory.

But as it turns out, I didn't have to finish my sentence out loud.

"You need a pretend boyfriend," Larry said, "so you'll be in a better bargaining position."

I felt a little sick in the pit of my stomach. "Yeah, sort of."

Pat came back and plunked down a ketchup bottle on our table and I waited, figuring Larry might need a little time to watch her move her stuff again for a moment but—*uh oh*—he was studying me instead.

"What?" I said.

"Paige. You know I'd do anything for you."

I waited for the wink but the expression on his face was . . . weird.

I dropped my eyes—this would get easier once I got used to it, right?—and fumbled with my cell phone. "So you'll help me out?"

"It's just that—Paige, this isn't like you."

"Of course it's like me, Larry." I glanced back up. "Stop looking at me like that." And I pretended I was checking my cell for missed calls or something.

"So what happened between you two?" I could feel his eyes on me still. "Long distance relationship thing stopped working for ya?"

"That's not exactly relevant," I said.

"It's extremely relevant. Did he break up with you?"

"No! Of course not."

"Ah, of course not. *You* broke up with *him*."

"No!"

"You broke up with him, now you want him to think you're seeing someone else, even though you're not. Either you're trying to twist the knife—"

"No," I said for the third time. "It's not like that at all. I still—"

"Or you're still hot for the guy."

Our eyes met again for a split second.

"I see," said Larry. "So you broke up with him for the dramatic effect, not because you really wanted to end it. He's an artist, I remember that much. Phil, right?"

"Gil. And I didn't break up with him. I just—"

"Ah. You didn't break up, you're just throwing your weight around. You've got him thinking he has a rival. And now you want to up the ante."

I did not like the way the conversation was going—not a bit.

"It's not as bad as it sounds," I muttered. "I just need a . . . friend. A male friend. To phone me or text me maybe, a couple of times, when he's around. That's all." His eyes were on my face again and I fought the impulse to squirm, and instead took a deep breath. "So will you help me, or not?"

He didn't answer right away. It was like he was thinking it over, which didn't make any sense.

Then he suddenly settled back in the booth seat and grinned like the Larry I knew.

"Well, babe," he said. "One thing I will say. You could have just toyed with me. Led me on without letting on what you were up to. So I have to hand it to you, you're playing it straight." He paused, and then went on. "So sure. Okay. It's a deal."

I unwrapped the paper napkin around my silverware and, under the table, wiped my palms with it to dry them. "Cool," I said. "Thanks, Larry. I knew you were the man to call."

And I relaxed and the pit in my gut started to loosen. Because first of all, Larry was the kind of guy who could make my idea work. It would be a game to him, the kind of game he liked to play, and he'd play it to perfection. And second of all, the fact is I kind of like Larry. When he isn't talking about sports or how he's going to screw (all in good fun, of course) some other clueless lawyer who's dared take him on, he's a real charmer. A good listener. And he's no groper. The seduction thing is an art for him. His passes are flirtatious and non-threatening and even chivalric, but never physical, or at least, not aggressively physical. I suspect it's because he's made it his business to pay attention to women. So he's got the timing down. I wouldn't be surprised if he leaves those wives he dates pretty fulfilled, if you want to know the truth.

Pat returned with our sandwich plates.

"Okay, then," Larry said. "When is the guy Phil due in town?"

"Gil."

"Right. When is Phil-Gil due in town?"

"I'm not sure, exactly," I confessed. "I got a kind of, uh, cryptic message from him . . . a couple of days ago. So I'm not sure when I'd need—when we'd need to . . ."

"Ah." Larry leaned back and loosened his tie, looking happily at his burger. "So I'm on call, you're saying."

Okay, that sounded just like Larry. And for some reason—maybe because I'd let my guard down a bit—him saying that made me blush for real. Fortunately he was salting his burger and didn't seem to notice.

"I thought it would be better to run it by you right away—you know, to make sure you'd be okay with it."

"Well, of course I'm okay with it, Paige. Whoops, need more coffee." He turned around and flagged Pat, then turned back to face me again. "It will be a pleasure to play boyfriend to a hot young thing like you."

Oh, boy.

He flashed me a mischievous smile. "You'll dress for it, I assume? I mean, for our dates?"

Double oh boy. Maybe this wouldn't be so easy. He was grinning at me again, now, totally enjoying himself. "Larry," I said. "I didn't say anything about going on dates."

He grinned. "We'll have to go on dates," he said. "Otherwise it won't come across as authentic. And I'll have to have your phone number for my little black book."

He doesn't really have a little black book—although I used to tease him about having one—his paramours' phone numbers are stored in his phone along with everything else.

Now he pulled it out of his pocket.

All those times he'd asked for my number. How I'd prided myself in refusing.

Hope this isn't an enormous mistake, Paige Newbury . . .

I gave him the number and watched him key it in.

"There," he said. "All set."

Yes. All set.

Gil would show up, and he'd realize that if he wasn't careful, he could lose me for real.

Problem solved.

Yeah. Right.

8

I was heading back to the office when I got a call from the 911 dispatcher.

Stolen cat.

Hmmm. That's a new one.

But who am I to argue? Stranger things have happened. Maybe it was a valuable cat . . . and anyway, my meeting with Larry had left me feeling unsettled.

I welcomed the distraction.

The guy making the complaint lived in one of the town's middle-tier neighborhoods, the sort of enclave my grandparents used to call "developments,"—built back when the developments didn't outnumber the pre-Kennedy era neighborhoods. The streets were serpentine, lined by silver maples. No sidewalks—if you wanted to take a stroll, you walked in the street along the curb.

The houses were all four-bedroom quasi-colonials with attached garages.

Skip (declined to provide his given name—I'm betting on Herbert) Wendt's place was painted gray.

I parked in the driveway.

His storm door was one of those classic old aluminum doors with scrollwork across the middle panel surrounding a flourish-y "W."

I took a step back when he answered the bell, pressed back by the smell of drugstore cologne and fried food.

Wendt was wearing grimy tan polyester pants and a white tee shirt.

"She's got my cat," he said to me.

"She?"

He pointed across the street. "Lady who lives over there, place with the wagon wheel."

I turned to look at the wagon wheel, sunk halfway into the lawn of a house kitty corner (ha ha ha) from Wendt's. The wheel formed a backdrop to a soggy brown rectangle where, presumably, flowers would bloom later in the year. Pansies, petunias, salvia, 99 cents a half-dozen on sale at Wal-Mart. Or Lowe's. "How do you know she has your cat?"

"Seen her open the door and let it in."

I looked at him. Pale blue eyes under a shelf of tangled gray eyebrows. He hadn't shaved very recently. With his extra weight his face was a bit hard to read but his shoulders were up and slightly forward. Another guy who expected people to do what he asked.

"I need a description of the cat," I said.

"Black and white. Big. Twenty-three pounds. His name's Fred."

I nodded. "Big cat. Male?"

"I said his name was Fred."

Of course. "Neutered?"

"I guess."

He guessed. Okay, file that one away for later. "Collar? Any special markings?"

"His ears got frostbit so they're raggedy."

"What's your neighbor's name?"

"Maddy. Maddy Ingersoll."

"Okay. I'm going over. She home, you think?"

He shrugged but said, "She's always home."

"Okay. I'll be back in a couple minutes."

I left my truck parked in the driveway and walked over to the neighbor's house. Rang the doorbell about five times, banged on the door about five times, and just as I was about to give up I heard someone calling "Coming!" from inside the house and a moment later I heard the sound of someone struggling with a deadbolt, and then the door opened and a woman with bright white skin and bright orange hair peered out.

"Hello, Maddy Ingersoll?"

"Yes?"

"I'm Paige Newbury, Brighton Animal Control Officer. I'm here about a cat."

"Yes?"

She had an anxious look on her face, but for some reason I suspected it was more a default expression, or maybe she wasn't used to people coming to her door at 2 o'clock in the afternoon on a weekday.

"Your neighbor, Mr. Wendt, is missing a cat and he thinks it might be here."

Something flashed across her eyes but she answered, "Oh, no, nobody's cat is here."

"May I come in for a moment?" I asked.

"Oh! I'm . . . busy . . ."

"Just for a moment. It's chilly outside this morning and I need to ask you a few questions so that I can fill out the paperwork. You know, since he's called us with this story, I need to fill out a report, you know how it is."

She fidgeted with the doorknob. Her hands were spidery thin. "It really isn't a good time."

Too late. She hadn't opened the door much more than the width of her face, but it was enough: I could see a big hunk of a black and white cat weaving figure eights around Maddy Ingersoll's ankles. "Ms. Ingersoll?" I said, looking pointedly at the cat.

"This isn't his cat," the woman said primly. "This is a stray. It's obvious. Look at his ears. He's been neglected. He was practically starved to death."

"When, uh—when did you say he turned up?"

"Three days ago."

For a starving animal, the cat had made a remarkable recovery in only three days. "Ms. Ingersoll, I'm sorry, but I think there's been a mistake."

Her face fell. "I don't know what you mean."

"This is your neighbor's cat."

"That isn't possible."

"Maybe not, but the cat matches Mr. Wendt's description and he says he saw it enter your house."

She bent down and stroked the cat to hide her face from me. Then she stood up. "I'm sorry. I had no idea. He looked so thin. I was sure he was a stray."

"That's okay. Mistakes happen."

The cat rode contentedly in my arms as I walked back across the street.

Mr. Wendt was waiting inside the storm door. "See? What did I tell you?" he said as he held it open for me.

Fred jumped down from my arms and disappeared into the house. "She thought he was a stray," I said.

He snorted. "Like hell she did. We've been neighbors for seven years. She knows damn well this is my cat. She feeds him all the time."

I decided to ignore this. No point in getting drawn deeper than I already was. "The important thing is that you've got him back."

"Yeah, right. And what about her? Doesn't she get fined or something?"

"I don't have proof that she knew the cat was yours," I said. "The important thing is that you got Fred back."

"Our tax dollars at work," said Mr. Wendt.

Argh. Taxes again. Time to nudge Skip Wendt a bit off balance. "Mr. Wendt," I said. "I'd *highly* recommend you keep your cat indoors. Statistically, cats kept indoors live two to three times longer than outdoor cats—"

"Huh. Cat would tear my house to shreds inside a week, if he didn't get outside."

"He's safer inside. He could get hit by a car—"

"He's too smart for that. He never goes into the street without looking first. I seen him do it hundreds of times."

Obviously another pointless discussion.

But at least he'd forgotten about his neighbor.

"Well, I'm glad it's turned out okay this morning, Mr. Wendt," I said. "Take care, now."

He said something else to me but I made sure not to hear it as I walked away.

Like I'm going to ticket that old woman for feeding a cat.

You see, when you decide on a career in animals, you might think you've found a way to make a living and escape people while you're at it. You'd be wrong. Unless you're a Jane Goodall, and even she was in a television commercial and has an Institute. I don't suppose you can be in commercials and have an Institute without being around people an awful lot.

The rest of us can't even get away from humans for a few restful weeks of field work. In fact, we barely escape humans at all. There are times, maybe I'm following up on a call about a wild animal acting strangely, I'm tromping around in someone's back yard—and then it's just me and nature—yes, nature in the contorted form it takes in the modern suburb, but nature all the same, sprinkling our yards with dandelions and Creeping Charley, lacing our hedgerows with poison ivy and buckthorn, lulling us with cute little chickadees and then slipping in those dens of coyotes all smacking their predatory lips for a taste of Domestic Cat—in those moments, I know why I wanted to "work with animals" for a living—because it's both immediate and yet so . . . otherworldly.

But domestic animals come with leashes, and at the other end of the leashes are people, with all their peoply stuff and peoply problems.

I bet there are folks in jobs like bookkeeping or software development, who have pets at home, who have a higher ratio of animal-to-people time in their lives than I do.

It would have been worse, I suppose, if I'd become a vet.

That was what I'd set out to do. First step: get my undergraduate degree at Cornell's College of Arts and Sciences. Step two, get into the veterinary medicine graduate program.

It seemed like a perfect plan at the time. There was the love-of-animals thing, and being a vet was a good-paying professional job, and last but not least my dad was a people doctor. In fact when I was little he used to tell me I could be an M.D. too when I grew up. Being a vet was the perfect answer.

It seemed even more perfect once I started school, because it gave me a way to keep my mind off that boy Gil. Cornell lets you apply to their DVM program during your sophomore year. But of course they'll laugh in your face if you do that and aren't pulling at least B's. Well, maybe not in your face personally, but I bet they'd make paper airplanes out of your application and then take bets on how many tries to fly it into the recycle bin. Ha ha ha.

Well, I wasn't going to sit by and see my application humiliated like that. No way.

I focused one-hundred-and-ten percent on my studies.

It was hard, but I'd had plenty of practice, and in the back of my mind I figured that come summer surely Gil would turn back up at Mike's again—he'd have to come back, right? To visit? To see his family?

That's what people do.

But then I got home in mid-May to bad news. It seems that Mike's mom found a patch cleared in the woods behind their house with about 30 marijuana seedlings spreading their little green fingers toward the late spring sun. And she may have been cool about kids drinking beer, but drugs—that was an entirely different matter.

Mike was given a choice. He could join the service, or explain his little agricultural enterprise to the police.

Mike chose the Army.

I admit, my reaction was terribly self-centered. Mike, first hard-lined at home, now sweating it out in boot camp. But what about me? His stupid pot escapade had left me high and dry. Not even a chance to find out what Gil was up to, whether he was even in New York State.

I talked it over with Char. She said there were other guys in the sea.

"Why Gil?" she said. "You could date anyone." She rattled off the names of some guys who I could date.

"Alan Armstrong?" I said. "Really?"

She nodded.

"I don't want to date Alan Armstrong," I said.

"You're letting your life pass you by," Char told me.

I didn't argue. What could I say? I didn't want other guys. I wanted Gil.

I took a second summer job to fill my time. Otherwise I knew the summer would do me in—too much time to brood.

It was a relief when August rolled around again and I was packing to go back to Ithaca.

And I made a decision, too. That would be my last summer at

home. Next year I'd find a job in Ithaca, and take courses over the summer. Maybe they'd even let me start my clinic internship.

I put Gil out of my mind.

I figured I'd never see him again.

I was wrong.

9

Never answer your cell if you don't recognize the number. It can only lead to trouble.

"Hey, Paige," Larry said.

"Oh. Hi, Larry."

Yep. Trouble.

I sucked in my breath. "What's up?" I said.

"Well, my dear. May I call you 'my dear'?"

"Uh—" I tried to laugh. This call was already making me nervous.

"Or 'sweetheart'? Let me call you sweetheart, Paige—"

"Knock it off, Larry."

"—I'm in love with you."

"Knock it off, Larry," I said again, and then added for good measure, "I—I, uh, I was just on my way out."

A lie, of course. Paige Newbury's evenings tended to be somewhat . . . dull. Larry had actually caught me standing in front of an open refrigerator. The smell wafting out was chemical-y with an overtone of garlic—the smell an empty refrigerator would give off, if it had been used lately to store leftover pizza. Which describes my refrigerator most days. I looked at the pizza box, alone on the center rack. An oily stain was spreading up from one corner of the box.

"No worries, Paige," Larry said. "I'm just calling to see what time on Saturday I should pick you up."

"Pick me up." I shut the refrigerator door, alarmed.

"We're dating now, remember?"

"Larry," I said. "We are *not* dating. You're just supposed to call me when Gil's in town—and he's not, right now."

"Well sure, Paige, but when he does show up, you want this to come across as authentic. Right?"

This was what I got for picking a lawyer to be my fake boyfriend. We hadn't even gone on a first fake date and I'm already losing ground, fast, in our first fake argument.

"And people who have been dating a while," he went on, "have a certain way of acting around each other."

"Sure, Larry. Of course they do. Because they like each other enough to date more than once."

"Well geez, Paige, we like each other!"

He sounded almost hurt and I felt bad. "I'm sorry, Larry. I didn't mean it that way. But—"

"Plus, it's not just because they like each other. They get into habits. For instance, what tone of voice will you use when I make my fake boyfriend call to you?"

"I don't know, Larry! I'll wing it—"

"Paige, you do understand—this could easily backfire. If he thinks you've staged it."

Argh. I opened the refrigerator again, removed the pizza box and put a slice of pepperoni pizza on a paper plate. Larry's argument made sense. I had to admit it . . . maybe I hadn't thought this through carefully enough . . .

"It needs to be very smooth, Paige."

Double argh.

"So, what time?" he said.

"I dunno, Larry."

"Paige," he said. "Don't go wobbly on me. You're in new territory here, you know."

Well. Sort of.

"Whereas I'm a lawyer," he said. "It's my job to know how to manipulate people."

I eyed the pizza. The cheese drooped soggily off the edges of the crust onto the plate.

"Paige?"

"I'm thinking," I said.

"Hey. It's up to you. But I'm telling you, do this half-ass and it could blow up on you."

"I don't buy it."

He laughed. "Okay, can't blame me for trying though, can you? So shall I pick you up this Saturday, say around seven?"

"Larry! Stop it. I never said—"

"Aw, c'mon Paige. As friends. We can go out as friends, can't we?"

I considered this.

And I considered something else, too.

I'd cast Larry for a major part in my big plan.

It wouldn't do to mess it up.

I had to humor him. I had to be nice.

"So how about it, Paige?"

I could have backed out right then. That was my window. Jump Paige, jump.

But I didn't jump. Because there was one thing I had to avoid at all costs, and that was for Gil to show up and find me just like this, alone and nuking the Leftover Pizza Slice of Life.

I needed Larry's help, no way around it.

So I agreed. "Okay, Larry." I swallowed. "Okay. You have made your point . . . I guess."

"Great. So I pick you up around seven?"

"This Saturday?"

"Yep. You're not busy, are you?"

"You mean—well, I don't know. I could be busy! I haven't thought about it."

The indignity of being available for a date on such short notice!

"Relax, Paige," he said. "Seven o'clock, okay?"

Nothing fazes that man.

"Okay, then, seven o'clock." Then I thought of something else. "One other thing. I'm not doing this unless we go Dutch."

"Cool," he said. "See ya then," and he hung up.

I took a bite of my pizza.

"Paige, you are gonna have to keep your eye on that guy every second," I mumbled to myself as I chewed.

10

Saturday night.

I figured the first step in my defense was to wear something that would send the right message.

So: khaki skirt.

Powder blue knit long sleeve cotton shirt from Gap.

One-inch heels, no stockings.

I checked myself out in the mirror. I looked like I was dressed for a job interview. A desk job, I decide. Receptionist. Medical transcriptionist.

I peered a bit closer. The ring, hanging from its chain, made an odd-shaped bump in the fabric of my shirt.

I tried wearing it on the outside.

Didn't work. It was a big ring—a costume ring. It called too much attention to itself.

I reached behind my neck, unclasped the chain, and dropped chain and ring into my jewelry box.

A minute later I stepped outside, pulling on my coat as I walked.

Larry, of course, looked me up and down.

"What?" I said.

"Didn't feel like dressing up, huh?"

"This is a fake date, remember?" I told him. "I don't need to try to impress you."

He laughed. "That's for sure."

"What's that supposed to mean?"

"That you impress me without trying, Paige." He leaned forward and brushed his lips on the top of my hair. "So. Where shall we go?"

"Boston Market."

He laughed again.

"I'm serious."

But when we got into his SUV, he turned toward the city instead.

"Mental note," I said aloud. "Next time, we both drive and meet at the restaurant."

"Now what's the fun of that? Some fake date you are."

I looked out the window and grunted. "This was your idea, remember."

"We're collaborating, Paige. Partners in crime. BASTARD!"

The sedan in front of us had stopped suddenly and was apparently planning, now, to parallel park. Its back-up lights were on. There was a stream of oncoming traffic. Larry, eyeing his rearview mirror, put his truck in reverse.

"I see you're not trying very hard to impress me, either."

"Mmmmm. Women love angry, aggressive men."

"Who told you that? Dr. Phil?"

"Never heard of him. Friend of yours?"

"No." The stream of traffic passed, giving Larry room to pull out around the parallel-parking car, which was now on its second pass.

I thought about asking where we were going, but changed my mind. "So, any good cases lately?"

"Depends on what you mean by 'good.'"

"Interesting. Colorful. Front page of the D&C." That would be the *Democrat and Chronicle*, Rochester's local daily, not the medical procedure.

"Not really. Got a nice fight going on over the Parsons building in High Falls. But it hasn't made the papers yet. Not the fighting part."

"Isn't that the building the city wanted to condemn?"

"They said they did. But they don't really. It's one of the jewels on their 'rejuvenate downtown' crown."

The High Falls district got its name from its proximity to the Genesee River's tallest waterfall. Now the 19th century-era industrial buildings that flank that part of the river are slowly being reclaimed as shops, restaurants, and bars, thanks to liberal doses of public seed money and tax breaks.

"But it's a mess, right?"

"Depends on if you are Party A or Party B."

"And also on who your attorney is, I'm sure."

Larry chuckled. "You got that right, babe."

We were sitting at a stop light. "So which Party is yours?"

"Party B. Party A just went through a nasty divorce and is trying to force a sale. Or get my client to buy him out, either one. Seems he's a bit short on cash."

"Why won't your client sell?"

"He knows that if the place is developed, it will be worth a hell of a lot more."

"It's empty now, right?"

"Yeah."

"But habitable?"

"Structurally, it's sound. Of course, it's a pain to keep the riffraff out."

I nodded. "Didn't someone start a fire in it or something?"

"Yeah. The city is still grousing about that one. They say it's not safe for their firefighters to go in."

"Well, what about the riffraff? Can't be safe for them, either."

"No. The city grouses about that, too."

I wasn't listening so closely any more: we were in the South Wedge and he'd turned down a residential street, and I'd realized where he was taking us. "Aw, Larry, no. Not here."

Rooney's.

He pulled into the parking lot: a tiny plot of blacktop that had once been a yard. "Hey, next time, you choose."

A valet opened my door and extended a hand to me. Oh brother. I declined the offer of help and rounded the car. "Larry," I hissed, "when I said this was going to be 'Dutch,' I expected we would pick something that wouldn't cost me half my paycheck."

"We'll go Dutch next time. This one's on me."

He took my elbow and steered me into the foyer.

I pasted a smile on my face and followed the maître' d to our table.

11

On the bright side, I knew a fantastic meal was in the offing—and I do mean fantastic. Rochester's got a lot of great things going for it, but if you're in this part of the country and you want to do restaurants, try, um, New York. Or Toronto. Which, by the way, makes our good ones all the nicer. Like diamonds in a pile of pea gravel. Or something like that.

The building was originally a saloon and the dining room isn't particularly large one. We got the last two-top, a table by the window in the front.

The maître' d pulled out my chair and I sat down, and then Larry sat, and flashed me a grin, and picked up the wine list.

He'd apparently decided to ignore my reaction to his little stunt.

So what the hell. I gave a mental shrug and relaxed. At least I wasn't paying.

"Red okay?" he said to me.

"Fine. Yeah. Uh huh."

He smiled at me again. The "gotcha" smile.

I pretended not to notice. With Larry, if you get flustered, he's won.

The server was standing at our table. Yeah, I said server, not sommelier. This is still Rochester, remember. We multitask here. "We'll try the 1998 Château Beauregard," Larry said.

The server said "very good" and strode off.

"It's a Pomerol, so ought to be nice and chewy."

"Mmmm."

"I love it when you let loose with your sarcastic 'mmmm.'"

I smiled sweetly. "Fake dates only get sarcastic 'mmmms.'"

"We could be having fun, you know."

I laughed. "Larry, I am having fun." And the second I said it, it was true. This was going to be one of the best meals I'd had in a long time. Animal control is a decent gig, but it doesn't pay a lawyer's salary by a long shot.

The server came back and poured a splash of wine in Larry's glass and then another in mine.

I took a sip. "Wow," I said, admiringly. "That'll give you a black eye."

"Would you care for an appetizer?" the server asked.

"Yes," I said quickly. "The smoked seafood plate, please."

Larry shot me a look and I smiled sweetly. "You chose, remember?"

"I should have known you'd rise to the occasion."

Larry raised his glass, and I clinked mine against it and drank another sip. "To our first fake date," he said.

"Mmmm." Not sarcastic, this time.

"You know, you could upgrade."

"Upgrade?"

"Make it a real date. There's still plenty of time."

Argh. I felt my cheeks get hot. I gulped another swallow of wine.

"You sure you really want the guy back?"

"What do you mean?"

"Your boyfriend."

I thought about the ring on its chain, resting back home in my jewelry box. "I'd rather not talk about it, really."

"Did you really dump him or did he dump you?"

"Larry—"

"Aren't you women today supposed to be all empowered, and not let men treat you like crap—"

"Larry!" I whispered it, albeit fiercely, trying to get my point across without disturbing the other tables. I saw a silver-haired woman glance over at us.

Fortunately the server picked that minute to came back.

"Your appetizer will be up in a moment. Would you like to order your entrées?"

Saved by waiter interruption. I picked the pan-seared scallops on basmati rice. Larry asked for a steak. Rare.

It gave me a minute to calm back down.

The server refilled our wine glasses and left.

Two more parties of diners had now been seated, and the air in the room had gotten warmer.

"Paige."

"Yeah."

"I'll back off. Leave you alone about what's-his-name."

"It's okay."

The server slid a basket of warm bread and petite little muffins onto the table, and from his other hand, the plate of assorted smoked seafood.

I reached over to lift a bit of salmon with my fork.

Just then, a movement outside caught my eye.

Loose dog.

12

I bet you've noticed this too, the way loose dogs catch our attention nowadays. It's because they aren't something we normally see. At least not in the city, where leash laws are the rule of the land. A dog on his own, these days, always looks out of place.

I jumped up.

"What?" Larry looked startled.

"Dog!"

"Huh?"

Hey, this is what I do, right? I grabbed a muffin from the basket, broke it in two, stuffed some smoked salmon inside, and darted toward the door.

Our server stepped aside graceful as a dancer to let me by.

The dog was already halfway down the block. Brindle, short hair, stocky. Moving, but not at a run.

He stopped to smell a tree, lifted his leg.

I whistled.

He turned and looked at me, but it was a long shot and I knew it: he kept going.

"Here, fella!" I said, keeping my voice relaxed.

I needed to close the distance between us. Always a chance that running at him would make him run, too, but I needed to risk it. And by the way, heels—even low heels—really, really suck at times like this. Like I'm reporting anything new. But damn. I had to do my best, run on my toes, trying to gain on the dog without losing those stupid pumps.

"Hey, want a treat? Want a cookie?"

He realized I was chasing him and picked up his pace a bit, so I slowed to a walk.

He stopped to sniff a lamp post.

I could see now that he was a young dog, and intact. Out on the town on a Saturday night. "Here, fella!" Keeping my voice happy. "Want a treat?" I tossed a bit of salmon.

I could see his ribs. And that his collar had no tags.

He must have caught of whiff of the fish because he paused to sniff it, and then as he licked it up I was able to get a little closer. I kept my head turned away, not making eye contact. "Want some more?"

From the corner of my eye I saw him pause and wait.

"Sit," I said.

He sat.

Told you it sometimes works.

"Good boy!" I tossed him another bit of salmon—he caught it in the air—then slipped my hand under his collar. He tensed but didn't bare his teeth at me. I could feel the muscles of his neck. Pit bull, or maybe pit bull mix. Strong dog.

"Goddamn it, Paige."

"Hey, Larry."

He'd pulled his SUV up to the curb.

"Duty calls, y'know?"

"Yeah," he said. "Well, duty just cost me a forty-five dollar steak."

"You chose." I grinned at him.

He didn't look amused. "Now, what?"

"Got to take this fellow in."

"And how do you propose to do that?"

I grinned at him again.

"Aw! It's leather, Paige."

"I'll ride with him. I'll keep him on the floor."

He sighed, got out, and opened the back door. A gentleman, that Larry.

"Want to go for a ride, fella?" I tossed some muffin into the Infiniti and the dog practically pulled me over, leaping after it.

I jumped in behind him.

"Where to?"

I hesitated. We were in the city. The dog really belonged to Rochester Animal Services. But it was a Saturday night . . . I decided to just fall back on procedure I know best and take him where I take my Brighton strays.

"Pittsford Animal Hospital isn't open Saturday nights. It'll have to be the emergency office. White Spruce Boulevard near MCC." That's Monroe Community College.

"Geez, Paige. Some fake date you turned out to be."

"Sorry." It was taking all my strength to keep the dog on the floor. He wanted up on the seat and he wanted it bad.

"You owe me a make-up date."

"Right." It crossed my mind to remind him that what had nearly happened tonight was a fake date, not a real date, but I let it slide. I had other things on my mind.

"Next Friday good?" he said.

"Sure, Larry." The dog squirmed and swiped a paw up at the seat. I started scratching his chest to calm him.

Larry looked at me in his rear view mirror. "You okay?"

"Uh huh." Well, except for the muddy paw prints all over my fake date finery.

And one other thing. Now that the dog was calmer I'd noticed his ears.

They'd been injured. The right one had been torn and healed some time ago. Scarred. The left one was still scabby.

Young dog, to have ears messed up like that.

Still scratching his chest, I petted his muzzle—cautiously— some dogs hate being touched on the muzzle.

But he was fine with it. The salmon had won his heart I guess. So I felt around with my fingertips.

He had another scar there, on the left, where his lip had been torn.

"Crap," I muttered.

"What now?"

"This dog's been in a fight." I stroked the pit's neck.

"I know the feeling."

"You don't understand." We were on the expressway now so the SUV had picked up speed. "Pit bull. Picked up in the city. Scars on his face and neck." I paused. "This dog's been used to fight other dogs."

I could see Larry's expression in the rearview mirror. "What, is he dangerous?"

I shook my head. "No—not to people. Their handlers can't have dogs around that might bite people."

And he wasn't the least bit dangerous. He was a gem, you could just tell. A totally normal and by the way potentially gorgeous dog—except for those scars . . .

"Well," said Larry, "then you've given him a new life, then."

I shook my head. "No. Exact opposite. This is his death sentence."

"I don't follow you."

So I explained. The local animal shelter won't put ex-fighters out for adoption. And who can blame them? They don't want some innocent family adopting a dog that has been conditioned to attack other animals.

What the shelter would do instead is hold the dog as long as they needed for legal purposes—dog fighting is illegal of course, so the pittie would be considered evidence—and then they would put him down.

Larry looked at me in the mirror again. "What do you want to do?"

I answered quickly so I wouldn't have time to think. "I've got no choice in the matter," I said.

And I didn't. All I could do was give that pit bull the nicest under-the-collar scratch that I could for the rest of the drive.

He leaned happily into my hand, oblivious to the fact that his evening adventure would be his last.

13

Every time I started to drift off to sleep, that night, I'd feel my hands stroking that pit bull's muzzle.

I could feel those scars . . .

So yeah. I had trouble falling asleep.

And normally, when I picked up a stray, I call the shelter the next day to check on him. Like with that Eskimo dog. His people had shown up the day after I'd caught him, ID'd him, and took him home.

His name was Blizzard, by the way.

But with the pittie, I put it off.

And put it off.

Until Thursday. I'd finished my morning rounds and picked up a salad to eat back at the office, and without letting myself think about it too much I picked up the phone and dialed the shelter— Lollypop Farm, it's called.

And I got quite a surprise.

Somebody had claimed the dog.

"Really?" I said to Laura, the gal who took my call.

It took a minute to sink in. A dog that's been used to fight— like I say, he's evidence of criminal activity. The last thing his owner wants to do is show up and say "hey, that criminal evidence? It's my property."

It invites uncomfortable questions.

But apparently, in this case, the owner had plausible answers. According to Laura, he claimed his neighbor has a dog, and imagine this. The neighbor's dog had jumped the fence and mauled the pit.

Bad neighbor dog.

"As far as we could tell, Paige, he was telling the truth," said Laura. "He had I.D."

"I see."

She told me the guy's name—yeah, I asked—and I thanked her and we hung up.

Okay then.

I couldn't really blame them for releasing the dog.

And I suppose I should have been relieved. After all, the evidence that the dog had been fought was circumstantial. An educated guess. A hunch.

So suppose I was wrong? Suppose there was a completely innocent explanation for that pit bull's scars?

Did I really want that dog euthanized for no reason?

Damn it.

On the other hand, if he was being used to fight, he was now doomed to some pretty horrific suffering.

This wasn't why I'd become a dog catcher. You see, veterinarians take responsibility for saving animals' lives. They have to make hard decisions, including—inevitably—decisions about euthanization.

Dog catchers save animals' lives too, sometimes—we rescue neglected animals, strays, that kind of thing—but it's different. It's black and white. You see a situation, you intervene, you're the hero, you're done.

I went online and ran a Lexis-Nexus search on the name and driver's license number of the guy who'd claimed the dog.

And guess what—I got no hits.

The guy was carrying a fake ID, apparently.

Which, again, could mean nothing. Lots of guys in the city are probably walking around with fake IDs.

Damn it.

I closed my browser and told myself to let it go. I'd done my job. Actually, I'd done more than my job—I could've just let well enough alone from the beginning, but I'd grabbed the dog, and hey, by grabbing him maybe I'd saved him from being squashed by a bus or something.

The situation with the pit bull was over. Settled. Case closed.

"He's not your responsibility, Paige," I said to myself. "You did your job. That's all you need to do."

I reminded myself that Blizzard's adventure came to a happy end.

Focus on the bright spots in this job and you can get by.

I suppose that's true of any job.

I suppose it's true for life, too.

14

"You're broody," Char said. "What's bothering you? Gil?"

We were going out for dessert, and were in her car, waiting at a stop light.

"No," I said, "not Gil. That pit bull."

"Paige," she said. "You did the best you could, given the circumstances."

"Things with Gil are fine," I said. "Remember how he turned up in Ithaca? It was a life lesson. I learned not to doubt myself."

Not entirely true—I do get doubts once in a while—but close enough. What had happened in Ithaca was this: after my sophomore year I'd decided to spend my summer there, instead of going home. I was living off-campus by then, splitting a place with two other life sciences students. And sometime around the middle of August, I was flopped across my bed, reading a textbook on livestock pathogens, and my cell rang.

Someone asks for Paige. I say I'm Paige. And then he says he's Gil, "Mike's cousin." I sit up, which knocks the textbook on the floor—hardcover book, hardwood floor. He asks me what was that, and I say nothing, and next thing you know, it's sinking in, what's happening. He's telling me he's moving to Ithaca. He's enrolling in the arts program at Ithaca College.

And he's looked me up because he'd heard I was at Cornell, and also did I have any leads on apartments.

And I answered yes, which was a lie. But not a big huge lie, because I did know all the spots around town where people posted photocopied ads looking for roommates, and so when we met later for a beer I had loads of phone numbers for him to try.

But I noticed he didn't pay much attention to the phone numbers. And that he was paying a lot of attention to me . . .

"I know what makes Gil tick," I said to Char. "If he came all the way to Ithaca for me then, he'll come all the way to Rochester for me now. And—" I grinned suddenly, pit bull forgotten. "Don't forget, he sent the ring."

We were headed to a coffee shop on the east side of the city. It's in a renovated car dealership, Deco architecture on the outside, hip loft-style interior, and other than making me feel a touch old—it's near the Eastman School of Music, and therefore is crawling with college kids—it's the sort of place where you could almost pretend you were somewhere else. Portland maybe or Austin.

We ordered—lemon raspberry torte for me, peanut butter fudge mousse for her.

"So let me guess," I said. "You've got another business idea."

Bingo. "It will be like Psychic Hotline," she said. "Only over the Internet."

The gal behind the counter handed us our plates.

I followed Char to an open table. I should have been ready for this topic of conversation, of course. It was near the first of the month, meaning her rent was due.

"Have you Googled it?" I said as we sat down. "It's probably already been done, you know."

I try to be supportive. She is my cousin. But she has a tendency to come up with these ideas and then not really think them through. And I have to admit, it made me uneasy to think about her doing an online psychic advice business. I mean, doing in-person readings is one thing. But Going National?

"I bet I could charge, like, fifteen bucks for a half hour reading."

I considered how to answer and decided I might as well be honest. She'd know if I was hedging, anyway. "Honestly, Char?" I said. "It sounds a bit . . . skeevy, if you want my opinion."

She wrinkled her nose.

"I liked your online jewelry idea better. Whatever happened to that idea?"

Charlene's mother makes a decent living making and selling

jewelry, actually. It would be a no-brainer for Char to do it too. But I suppose she wants to go her own way.

"I'm a psychic," she said. "I wouldn't have this gift if I wasn't supposed to use it."

"Well," I said. "You asked my opinion."

I swallowed the last bite of my torte, feeling a touch nauseous from all the fat and sugar. Food karma. Yech.

We went out to her car.

"Do me a favor," I said. "I left my cell phone charger at the office. I'd like to swing by there and get it."

"Sure."

We pulled around behind the Town Hall. That's where my office is, along with the courthouse and the police department. Char parked, and I got out and was halfway down the sidewalk to the door when I heard her voice. "Paige!"

I turned around. She was getting out of her car. "Looks like you got a present!"

I backtracked so I could see where she was pointing.

A black lab was tied to the trunk of one of the skinny ornamental trees planted alongside the lot.

"He's FAT!" Charlene said.

"Oh, cripes," I said. "Bet it's Lady."

"Lady?"

"Yeah. Not fat. Pregnant."

Charlene chuckled.

"Not funny," I said.

"Funny!"

"Not funny."

The dog was tied to the tree with a piece of rope. No note.

"How did you know her name?"

"Her owner called me, wanting to know what I was going to do about her condition."

Lady was glad to see us. She flattened her ears and gave a doggy smile as I stroked her head.

Charlene was still chuckling. "And you said, 'oh, just drop her off'—"

"Yeah, that's right, that's me. Paige Newbury, dog obstetrician."

"You going to call the owner back?"

I fingered Lady's collar. No tags, of course. "She didn't leave a number."

"Oh."

"So I guess it's to the emergency clinic for Lady." I winced as I said the words.

Just like the pit bull . . .

Char looked at me a second, then said, "Okay. Want to go right now?"

"Sure." I untied the rope and Lady followed me—very ladylike, incidentally, or as ladylike as she could be, considering her advanced condition—to Charlene's car.

I opened the back door. Lady lifted a paw and put it onto the floor of the car, then swung her head back and looked at me.

Charlene giggled again. "I think she wants a boost."

"She's huge."

"She looks like she swallowed a sea lion."

I frowned. "Here, go around to the other side and I'll toss you the rope. Maybe she'll get in herself with a little encouragement."

It worked. Lady might have preferred a boost but was too polite to protest the inevitable.

Charlene pulled out onto Elmwood, heading toward Henrietta. I turned around and looked at the dog. She had started to pant.

"She sounds hot," said Char.

"I was just wondering how long she was tied out there."

That wasn't exactly true. The truth was, I was having flashbacks to the other night, riding with that pit bull in Larry's SUV.

"You're having second thoughts, aren't you," Char said.

I sighed.

"You gotta make up your mind, Paige."

"I don't know what to do."

Only I did. I knew just what to do. The dog would be fine at the vet clinic. They handle this sort of thing all the time.

But.

I looked at her again. It seemed like her eyes hadn't left the back of my head.

I'd done "the right thing" with that pit bull . . .

We'd passed the turn to my apartment.

"Look," I said. "Sorry Char but—I, uh, I want to at least give her some water. They might be busy at the clinic. And she could have been out there for hours, for all we know."

Back at my place, Charlene pulled the stuff out of my broom closet while I went upstairs to get an old blanket. When I came down, Lady was still lapping from the mixing bowl of water I'd put on the floor.

"Her skin is flakey."

"Diet, maybe," I said.

"I've never understood why you won't get another dog."

"Well if I ever do, it won't be a pregnant one."

"Mmmm. Want me to run to Tops for some food?"

"You don't mind?"

She shrugged. "I'm out of paper towels—I need to go anyway."

Good ol' Char.

Lady walked over to the broom closet—or rather, shuffled over, enormous stomach swaying as she moved—and sniffed at the blanket I'd folded and put on the closet floor. I patted it and she pushed her head under my forearm, asking to be petted.

"Okay. I'll be back in ten."

"Right."

"Paige?"

"Yuh huh." Lady was pawing at the blanket now and circling, getting ready to make herself comfortable.

"How many puppies you figure are in there? Fifteen?"

"That's not really funny."

"Twenty?"

"Glad you're having a good time."

"Twenty-five?" she called as she closed the door behind her, still giggling.

15

There wasn't a doubt in my mind that Gil had come to Ithaca because of me.

The stuff he told people about why he'd come—about his parents threatening him ("they said no more money unless I got a degree")—it was all a cover. He could've gone anywhere, to college. There's a reason he picked Ithaca.

Me.

And it changed everything, when he turned up.

It changed me. Because it was one thing to be a kid at a party, angling for a kiss from the cutest guy you'd ever seen. But now—now I was out in the world, my life was really underway, and the game was for real. For keeps.

Plus, I now knew for certain: the pull I had on him wasn't my imagination, and it wasn't circumstantial, either, not entirely.

It was there when he was sober.

It was there when I was out of sight.

He'd show up at my apartment. "What are you doing?" "Studying." "Are you kidding me? It's Friday night!"

I'd hide how glad I was to see him. Not entirely hide it, more like cloak it. But I'd let him talk me into going out. I'd let him take my hand and pull me out of the apartment, out onto the sidewalk, and then he'd lead me to some party.

Don't get the wrong impression—none of this was calculated, exactly. I wasn't consciously trying to manipulate him. It came naturally to me, it was instinct. I wasn't manipulating him, it was pure, I was being purely feminine—I was a female bird when a male struts past her and fans his tail, a lioness when the male lion approaches and calls to her, and she drops her belly to the ground and calls back, deep in her throat, and raises her haunches.

It was nature, it was my nature—it was Nature moving through me.

The only reason I was more aware of it than most girls is the work I'd done with dogs—what I'd learned about body language, about how much we communicate without words.

He'd walk me back to my apartment. Downtown Ithaca is settled comfortably in the flat-bottomed notch at the southern end of Cayuga Lake, but the rest of the city is stacked up against the steep, steep hills that flank the lake to the east—so when you're a student and don't have a car, every place you go, eventually you have to climb a hill. A steep hill. It seemed almost straight up, the climb to my apartment. We'd stand in front of it, catching our breath, and kiss, and in the pinkish streetlight I'd see the look in his eyes, and it was almost panic—that's how much he needed me.

It was time.

My roommates weren't home.

We went straight to my bed.

His belly was flat and hard and when he was on top of me it pressed against me in a way I could never have imagined.

"You were so . . . ready," he said afterward, before he fell asleep . . .

Char called me the next morning. She'd come out as a psychic by then and I was getting used to it, her calling me because she'd "picked up on something."

"Are you okay?" she asked.

I told I'd never been better, but when she asked me how school was going I let it slip that my grades weren't all straight A's any more.

She knew things were getting hot with Gil, of course. "I told you," she said. "You pretend for years that you have no sex drive whatsoever—and now look."

"I never said I didn't have a sex drive!"

"Well, still. You sublimated it."

I laughed. "No New Age pop-psy session, please, Char!"

"Do you love him?"

"I'm *in* love with him," I said.

"As long as you're happy."

"Enough about me!" I answered. "What's new with you?

16

I called one of my vet school friends, Sandra McInroe, and she came by the next night to give Lady a once-over.

I watched her examine the dog, thinking to myself that I was most certainly out of my mind.

I'd broken two of my rules.

First rule: no dog.

Second rule: don't even *think* about a dog.

But I'd done it. And not just any dog. Oh no. I'd picked a walking population explosion. A dog who would soon turn my apartment into the lab-cross remake of Trouble with Tribbles.

Sandra's professional opinion: puppies due sometime real soon.

I didn't need a degree to figure that out.

"How soon?" I said. "Like tonight, soon?" I was thinking of my make-up fake date with Larry.

"Nah," said Sandra. "She's too relaxed."

So much for an excuse to break the date.

"You have a thermometer you can use?"

Dog's temperatures drop a bit when they're about to whelp.

I shook my head. "I don't have any of that stuff anymore."

"I'll lend you one," said Sandra.

Then she left and I went back and looked at Lady again, curled up on her blanket in the closet.

Her tail thumped the floor.

Well. At least my third rule was still intact. Don't get attached. I was *involved*, yes. Obviously. But I wasn't attached, and as long as I stayed unattached, it might work. All I'd need to do was take care of the puppies until I found them homes.

I checked the time on my cell.

There was still plenty of time to break the date. After all, Sandra *could* be wrong about when the puppies would come.

Larry picked up on the second ring.

"Hey," I said. "It's me. I have a little situation, here."

"Mmmmmm. Again with the situations. Well, you've called the right guy, gorgeous."

"Larry, I'm serious. I've got a dog at my place who is about to have puppies."

He laughed. "Are you kidding?"

"Nope."

"What do you mean, like she's going to have them tonight?"

I hesitated for a second. "Well—not necessarily. But still. I don't know if I should leave her alone, you know—"

"She'll be fine. Just give her your cell number."

"Larry!"

"Paige, relax. We'll only be gone a couple of hours. You're not planning to watch her 24-7, are you?"

What did I say about picking a lawyer?

"Okay." I sighed. "But no Rooney's this time, got it? And I'm wearing blue jeans and sneakers."

"Good, you'll be prepared, in case you need to run down another pit bull."

Yeah. The pit bull.

"See you in, say, about ten minutes," Larry said.

Right. More like two minutes. Because I was about to wash my face—preparing for a fresh bit of make-up—when the doorbell rang.

Larry, early.

I went to the window at the top of the stairs, opened it and yelled down, "It's open, c'mon in."

I heard the door open and called down again, "You're early! I'm cleaning up. Lady's in the kitchen, go on in and say 'hi.'"

He said something back but I'd already shut the bathroom door by then and couldn't make it out. And I must have been hurrying a bit, because next I grazed my cheekbone with the mascara brush. And as any top model will tell you, you can emphasize your eyelashes all you want, but if you also head out with slashes of mascara goo on your cheeks, that's all your potential admirers will notice. Also, a scrap of toilet paper sort of works to scrub misplaced mascara from skin, but not all that well, and at a great price.

I stood for a second, looking at the pink blotch on my face.

Well, nothing to do but go downstairs. After all, I consoled myself, it was only Larry.

Only it wasn't Larry.

I realized it when I was about five steps from the landing. I could see into the kitchen there. And someone was crouched down in front of the broom closet.

I froze.

It most certainly wasn't Larry.

It was Gil.

17

"Nice dog."

I didn't answer. I couldn't. Talking may not require the use of many muscles, but on some occasions it can make you lose your balance, and I was, you remember, still standing on the stairs.

He turned his head to look at me without standing up, and even though he was all folded up in that crouch I could still see that body I knew so well, all tall and cowboy-loose. His hands were still stretched out into the closet, on Lady, who I'm sure didn't mind a bit that he had his eyes on me as long as his hands were still on her.

The doorbell rang.

My brain, playing catch-up, reminded me that the doorbell, ringing, most probably meant that Larry was there.

For our date.

My stomach, still plunging at the site of Gil, plunged even more wildly.

Gil stood up.

"Gil," I said. "Gil—I need to get the door." And I kind of kangaroo'd down the last few steps and darted to the door—I had this crazy feeling all of a sudden that Gil might answer it and then—and then, I didn't know . . .

It hadn't occurred to me yet that, no matter what, the two were about to come face to face.

I threw the door open. "Larry!"

He gave me a funny look. "You okay? What happened to your cheek? Bump into a rogue camel at work today?"

"No. Uh, rogue mascara stick." I'm sure I was looking about

wildly. "Ready to go?" I took a step at him—I must have thought I could just walk out, shut the door behind us, and Gil would be none the wiser.

"What, I don't get to meet your new buddy?"

"My buddy!"

"Paige, you okay? The dog'll be fine."

"Oh! Yeah, Lady! Yeah. Well. Not now. I mean, we have to go. I mean, I can't go. Larry, I—we have to call this off."

Larry looked at me like I was talking crazy. Which, I suppose, I was. "Paige, you okay?"

No. No, quite the opposite. I should have been in complete control of this situation and instead I was on the verge of a full-blown panic attack. And I knew why: I was caught—and I had the feeling that Larry might not be keen on playing along.

Moot point in any case. Larry was no longer looking at me—he was looking past me, and I think I saw his mouth tighten just a bit, and then he looked at me again—

And he winked.

"So!" he boomed out. "You must be PHIL!"

Oh, Gawd.

I felt him catch my elbow and turn me around so as to make us a proper threesome. "Paige said you might turn up."

Gil glanced at me but his expression was unreadable. Or maybe I didn't dare try to read it. "Gil," he said. "And you are . . ."

"Larry Crawford." Larry stuck out his right hand and put his left arm around my shoulder to give me a quick boyfrienderly squeeze. "You just get into town?"

"Larry," I said, "maybe we should—"

I was shrugging my shoulder slightly in the hopes that Larry's arm might fall off but he didn't let go.

"I see," Gil said.

He turned his body sideways to get past me in the doorway and I could smell him. And yes. He smelled like Gil.

Gil.

I nearly lost it.

What the hell was I doing? What the hell was I thinking?

"Gil, I—"

He glanced at me again. "Sorry to interrupt."

Dammit! He was leaving? Walking down the front walk now, and I saw an old beater parked there, some old blue four-door thing and was that an oversized mermaid ornament perched on the hood?

I should have handled it differently, I should have played it cool no matter what. Don't chase the guy, don't chase the guy, act cool, let him come to you . . .

But I wasn't properly prepared. I wasn't in control. On the contrary, I felt frantic. I think I actually may have said something like "Gil, where are you going?"

He said something in return but I couldn't make it out and then he was in his car.

I watched stupidly as it pulled away.

Larry touched my shoulder. "All right, Paige! You did great!"

I stared at him. "What?"

"You did great!"

"What . . . are you talking about?"

"You want to make him jealous, right?"

"No!" I said. "I mean—I don't know. But I didn't expect— Larry, what are you trying to do, here?"

"Babe, you don't know the half of it." He gave me his most charming smile and pulled the door closed. "Now how about you introduce me to this dog of yours."

I opened my mouth, then closed it again. It was starting to sink in that I was, quite possibly, about to be righteously pissed off. "You just *deliberately* chased him away."

"Aw, c'mon—you don't believe I'd do that."

Argh! "Larry. This is my thing, okay? You need to let me—"

"So what's her name, did you say?" he interrupted me and stepped over to where Gil had been standing by the broom closet.

I could hear the thump of Lady's tail against the wall.

"Larry!" I said, following him. "Are you even listening?"

Larry turned and arched an eyebrow. "Let me tell you a little story."

I glared at him.

"Guy I know, married to this absolute hottie. I mean, she's so hot, you could serve cheese fondue from her cleavage."

"That's not funny."

"It's very funny. Anyway, he's an attorney, so we run into each other socially from time to time, and this woman has never bothered to hide the fact that she'd love a roll with me."

"You're quite sure that's not all in your imagination?"

He laughed. "Nope, and I have the lipstick on my collar to prove it, my dear. So meanwhile, she's got this friend, nothing special to look at, who seemed like maybe, just maybe, she was also interested in my stuff, but I could never tell for sure."

I rolled my eyes.

"Listen up, Paige, this is the important part. Guess which one I went after?"

"Knowing your standards, Larry, I'd say probably the closest one."

"Nope," he said triumphantly. "In fact, I peeled Ms. Hottie off me one night just to chase her friend around a buffet table."

I stood up. "Larry, if you think it's helping me now to picture you nailing some married woman on a buffet table—"

"Paige! Show some respect! I didn't nail her on the buffet table, I held her plate for her and filled it with tidbits!"

"Oh, you nailed her later."

"Well, maybe so, but the point is—"

"And you never, ever, nailed Ms. Hottie?"

"Paige! Are you deliberately missing the point?"

"Oh, I know what the point is, Larry."

"The point is that I wanted the other one more. I wanted the one who—the one who seemed to change her mind about me."

"I get that, Larry," I said. "Why d'ya think I wanted him to think there could be someone else? Only—"

"Exactly. So why are you so upset? Things are going just like you planned."

I felt my shoulders drop. What could I do? "I didn't expect—this," I said. "You guys going head-to-head. You chasing him off—"

The stress of it all suddenly washed over me and I felt like I might start to cry.

Larry put his arm around my shoulder. "Aw, Paige," he said. "It's not like that—not at all."

"I shouldn't have done this," I said. "I should have—" I tried to stop myself from continuing, but it popped out anyway. "I love him, Larry."

"Sure you do, Paige. Don't cry. It'll work out. Trust me. C'mon, let's go get something to eat, okay?"

I pulled away and passed my shirt sleeve over my eyes to wipe my tears. "I don't even know where he's staying."

Larry arched an eyebrow.

"Larry," I said. "He and I were . . . practically engaged. When he is in town—"

"Ah." He nodded. "Su casa is his casa."

More tears.

"Hey." He took me in his arms for real now, stroking my hair. "Hey."

I glanced at his face. He looked upset now, too.

"Do you really think this will . . . do you think he will . . ."

"Paige, you're smart, you're interesting, you're attractive—"

I forced something out that approximated banter. "Ha. You don't have to lay it on that thick, Larry."

"And he found you just the way you wanted to be found. Besieged by a handsome, successful attorney."

I wiped my eyes again. "Right. At least your opinion of yourself isn't *too* high."

"Hey, I'm confident," Larry said. "It's part of my charm. Women love confident men. So how about it, what are you hungry for? Name your cuisine."

My sleeve was now smudged with mascara. So much for the eye makeup.

I shook my head. "No," I said. "No dinner. I couldn't eat anything now."

"You have to eat! Come on."

I felt another sudden flash of anger. "Enough, Larry," I said. "Please just leave."

And must be, this time, he knew that I really meant it, because he stopped pressing me. "All right. Just, whatever you do, sit tight. Don't run after him."

Argh.

As if I needed to be told.

I waited until his SUV was gone, then snapped the leash onto

Lady's collar and took her for a walk, and then when we got back I knelt by the entrance to the closet and petted her for a minute.

Dogs are such predictable animals! Even the ones we call unpredictable really aren't—you just need to figure out their triggers. What they want, what they don't want . . .

Figure that out, and you'll always have a pretty good idea of what they'll do.

And men . . . the thing is, they're predictable, too. But you have to get it right.

"I've got Gil pretty figured out, Lady," I said, and her tail thumped the floor. "But man. Did I screw it up with Larry."

18

We'd had a dog.

Me and Gil, I mean.

Trixie.

She was a stray.

I found her running alongside Route 13.

It was a year after Gil had enrolled at Ithaca.

We were A Couple by then. "Gil-n-Paige."

Rolled right off the tongue.

It didn't happen overnight. And especially at first, I had to get used to him. He wasn't the kind of guy who kept with the pack. We'd be hanging around with a group of his art buddies and they'd all decide to go to some club or party or a place like Castaways for the music. You'd think Gil was planning to go along, but if you weren't watching he'd suddenly vanish and you'd find out later that he'd gone somewhere else instead. Without saying anything to anybody. Maybe back to his apartment or for a walk or he'd end up at Chappy's drinking beer with some professor.

I had to condition myself to accept that—to accept that he might disappear, but if he did it was nothing to get upset about. It's just how he was.

And no question, we had chemistry. Three or four nights a week we'd end up at his place, and when everyone else was gone he and I would go to bed together, and the next morning I'd help clean up or we'd make breakfast together.

It was perfect.

And after a while everyone in our circle thought of us as attached.

I knew better than to make a big deal out of it. We were meant to be together—no question about that—all I had to do was keep my cool. Keep it super low-key.

Keep his interest—as long as I kept his interest, I kept the guy.

Things went on that way for a year or so. My grades had slid from As to Bs but I was still thinking vet school, only now I was also thinking marriage. I know, not very feminist of me. But my plan was to do both. Have it all.

And also, wasn't it time we got a place together?

Of course it was.

Only I had no idea how to pull it off.

Meanwhile my roommates were gradually driving me nuts. One thought everyone should act like her personal therapist. Yech. The other started dating a divorcé who turned out to be a bit of a perv. Double yech. Then I heard about this place that was supposedly going to be freed up starting June—the guy renting it was going to Europe. A little one-bedroom. More expensive than sharing an apartment but my dad said he'd do it if it would help me focus on my studies.

I thought, okay, I'll take the place, then figure out how to get Gil to move into it, too.

I gave my notice to my roommates.

They arranged for another student to have my room.

Then the guy with the studio changed his mind about moving out.

I was about to be homeless.

I couldn't believe my luck.

"I need a favor," I said to Gil.

I'd picked my timing carefully. We were in bed, his arm was looped under my neck and he was all post-sex relaxed and starting to doze off.

"I need a place to stay."

And he said sure, I could move in with him, no problem.

We were totally compatible. We were hot for each other. We were splitting expenses.

It was perfect.

I'd bagged the guy everyone said would never commit.

And Trixie—to this day I don't know how she didn't get hit.

My first glimpse of her was when she darted across all four lanes. I pulled over and put on my four-ways and waved my arms screaming at the cars to just stop. Just stop. Finally a few did and that meant other cars approaching had to stop, too.

I wasn't as experienced with dogs then but as luck would have it there was a piece of rope tied to her collar and I was able to get close enough to her to step on it.

She was a Shepherd mix, brown, with a grizzled muzzle.

An old gal.

Our dog.

19

Char opened her apartment door and took one look at me and grabbed me by the arm.

"Paige! What happened?"

I stepped inside. "It's Gil," I said. "He showed up at my place—"

"So why—"

"Larry dropped in, too. At the same time."

She stared. "Oh dear. Then what happened?"

"I don't really want to talk about it," I said, avoiding her look.

I knew she wanted to press me to talk. But she's not stupid—she knew better than to try to force it. "I'm so glad you're here," she said instead. "I have something I wanted to show you. Have you eaten?"

I noticed then how her apartment smelled—curry—but I shook my head, shrugged out of my jacket and sat on her couch. "Not hungry."

"Wait here."

She went into the kitchen and came back with a spiral notebook.

She was wearing a sari, which flapped the air behind her like a butterfly wing as she walked.

"See?" She opened the notebook and handed it to me. "I'll set this up somewhere downtown and give readings to people."

I looked at the drawing. It was a kind of booth. Very much like the one with the automaton fortune teller in the movie *Big*. "What color will it be?" I said.

"Mauve."

"Not too dark." I was picking my words carefully—still trying to be supportive. "You don't want to scare people."

"Oh, I'll keep the curtains pulled back."

That would help, I thought. "Where are you going to set it up?"

"Oh, downtown somewhere."

I considered asking her whether she would need a permit, but I changed my mind. "It looks . . . large. How are you going to move it?"

"Oh. It will be easy to break down. You know. Hinges on the corners, that sort of thing."

"You'll be able to fit it in your car?"

"Well," she said. "Stash said he'd help me move it once it's built and everything." Stash, a friend of Char's, is a heating, air conditioning, and ventilation technician, so he drives a pretty big pickup. "But could you help me pick up the plywood from Home Depot? I'm not sure exactly when yet—I need to pull together the money—and Stash might be able to do it, but sometimes he's hard to reach during the day. When he's on a job."

"Uh, Char. I don't know about that. My truck isn't really mine. It's the town's. It's not for personal use."

"How is work, by the way?" she asked. Changing the subject so she wouldn't get a "no."

"Same old," I said. "I've got this guy who's convinced his neighbor is trying to steal his cat."

"No kidding, really?"

"Only all she's really doing is feeding it. But he keeps calling me so I have to keep going out." And I told her how I'd been back just that afternoon, and how Maddy wouldn't answer the front door.. But while I was ringing the bell I heard the back door slam, and a moment later Fred came strolling around the corner of her house.

I'd carried him across the street and handed him to Skip, who told me he was Exceedingly Dissatisfied with how I was handling it.

He wanted action. Arrests. Jail time.

Char stood up, I guess to put her notebook away. She was still smiling, but then looked like she was going to say something.

"What?" I said.

"Sounds to me like those two are in love."

"What are you talking about? *Seriously?* Skip and Maddie? They despise each other!"

She laughed again. "You mean, you don't see it? What's really going on?"

"Old people in the suburbs are losing all their marbles?"

"Nope. He wishes it were him she was taking in and feeding and petting. It isn't about the cat at all. They're both just afraid to admit that they need each other."

I was a little worried about even trying to answer. It can be dangerous to encourage Charlene, even a little. But I decided to try. "Char," I said. "You don't understand. If these two are meant to be together, there's only one reason—to get straight to the divorce. Do not pass Go, do not collect your pre-nup."

Char just smiled. "Oh, you wait," she said. "It's simmering below the surface. One of these days—"

"Yeah, one of these days is right. Let's just hope ol' Wendt there doesn't have a pistol permit, or it won't be me who gets called to the neighborhood."

"Wow, you are stressed out, Paige. Hang on." And she disappeared into the other room again and this time returned with a coupon. Good for one free 15-minute massage at a New Agey spa where she sometimes does psychic readings for people.

"I don't want a massage."

"Take it," she said. "My friend Donna—you remember Donna, right? The coupon was her idea. It will help you get centered."

"Of course I remember Donna. But I don't want—"

"Take it."

I took the coupon and she smiled and then I followed her into the kitchen. She handed me a plate and took the lid off a pot of basmati rice. I spooned some rice onto my plate and then she handed me another spoon and took the lid off the second pot. The sweet spiciness that wafted across my face should have smelled delicious—when had I last eaten? Breakfast?

"Well," said Char. "As far as Gil goes—you wanted him to think he might lose you. So I guess he does, now, right?"

"Yeah." I spooned the orangey saucy stuff—with what looked

to be squares of cheese or tofu or something in it—onto my rice. "So?"

I handed her the spoon. "He walked away, Char. Without telling me where he's staying or—"

"Oh," she said. "Well, can you call him? Talk to him?"

I set my plate on the table and sat down. "What would I say? 'Hey Gil, ya know that guy you saw at my place? I'm not dating him—it's really just a setup to make you jealous."

Char sighed. "You want a glass of wine?"

"Oh, please yes!"

She opened her fridge and took out a bottle. "Well. You've got yourself into a little pickle of corner."

She poured some white wine into a couple of glasses. "I could read the cards for you," she said as she took her seat across from me.

She meant Tarot cards. To tell my fortune.

I sighed. "Char, I love you, really, and I think it's great that you've got psychic powers and all, but you know me. You know I don't believe in that stuff."

"Aw, Paige, don't cry." She got up, fetched a box of tissues from the counter, and set it next to me. "He's got your number. He'll call . . ."

20

I don't make a ton of money in my job. And nobody would have blamed me for feeding Lady cheap dog chow. But that was obviously what she'd been eating, and her coat showed it, so the next day I decided that as long as she was under my roof we'd do a little better.

There's a pet food shop in the South Wedge that specializes in the high quality stuff.

So as I was finishing my afternoon rounds I decided to swing up Clinton Ave. and invest in some decent kibble.

Then, on the way back down Clinton, it happened.

There are probably thousands of pit bulls in Rochester. Hundreds of them are brindles.

But I knew him instantly.

I hit my brakes and pulled over to the curb and switched on my four-ways.

I jumped out of my car.

He was on a leash that had been looped around a street sign post outside one of those neighborhood grocery stores that you see all over in the city.

His collar was new, black leather with pointy silver-colored rivets.

I didn't touch him, just spoke quietly, "good boy, what a good boy. I'm the one who gave you the salmon, remember?"

And he recognized me. He flattened his ears and grinned when I spoke to him and his tail moved.

His shoulder had a fresh cut. Bits of dried blood stuck to the fur around it. And his right ear had been torn again.

A Hispanic kid came out of the store now, stuffing a pack of cigarettes into his jacket pocket. Well, I say "kid." He could have been in his early 20s, but his scraggly facial hair made him look more like a teenager. His face didn't change when he saw me but I noticed his eyes flick to my truck and back.

"Afternoon," I said to him.

I didn't smile.

He didn't answer.

He took the dog's collar, unhooked the leash from it, and started unlooping the leash from the bike rack.

"This your dog?"

He grunted.

"You know it's illegal to use dogs for fighting."

His voice was surly. "I dunno what you talkin' bout."

"You heard me."

He shrugged. I'm small, white, alone, and a woman. Of course he wasn't going to take me seriously.

"I could have you arrested right now," I told him.

A lie, pretty much, but it's all I had.

He finished fumbling with the leash. "I don't fight my dog."

"How'd he get all cut up, then?"

"Neighbor's dog jumped the fence."

I'd heard that one before.

But before I could say so, aloud, two other guys emerged from the store. Older guys, mid- to late-40s.

Both looking at me.

"Problem?" one of them said. He was about 5'9" and stocky, and close enough to me that, in the moist April air, I could smell the malt on his breath. His buddy was a shade taller and wiry, and carried a 12-pack of Miller.

I made a split-second and probably not-too-smart decision to press my luck.

"This dog's been fighting," I said.

"Prove it," the young one muttered. He was now standing about three paces away, holding the dog's leash. The stocky guy had his chest puffed out, ready to stand me down, but it was his buddy who really worried me. His eyes were pretty hard.

I tried to make my eyes hard, too. "One of you the owner?"

"Nah." Stocky Guy was talking. "The dog is my sister's dog."

"Do you have an ID on you?"

Stocky Guy shifted his weight from one foot to the other. "Not me. Just stepped out to the store."

I looked at Wiry Guy.

He didn't say a word. He didn't need to.

I hated to back down. But it was one thing to detain the kid until the RPD showed up. These other two—they wouldn't be so easy.

And the young guy was now about six paces away. Leading the dog away.

No question. If I called this in, they'd be long gone by the time I got a cop there.

"The dog's been in a fight," I said. "And so you know, I'm an Animal Control Officer with the town of Brighton, and I'm going to report this, and my buddies in the city are going to be keeping an eye out for you guys."

A lie. And they knew it. The wiry guy's eyes switched from hard to sneering. And Stocky Guy had already started walking away to join the kid.

I got into my truck and watched their backs in my side mirror.

And you know what, I felt like total crap. For the dog. And for the other dogs.

Because, you know, it takes more than one to fight.

I sighed and checked my other mirror for traffic.

Just what I needed. To spend the rest of the evening all miserable, again, about a dog I wasn't meant to save . . .

I was just about to pull out from the curb when my cell phone rang.

It was a local number.

I didn't recognize it.

But I knew that when I answered, it would be Gil the other end of the line.

21

Of course, it would have been better if I'd had a chance to prepare. Instead, all I could do was react to his voice, and I suppose more than anything I sounded like a teenager again.

"Gil!" I said, wrestling myself under control. "What's—where are you calling from?"

"Work," he said.

"Work?" But he was calling from a local number. Which meant . . . "I didn't realize—"

"Yeah. Men's department, Lord and Taylor."

My brain almost couldn't take it in. A retail job? Gil? "Well," I fumbled as best I could, "as long as it leaves you time for your art."

He grunted. "I'm on a bit of a hiatus, actually."

"A hiatus?"

"I'm taking a little break."

From his *art?* Okay. This was now beyond weird.

But before I had a chance to consider how to respond to that bombshell he hit me with another one. "I have a question for you, Paige."

I guessed immediately what it was. Or anyway what it was about.

Larry.

"It's not what you think," I heard myself say, and then wanted to kick myself. Sounded like a frigging line from a frigging sitcom. But what could I do? "I'm not dating him. I mean, he wants to date me but believe me, he's only a friend."

"Ah. Yeah. I noticed how he was acting around you. Exactly

like a friend."

Ouch.

But the only way through situations like this is straight ahead.

I kept talking.

"He—" I searched my mind for—I admit it—a plausible lie. "We met through work, okay? And he knows I was upset about things and he was trying to be supportive, is all. He was out of line, though, the other night."

There. It wasn't even really a lie. A half-lie, maybe.

"Whatever, Paige."

"He doesn't mean anything to me," I said.

"It's okay. You were tired of waiting, you were ready to move on. You don't need to lie about it."

I felt sick. "It's not like that."

He didn't answer, and the silence between us seemed to drag us both toward something neither of us wanted. At least, I didn't want it.

"Gil?" I said—anything to get him to talk, again.

"Yeah Paige. Well, the reason I called, big surprise, was not to discuss your . . . friend."

OMG are you kidding me you mean to say I . . .

"That dog of yours—what are you going to do with the puppies. You got homes for them?"

PUPPIES? He was calling about—

I somehow kept from choking. "No!" I said. "No, I don't have homes for them—as a matter of fact—"

"My boss' daughter wants a dog."

I wet my lips so the words might have a halfway decent chance of sounding natural. "Right. And sure, yeah, I'll definitely be looking for homes for—of course, they'll have to be good homes—"

"I mentioned to him that I knew someone who might have puppies."

"That's great, Gil," I said. "That is . . . so cool of you." I forced a stupid little laugh. "You, uh, get the prize. First puppy placed."

He grunted again.

He's gonna hang up he's gonna hang up.

But he didn't.

"You gonna be around later?" he said.

"Yes—yes!"

"Alone, I hope."

To my discomfort, I felt a little flare of anger at that. But I suppose ultimately it was anger at myself. For putting myself in this position. "Yes," I said quietly. "Alone."

A moment later, I set my phone on the passenger seat.

My hands were shaking so hard that the truck's steering wheel vibrated as I pulled out from the curb.

Talk about a close call. To assume he was calling in order to discuss Larry! Of course he wasn't. He was a guy. He'd never do that—pick up the phone to ask me some girly style question. *Hey, ya know that guy who was at your house, d'ya like him more than me?*

Horrible mistake, Paige.

Horrible.

Calm down.

Yes, calm down. Because okay, I'd screwed up. But he was coming over—he was coming over!

I turned onto my street. Pulled into my drive. Checked my mail and opened the front door.

And stared at Lady.

She was acting funny.

She was pacing.

Oh Gawd!

I took my cell out of my pocket and dialed Sandra.

"I think Lady's about to have those puppies."

And then I hung up and thought well, crap. So much for my night with Gil . . .

22

Newborn puppies don't really look like puppies. They look more like . . . furry little sausages.

I'd been in touch with Sandra by phone on and off since I'd gotten home the evening before..

Now I crouched next to her in front of the closet while she gave her post-partum exam. It was all pretty routine. She checked Lady's gums to confirm that they were pink—whitish gums are an indicator of shock—and palpated her gut to make sure she'd delivered all of them.

She had.

Nine puppies.

"Everything looks just peachy," Sandra said, standing back up.

It was the first time I'd ever seen Lady interested in something else besides being petted. She was nuzzling and licking the pups intently, moving her muzzle from one to the other as if she was counting and recounting them.

"So I just watch for the normal stuff," I said. "Eating and drinking, that sort of thing."

"That's the idea."

She left, and not two minutes later Char buzzed the doorbell. I ran over and threw the door open. "There you are!"

She just grinned at me. "How many?"

"Nine!" I said and she followed me to the closet where we stood together, looking down.

"Dontcha want one?" Char said mistily after a minute.

"I've got NINE, Char," I reminded her.

"Mmmmm. I mean a baby. I can't wait to be a mom."

I suppose I was feeling a bit sentimental myself. "You'll be a great mom, Char," I told her, and she sighed happily and knelt down to stroke Lady, whose tail thumped the closet wall. "How about some tea?"

"Sure."

The kettle was whistling when she came into the kitchen.

"Mint okay?" I asked.

She nodded and I dropped tea bags in our mugs, and the bright smell of the mint hit my nose as the steam wafted up from the mugs.

"So what's next?" Char said.

I held my mug up next to my face, breathing the minty scent, and then sighed. "Now," I said, "I have to find homes for nine puppies. I mean, eight. Want one?"

Kidding. I knew she couldn't have a dog in her apartment.

"My friend Candace might take one, actually."

"Really?" I blew on my tea, watching it ripple toward the far side of the mug, and took a cautious sip. "I should invite her over."

"You should invite a bunch of people over."

"A puppy party."

We looked at each other. I'm not the sort of person who likes throwing parties. But I was thinking about Gil.

"What did you mean just then, you need homes for only eight? Are you keeping one?" She grinned at me.

"Nope. It's Gil. Apparently he knows someone who might be interested."

She laughed. "Even after last night?"

I smiled wryly. Gil had come over, of course. But I was so distracted and worried about Lady. And he had to get up early the next morning—he'd only stayed about an hour.

Every time I turned around, lately, dogs were interfering with my dates. Only last night the date was one I'd wanted. On the other hand, it wasn't necessarily a bad thing that he'd left my place wanting more than he'd gotten.

It meant he'd be back.

"By the way," I said. "Get this—he's taken a job. A real one. Department store, men's clothing."

Char's eyebrows shot up. "Are you joking?"

"Nope." I shook my head. "Not joking."

"Is he—"

"Thinking of settling down?" I grinned. "Kinda looks like it, dontcha think?"

She gazed back at the puppies again. "See, Paige? It's all working out.

"Yeah," I agreed—and I felt so good, in fact, that I did something a bit out of character. I asked her to use her psychic powers to help with the party planning. "So, uh," I said. "Help me figure out who to invite so we can, uh, balance the energies and all that."

It was all the encouragement she needed. "Well," she said. "First we figure out how many to invite. Too few and the energies will be diluted, too many and their energies won't harmonize."

She closed her eyes.

I waited.

She opened them. "Ten to twelve should be about right," she said.

"Lemme get a paper and pencil."

I came back and started writing down names. Me, Char, Gil, Candace, and Candace's boyfriend, Zach.

"I'll bring Stash," Char said.

I sighed. I like Stash okay, although I'm not particularly big on body art, myself. His nickname refers to a tattoo of a handlebar moustache that adds, er, a "touch of whimsy" to his belly just below the beltline. Yeah, I've seen it. Stash likes to show it off. In fact, I've seen it often enough that I'm always ready now—I'm the one yelling "OK, Stash, that's far ENOUGH!" if he seems to be forgetting the brakes as he's lowering his pants.

"Who else?" Char was saying. "How about Doug?"

I pictured drifts of granola bar crumbs on my couch. "Nah. With all those kids, if he's going out on a Saturday night, it had better be somewhere nice, with his wife."

"Absolutely. So, there's Donna."

The gal that works at the massage place where Char does readings. Not my favorite person to hang out with. Oh, she's nice enough, but kind of . . . flamboyant. She likes to call attention to herself. My total opposite, in other words. But in a party situation, where she can float a bit, she's fine.

"Sure. Donna," I say. "That makes seven."

"We'll have her bring a date," Char agreed. "That's eight."

"How about Aunt Judy and a date?"

Char gets along with her mother like they're sisters. "Okay," she said. And then, "I'll make the invitations. I'll need a snip of Lady's hair."

I didn't ask why. I assumed it was for some graphical effect for the invites, not a spell, but who knows?

"So what's a good day?" Char said.

I thought it over. "It has to be at least two weeks away—so that the puppies' eyes will be open."

I looked at the calendar on my phone, then thought of something else. "Suppose we picked a day, and it's bad for Gil?"

Char was rooting around in my junk drawer. "Call him and ask what night works," she said. "Where are your scissors?"

"They should be in there somewhere." I picked up my phone. One ring . . . two rings . . . three rings . . .

And then it was him. His voice on the other end of the line—"Hiya, Gil," I said. "It's Paige."

"Hey."

I kept my tone light, girlish, happy. "You'd never believe it—Char and I had this great idea—we're going to have a puppy party . . ."

I found Char again a minute later. "We're all set. Second Friday in April."

I watched her drop a snippet of Lady's hair and drop it into a junk mail envelope from my recycle box. Then she shook her head and said, almost like she was talking to herself. "He took a job. How odd."

She looked at me. "Almost like how you decided you weren't going to become a vet."

23

When I first began having doubts about my career plans, I kept it to myself.

I was worried people might blame it on Gil. I was so obviously besotted by him. And my grades had slipped another notch, I was getting B minuses now instead of B plusses. So maybe I was a bit distracted.

I finally broke down and mentioned my grades to Char over spring break, and sure enough, she thought it was my love life. She said, "Paige! You're a romantic after all."

But she was wrong. The exact opposite was happening, in fact.

Some things about being a vet were starting to sink in, and it was bothering me.

Nature was bothering me.

You'd think I would have figured this out sooner. I'd been around veterinary practices since I was 16. But the work I did as a teenager was all back in the kennels. I led dogs to the outdoor kennels so I could clean their crates, and then led them back and fed them. I scooped poop and scrubbed the kennel floors and hosed it off. I emptied litter boxes and replenished supplies.

But then I got a job with a different animal hospital, one near Ithaca—not easy to do, there were tons of applicants—and because I planned to become a vet they gave me more responsibilities. Checking stool samples for worm eggs, holding animals while they administered injections or medications. And during office hours I joined the vet and the techs in the exam rooms, to give them an extra pair of hands.

Then one Saturday afternoon this lady brought in an old

Beagle. He was a standard Beagle, black and tan—and old. His face was completely white, and he was fat—he waddled—and he moved really slow, arthritis probably, and he had a fatty tumor—a lipoma—on his back.

But what was really weird is that for a second I thought he was another Beagle—a Beagle I'd seen before, at my last job.

Snoops.

Snoops had been a regular patient my first summer working, so I'd gotten to know him pretty well. He was in once to have some rotten teeth pulled and in another time when he had a bout of diarrhea and since he was so old they kept him overnight to keep an eye on him and give him IV to make sure he wasn't getting dehydrated.

And then here all of a sudden was a Snoops lookalike.

Even the tumor looked the same.

Only of course it had to be a different dog.

Snoops was dead.

And then I thought, my God. Being a vet, that's what it comes down to—trying to fend off death. And you can never win.

Nature wins.

Nature wins.

I left work and went back to my apartment. Gil was off somewhere, I didn't know where. And wow, I felt low—lower than I can ever remember feeling. Nature had always seemed like a sort of resting place, a place where things were simpler and easier and calming—now suddenly I knew that wasn't true.

Nature is relentless.

So whereas before it seemed interesting and fun to know that humans are animals, too—that human behavior can be deciphered the same way a dog's behavior can be deciphered—suddenly it didn't seem like so much fun. It seemed like a sentence.

And there was no getting out of it.

We all hold a losing hand.

And gradually, gradually I started to see that to be a vet I'd need to pretend that I didn't know that. I'd have to pretend we can beat Nature. I'd have to lie.

The vet I was working for at the time was a brilliant man. Freakishly intelligent, broad, high forehead, garrulous, paunchy, the most upbeat man you've ever met—except when he lost his temper, which he did from time to time, without warning. So I was always a little nervous around him—I thought, he's a perfectionist, he loses his temper when people screw up. I was nervous I'd screw up and make him angry. But then I realized it wasn't that he was a perfectionist, exactly—it's that all these people bringing their pets in to him thought he could beat Nature, and he couldn't. It was an illusion. He wanted to be their savior. He wanted to cut in the right place, or prescribe the right medicine, or give the right advice and voila, your pet will never die. And many times—eight times out of ten, nine times out of ten—the pet wouldn't die, the procedure or advice he gave would save the pet's life. But it was only a temporary reprieve. And then would come the pet who couldn't be saved, and the doc would know it. He'd know that he was powerless. And it ate at him. And so from time to time he'd blow up—you can't blame him, he was in an impossible position.

And I didn't want to be like him when I grew up.

Oh, I admired him! He was brilliant. People came from everywhere—from New York City, which is like a six-hour drive—that's how good he was, the reputation he had. He was brilliant, he did brilliant things for peoples' pets. He kept up on the latest science, I saw the piles of journals and books he'd take home with him after calling hours, a man who'd been practicing for twenty years and he was still studying, learning.

And failing—still failing.

Not his fault. Not his fault. Nature always wins.

Sure, Gil was a factor—but it wasn't because he was pulling me away from my career path but because I'd known for so long that I was going to be a vet, and now—now that was gone.

What I was going to be?

A wife?

The thought popped into my head, of course, and of course I recoiled from it. That's not what women do! Not smart women. Not women with ambition. Not women who plan to be self-realized adults in charge of their destinies.

Ugh.

I needed to buy some time to think it over. But I also needed to adjust course a bit. So I floated things to Gil, finally, only casually, obliquely.

"I've been thinking about after graduation," I said. "I've been thinking instead of going straight to vet school, I'll take a year or two and work."

I watched him from the corner of my eye. He was eating chicken wings. I could smell the sauce and the blue cheese he was dipping the wings in as he ate them.

He didn't stop eating.

"I'll get a job, of course," I said when he didn't answer. "That way, if you want do focus on your art you can. Without, you know. Worrying about how we'll eat or something."

He stopped chewing then, and looked at me, then shrugged and swallowed and picked up another wing.

And I reached over and took a wing myself. Because with things like that, and a guy like Gil, what you want is no reaction.

Which exactly is what I'd gotten.

24

I once mentioned to Char, quite a bit later, the whole thing about how Nature wins. She'd gotten the Tarot deck by then and had read her own fortune and was talking about Soul Mates. And it bothered me a bit so I told her I didn't believe in Soul Mates, I believed in Nature, and that Nature always wins.

It stopped her dead—the tone of my voice, probably. And I told her about Snoops I and Snoops II and that I wasn't going to be a vet because I wouldn't be able to stand it, not being able to save them. And she said maybe it was that I was grieving, still, about losing Trixie—she'd died suddenly, only a few months after I found her. Her heart, probably. Like I said, she was an old dog.

But Char's words didn't help. They actually proved my point.

25

With the puppies now a reality—a squirming pile of furry black sausages in my kitchen closet—I had switched into high gear. Because puppies grow fast. Right now Lady was taking care of everything, from feeding to cleaning—but pretty soon those responsibilities would fall to me.

I needed collars and a food dish . . . and it would be nice to have an indoor pen.

Without having to buy one.

So I tried Vicki, a local dog rescue volunteer, and asked if she had one I could borrow. Turns out she did (yay) and even offered to deliver it.

How could she resist if it meant she could see a bunch of newborn pups?

"I'll bring some newspapers, too," she said, and laughed. "You're gonna need them."

"Thanks."

"Lady's a very lucky dog," she added before she hung up.

And I thought, yeah, Lady's lucky. But that pit bull . . .

I glanced at the clock.

I had forty five minutes—then I had to be in the city to testify in court.

It was a bit of an oddball case. Some guy got the bright idea that he'd hatch out some chicken eggs—you can get hatching eggs for two bucks or so apiece, if you want to raise a legit flock of chickens, although I suspect he was getting them for less than that—dye the chicks pink and blue, and sell them right before Easter. It was a dumb idea for a lot of reasons, including the fact that it's illegal in New York State to dye chicks, no exemptions for using Kool-Aid, dude. Plus you can't possess farm animals in a residential neighborhood in Brighton. Not even if you have a business license, which he didn't. Plus the age-old point that nothing good can come from someone buying a baby chick as a pet, since it's going to grow into a chicken, and what kid really wants a full grown chicken in their room? It's not like having a hamster. They're messy. Plus, they peck.

It was the "bad pet idea" bit that got him caught. He set out a box of pink chicks at a weekly farmer's market in the next town over. Note to any budding capitalists who think they'll make some quick cash exploiting cute little animals: don't set up shop where the density of animal rights activists is bound to be about six times over the average. Farmer's market = ex-hippy baby boomers = people with a nose for injustice and the resources to do something about it. Within a half hour, his entire stock had been bought up by an impromptu alliance of market-goers who'd collectively decided to rescue first, ask questions later.

Then one of the gals at the market followed the guy him home in her car. How did she manage that, you ask? Simple. He'd invited her. She'd pretended that she wanted to get into the business with him, so he took her to see his set-up. Clever gal. So by the next morning, she was sitting across from me in a conference room at the town offices, dropping digital prints of pink chicks, and photocopied notes, and an ASPCA handout on chicks as Easter gifts onto my desk, telling me I needed to put a stop to him. And she didn't even know about the dyeing law yet.

It would have all been over within a few weeks, except as I said, guy's bit of an oddball, and decided to fight it. I didn't follow it all that closely, to tell you the truth, other than to respond to requests for affidavits a couple times. But now, a year later, it was finally before a judge.

It was a huge waste of my time, not to mention the judge's and the rest of the court staff. But I suppose with a 400 percent mark-up in the offing, the guy thought it might be worth it to get a judge to rule against the anti-dyeing law. Millions to be made, if only he could get permission to dunk chicks in artificially colored kid's drinks. Or should I say, if only he could convince a judge to stick out his political neck for nothing.

Of course he lost.

I found out later—I left after I'd finished my testimony. Then I walked out past the guards and metal detectors and down the steps into the glass pergola-style foyer between the courthouse and the parking garage, and someone called my name.

Larry, dressed in one of his beautiful imported suits.

He stepped from the elevator and strode toward me, brandishing his cell phone in one hand and his briefcase in the other like a modern day knight's sword and shield.

"Hey, gorgeous!" He kissed me on the forehead. "At long last!"

I sighed. "Not that long, Larry," I reminded him.

"Aw, you're not still upset about the other night!"

I set my teeth. "Yeah. About that—that arrangement we had— it's good we ran into each other, because things between Gil and I—they're fine again, now. I don't really need your help anymore."

"I see, Paige. Well, that's good news. Phil come crawling back to you?"

I frowned. "Not exactly, but—look Larry, I don't really want to talk about it. And his name is Gil."

"Right. Have you had lunch? I'm about to get a bite to eat."

I ignored the question. "We love each other, Larry." It sounded funny saying it aloud like that. "But anyway, thanks for trying to help me out—I had a good time hanging out with you and everything."

"Paige, are you okay?"

I looked away. "Of course I'm okay," I said, and then, quickly—before he could ask me about lunch again, "Oh, I don't think I told you—you know that pit bull you helped me catch the night of our fake date?"

My diversion tactic worked. "How could I forget?" he asked.

"Well first of all—somebody claimed him. From Lollypop."

"I thought you said they'd put him to sleep?"

"Apparently the guy had a plausible story," I said. "And good enough fake ID. Well get this—I saw the dog again. Tied up outside a store on Clinton Ave."

"No kidding."

"Talked to the owners. Hispanic guys."

"Nice guys? Friendly?"

"Yeah, very well-brought-up. They fight that dog, Larry."

"Yeah, that's what you said. So what happened?"

"Oh. Nothing. There's nothing I can do, really. Unless I intend to patrol the South Wedge on my own time, on Saturday nights, looking for the fight."

"I hope you don't mean that, Paige."

I frowned again. "And your objection would be—what?"

"You know what. You could end up getting in way over your head."

"I'm not stupid," I answered coolly. But I'd started to fidget a bit as I said it.

"No. But that sort of thing really isn't your area."

Oh, brother. "Larry, there's an innocent dog involved here. Actually, more than one innocent dog, if you count the ones he's been forced to fight."

"That doesn't mean you have to put yourself in danger."

I don't know why that got me so angry. Maybe because I knew in my heart that this discussion was completely theoretical. I didn't have a choice, because no matter how sorry I felt for that dog, there wasn't a damn thing I could do about it. "If I thought for one second it might get me somewhere, I'd spend every free minute cruising the South Wedge, thank you very much. But the fact is, I have nothing to go on. The guys weren't exactly cooperative. I didn't have grounds to just seize their dog. And unless they're into organized fights, it's not like there's much hope of catching them in the act."

"Well," he backtracked slightly. "You have to do what's right, of course. But you could run into problems if you got tangled up with—"

"Like I don't know that."

"Look, Paige, I didn't mean to make you mad."

I sighed. "I know you didn't. It's just hard, that's all. I hate not being able to do something to help that dog. And . . ."

I paused.

"And what, Paige?"

"Well, the thing is . . . I could have just kept him, that first night."

He nodded. "Yeah, you could have. But you know, Paige, it's not your job to save the entire world all on your own."

I sighed.

"Nobody can. And look what you're doing for that other one—hey, did she have her puppies?"

"Yeah. Nine of them."

"Hah. Well—how about lunch?"

"No—I have to go check on the pups and get back to work."

"Okay. If you're sure." His eyes held mine for a split second, and then he turned slightly and asked, "Where are you parked? This way?"

I nodded and we walked out to the garage together.

But just before we parted he turned to me again, and this time his voice was thoughtful. "Say, Paige. Question for you. If these guys are fighting that dog, you don't know where they're doing it, right?"

"No idea. I talked to Rochester Animal Services, but if they know of anything specific, they aren't sharing."

"So it could be anywhere. Anywhere."

"Larry," I said. "What are you thinking?"

"Well . . . nothing, really."

Yeah, right. I could tell he was going somewhere . . . and it had something to do with my pit bull. "Larry," I said. "Do you know something about any of this?"

"Nah. Just wondering how much cash a dog fight might bring in. You know, if someone got into it seriously, as an organizer."

I wasn't entirely sure he was telling the truth. But I played it straight. "Lots," I said. "Tens of thousands, maybe hundreds of thousands. Plus there's often a lot of other business being conducted along with. Drugs. Maybe guns."

"Interesting."

"I . . . yeah. Look, Larry, unless there's something else, I've got to go."

"Sure, babe. But Paige, any time you need my services again, you have my number."

I should have felt relieved, but wow. The day wasn't half over and I'd already been twisted in fifteen different directions. Which wasn't fair. I was putting things back on track with the man I loved. Things were going just like I'd planned. And instead of feeling happy about it I felt . . . weird.

I found my truck and wove it back out to the garage entrance—but then, instead of going back to Brighton I headed to Verona Street, where the Rochester Animal Services has their offices.

I had no rational reason to make the visit. Char, of course, likes to say we should follow our intuition, but frankly, I wouldn't know my intuition if I tripped over it. On the other hand, I knew what I wanted, and what I wanted was to go back in time and do something differently the night I picked up the dog. Since even Charlene's powers aren't sufficient, as far as I know, to turn back time, I settled for the futile gesture. At least it made me feel a little better. For a few minutes.

The RAS staff were sympathetic enough. They led me back through the rows of kennels where they house their unclaimed dogs.

There were a dozen pits or pit-looking dogs. American Pitbull Terriers or mixes.

My brindle wasn't one of them.

I gave them a description of him anyway, and told them about the three men I'd seen with him.

They said they'd keep their eyes open. Dog fighting, they said, goes on all the time. Mostly it's impromptu stuff—couple of dogs set on each other on a street corner or in someone's garage.

"Sorry we can't do more," they said.

So was I . . .

26

When I was a kid, I methodically read every novel in my middle school library that had anything to do with animals. Many of them, I read more than once. Some of them I learned later were classics, others I haven't thought or heard of in years, until tonight, when I Googled them. *The White Panther,* by Theodore Waldeck. All the John and Jean George books. A bunch of collie books by Albert Payson Terhune. Jack London's *Call of the Wild* and *White Fang.* All of Jim Kjelgaard's Irish setter novels. *Bambi,* of course, which depressed me, not because of the mother dying thing, but because as young as I was at the time it seemed so awful when Bambi, in the closing chapter of the book, chose survival over love. *Moby Dick,* which also puzzled me, as it seemed to have precious little to do with a whale. "This is an ANIMAL story?"

In fact, in retrospect, I didn't really "get" a lot of what I was reading at the time. I know now, for example, that at least some of them were more animal rights tracts than novels. *Black Beauty* isn't really about a horse, but about how people treat horses. And Terhune wasn't above some serious preaching in his books, like *Lad, A Dog,* and for that matter, neither was Jack London, in his way.

It wasn't only my naiveté as a reader that made me oblivious to this messaging, although that was part of it. But mostly it was because I was in complete agreement.

Of course, we should be kind to animals.

Isn't that a given?

Nowadays, of course, a lot of the practices that these novels decried are illegal. But not all of them, and even making them illegal doesn't always stop them. Which makes you wonder, sometimes, whether other people are living in a kind of ethical past—they haven't been through the *Black Beauty* stage yet.

Or maybe it's something even darker than that . . .

27

Char came over early to help me get ready for the puppy party. It seemed like a good idea at first. I'd decided to serve stuffed mushrooms and they take forever, all that chopping and stuffing and cleaning up the counter afterward. Plus she was still bugging me to help her pick up her plywood and stuff to make her psychic readings booth. So it was a fair trade, sort of. She helps me chop celery, I help her with one of her zany money-making schemes.

"We'll get your plywood during my lunch break, okay?" I told her as she peeled the paper off an onion.

Then she mentioned that she wanted to smudge the place. I asked her what was that and she said it's a Native American purification thing. I said that "smudge" didn't sound particularly pure-ish. And she said wasn't I going to go change my clothes?

So I sighed and left her to do her thing.

My third mistake, after the mushrooms and letting Char smudge, was my outfit. Jeans—that was a no brainer. High heel mules—round toes, the look is maybe dated, but I'm in my own apartment, I can get away with it. But when I came to the top, things got tricky. I needed just the right degree of sexiness. It's like salt and soup. Too sexy, and your guests will make funny faces they try to cover by being polite. Not sexy enough, and the soup just falls flat. All that work for nothing.

I pulled out about eighty different tops and tried on about forty of them—okay, so I'm exaggerating, but the point is, I couldn't make up my mind and before I knew it I heard the doorbell and I panicked and decided to go up the scale and wear a cashmere sweater. It wasn't a bad choice, I figured, because the neckline was cute and it was the right color: a pinky red. Call it wolf whistle cranberry.

I thought for a second about the ring on its chain but wouldn't that be awfully obvious . . .

No. No ring.

So I was finally dressed and coming down the stairs and what did I hit on the way down but a wall of smoke. I thought oh crap, something's burning, the mushrooms! But it didn't smell like mushrooms, exactly, and then I saw Char standing with a clump of something in her hand, she was waving it through the air, and as she waved it I could see one end glowing and smoking.

"Char!" I said.

"Almost done," she said. "Donna's here," and around the corner from the kitchen came Donna.

I forced my face into what I hoped was a gracious smile. "Hey, Donna. Where's Walter?"

"Oh, Paige!" She flourished her burgundy-tipped fingers at me. "Didn't Charlene tell you? I am soooooooooooo single right now! That Wallllter! What a loooooser! This is Marguerite!"

She flourished her burgundy-tipped fingers and another woman appeared behind her.

The woman's head came to about Donna's shoulder and looked nervous as a deer nosing out into a clearing on opening day of hunting season.

"Hi, Marguerite." I cast around for something small-talky to say that might put her at ease. "I hope you like puppies."

Donna held out a paper bag-covered bottle. "Kitchen?"

I nodded.

Don't get me wrong. I like Donna okay. She just . . . female in a way that I'm not. So is Char, really, but Donna . . . I watched her derrière waggle luxuriously toward the kitchen—how can anyone make jeans look like that? And the black and gold lamé sweater . . . my cashmere suddenly felt like an Old Navy sweatshirt.

A too-warm Old Navy Sweatshirt.

I sighed and followed lamé sweater into the kitchen, where Char was standing over the sink, dousing her smudging stuff in water—much to my relief—as I suppose even a Native American purification ritual is scant protection against a house fire.

"White or red?" I said to Donna.

A phone rang.

"Is that your cell?" said Char.

It did sound like my cell—where had I left it? I put the corkscrew down and pawed some unopened mail on my counter and there it was.

I picked up it up and frowned.

Larry.

What could he want?

But apparently I hadn't learned my lesson, yet, because instead of ignoring the call I took it. The fourth mistake of the evening.

"Paige," he said. "You home right now?"

Oh dear. "I'm kinda busy, Larry."

"I'll take that as a yes—see you in about two minutes."

What?

"Larry!" I said it kind of loud and Donna peaked around the corner from the kitchen. I turned my back to her and kind of hunched over my phone and lowered my voice. "Larry! Tonight is not—I have people coming over—"

"What people?"

"People!" I said. "I'm throwing a little party, and—"

"Perfect," said Larry. "I'll blend right in."

He must have known Gil was one of the "people." Of course he did . . . how could he be doing this? "Larry," I said for the third time. "I'm telling you—this is not a good time."

"Everything okay?" Donna asked.

She'd come up behind me without my noticing—I nearly jumped out of my skin. "Yes!" I answered, nodding, "Fine!" And I walked quickly away from her toward the other end of the living room. "Larry—"

"It's about your pit bull," he said.

Huh?

"My pit bull?"

"That's what I said."

"What about my pit bull?"

"I'll be there in two minutes," he said, and hung up.

I turned around and now Char was standing next to Donna. Both had question marks in their eyes. But before Char could say anything, Donna held up a bowl of chips. "Where should this go?"

I noticed again that I was a bit too warm. The cashmere.

"The living room, Donna," I said. "Anywhere's okay." Then, in a low voice to Char, "It's ah—nothing—Larry's stopping by."

"What?"

"He said he's got to tell me something about the pit bull," I said.

"Well," said Char. "This should be . . . interesting."

"He's a friend," I muttered. "He's coming as a friend."

And I no sooner said the words when I heard the door open. I kind of skittered around the corner.

Larry. Guy must have been calling from my driveway.

"Wow!" he said, raking me up and down with his eyes. "Paige, you look fantastic, what's the occasion?

"Quit it, Lar," I muttered. I was beginning to sweat, now, and I hadn't even had any wine yet.

He didn't seem to notice. He grinned and winked at me, then sniffed the air. "What you girls doing, smoking POT?"

I glared at him. "That's it, Larry. We've just smoked a joint. Too bad you missed it."

Donna had returned from distributing the bowls of chips. "Pot?" she said. "Please tell me you're joking!"

"I'm joking," I told her. "It's Char's smudgy thing."

"She was burning sweet grass." Marguerite's voice peeped up from somewhere within Donna's shadow. "It gets rid of evil spirits."

"You sure it's not for fleas?" Larry winked at me again. "Smells like it should kill fleas. And who might this be?"

Of course—he'd seen Donna. I repressed a sigh.

"Donna, Larry. Larry, Donna. Donna is a massage therapist—"

"Was," Donna breaks in. "I'm going back to school, now—RIT—I'm studying ar—"

"Massage therapist, huh?" Larry laughed. "Didya bring your table?"

Donna paused a split second and then giggled, "Oh you mean like in Seinfeld! I loved that show!"

I leaned quickly to Larry's ear and murmured, "Down, boy."

He winked at me and I rolled my eyes.

"So Larry," Donna was saying. "What do you do?"

That's it, Donna. Glom onto him. Let Gil see Larry for what he really is.

The door was still open and now through the screen I saw Stash coming up the walk, chatting with Aunt Judy and her boyfriend, and beyond them—Gil's car.

And the driver's side doorway was opening.

My heart hit my stomach like a rock. I barely had time to think—all I knew was that I didn't want to be standing there—next to Larry—when Gil walked in the door.

"Hey," I yipped happily, "this is a *puppy* party, you guys really need to be in here with the *puppies!*" and I grabbed Donna with one hand and Larry by the other and dragged them both toward the kitchen, poor Marguerite fleeing in front of us, practically bleating in fear.

"Char!" I called over my shoulder. "Could you please get the door, please?"

How could this be happening?

"They're in the closet," I said to Donna and pointed and she and Marguerite went over to take a peek, then "Larry, give me a hand with the wine, okay?" to get him over to the other side of the room.

I could feel him looking at me.

"What's the matter?"

"What'dya think?" I said.

I grabbed a bottle of Chardonnay, and Larry watched me stab the cork a couple of times with the corkscrew. I couldn't seem to get it in started in the right spot. Then he stepped over and took the bottle from me and said, "Slow down, babe. You *know* we have all night."

"Not funny," I muttered. "I'm boiling hot. I need to change into something cooler."

"Please don't," he purred. "Hot is good."

"Larry." I hissed, glaring at him. "I told you. Knock it off."

There was stomping in the foyer. That would be Gil. He always stomps when he enters a house, as if he's got snow on his feet, doesn't matter if it's 90 degrees outside. His mother must have harassed him about tracking. All that imaginary dirt.

I forced myself not to look in that direction.

What if he headed to the kitchen first?

Please, Char, read my thoughts—keep him in the living room!

Larry had extracted the cork from the wine bottle. Now he said, "Wine, ladies?" and carried two glasses over to where Donna and Marguerite were cooing at the puppies. Then he filled another two—he finished the pour with a little twist of his hand to keep the bottle from dripping—and handed one to me and gestured at me with the other to initiate a toast.

So much for thinking he might say what he came here to say and leave.

I opened my mouth to ask him about the pit bull but winked at me and said, "Let's have a look at the pups."

I gritted my teeth and trailed behind him, reminding myself that I was doing this for the pit bull, and what could I do except play along until I could get rid of the guy?

Lady looked up and thumped her tail on the floor, as beatific as ever in her sappy-eyed sort of way.

"So," I said in my oh-so-natural voice. "Have you ladies picked out which ones you'll be taking?"

Donna giggled but Marguerite didn't, and I realized she was actually considering it.

I wondered if she and Donna were roommates. I wouldn't trust Donna to look after a dog in a million years.

Then Aunt Judy—who looked like a stockier, brunette version of Char—came into kitchen, followed by Stash, who shouldered his way to the fridge, 12-pack of Budweiser hoisted overhead. Gil, on the other hand, was still . . . where? I leaned forward and snuck a glance around the corner and there he was, still standing in the foyer.

He wasn't looking toward me.

Did he sense I had peeked out at him?

Just go the other way, Gil . . . don't come into the kitchen . . .

Char, where are you?

I became aware that Marguerite was asking me questions. Something about "when was it best to take a puppy from the litter," and was it true about a fear period at twelve weeks. The questions were long and complicated and she was being very thoughtful, and I utterly failed to follow what she was saying.

"Hold that thought," I said finally, "I'd better go greet the rest of the guests."

Candace and Zach' had shown up, too—I could hear their voices—Gil had been pushed out of sight into the living room.

Something crossed my mind. This is what happens, when you have too little contact with someone, everything becomes epic. He was only around the corner. But it felt like—he may as well have been in Seattle again.

And I didn't want him out of my sight.

28

If I could have, I would have kept Larry trapped in the kitchen and Gil trapped in the living room for the duration of the party, and for a few crazy minutes I half-believed I might be able to pull it off.

But of course I couldn't. I thought Larry was caught in a conversation with Marguerite, and I snuck away to the living room—and there was Gil, standing over in the far corner with Zach and Stash. I gave a stupid wave and then behind me—good old Donna yelped "Larry!" and started laughing.

And of course Gil heard it, too, and he shot me a look and oh man, why had I chosen cashmere of all things? And what was Donna yelping about—and then in came Donna with Larry behind her and I had no choice but to do the introductions.

So Larry, of course, pushed by me toward Gil and said "Good to see you again."

Gil ignored Larry's hand.

Great. Just great.

By instinct I used my shoulder to separate them, stepping between with my back to Larry, blocking him out. "So how are you doing?" I said to Gil and to my relief from the corner of my eye I saw Larry fall away, return to Donna on the other side of the room.

That's it, go after Donna . . .

"What's that guy doing here?" said Gil, giving me a hard look.

"It's—it's for a work thing, actually," I said, but I knew damn well my explanation wasn't the least bit plausible—how could it be? This was a waking nightmare. "Can I get you something?

Wine? Beer?"

"Have a beer, man," said Stash and held out a can.

Gil took it from him.

"Who's the hottie?" said Stash, and I followed his glance. He was looking at Donna.

"That's Char's massage therapy friend," I said.

Stash was staring at her. She was leaning toward Larry, now, saying something directly into his ear.

I turned back toward Gil but he'd moved away, over to the couch, and was settling back into the couch now with his beer in one hand and a handful of chips in the other.

Well, so that was that.

And how could I blame him?

The oven timer buzzed in the kitchen.

I smiled a big false smile. "Mushrooms are ready!" I said and fled to check on them.

Char was bent over in front of the oven when I got there. She stood up and set the pan on top of the stove.

"How ya want to serve these?" she said.

I took a platter out of the cupboard. "This is a disaster," I moaned. "Char, I need a huge favor."

"What?"

"I need to talk to Larry, and I don't trust him to behave himself in there." I gestured toward the living room. "I'm worried he'll make it look like we're flirting."

"So you want me to get Larry in here, without Gil noticing."

"Yeah."

She began picking mushrooms up off the pan with her finger tips and dropping them quickly onto the platter.

"Not with your hands," I said, "hang on, here's a spatula."

"Gil's not stupid." She took the spatula. "Don't you think he'll wonder why you two are off together in the kitchen? But I suppose I could get him talking to Stash, first . . . that's enough to distract anybody."

"That could work," I said. "You do know you're the best cousin ever, Char?"

"And then I suppose I need to keep Gil busy until you two are done. This is probably bad for my karma, you know."

I nodded. "I know," I said. "Thank you, Char. I owe you. Big time."

"Right," she said and hoisted the platter of mushrooms and made for the other room.

29

It seemed like hours before Larry finally ambled back into the kitchen.

I was standing by the sink, scrubbing the bits of baked-on mushroom stuffing off the cookie sheet.

"Hey, babe, somebody said you wanted me?"

He emphasized the word "wanted" ever so slightly.

"Larry," I answered. "Now that you've managed to muck things up between Gil and me, *again*—"

"What did I do?" He widened his eyes. But it wasn't innocence in his face.

I scowled. "Don't play games with me."

"He'll be fine, my dear." He picked up another wine bottle someone had opened and refilled his glass. "You're empty-handed," he said. "What are you having?"

"Nothing."

"Aw, come on. Here." He'd found my glass where I'd left it on the counter, and refilled it and handed it to me. "Now. Where were we?"

"Let me see." I took the glass but didn't drink. "Oh, that's right. You crashed my party on the pretense that you had some earth-shattering information about that pit bull."

"Wow, you are PO'd at me, aren't you."

"Bingo."

"I'm here because I care for you, you know," he said.

"Right," I said. I glanced toward the door. I could hear talking from the other room. I couldn't make out any voice in particular—no way of telling if Char was successfully keeping Gil in one place. I looked back at Larry. "This had better be good, is all I can say."

"Oh, it's good."

He looked me in the eye and for some reason I felt a little chill tickle the back of my neck. Which was weird, considering a second ago I'd been melting in that stupid cashmere sweater.

"You said the dog was used to fight, right?"

I shivered and took a sip of my wine. "Yes. No question in my mind."

"So you know that one case I've got, the one about that High Falls property?"

I nodded.

"Kyle Warren—that's the guy who's trying to screw my client—shows up for a hearing the other day, and rolls up his sleeve—and his damn forearm looks like he'd got it caught in a damn chipper-shredder."

"I don't see what that's got to do with my pit bull."

"I'm getting to that. I say to him, what the hell had happened, and he says, 'I got bit.'"

That got my attention.

"Bit?"

He nodded. "I say, 'Kyle, you got one hell of a poodle there.' And he says 'yeah, a pit poodle.' And Dominique—that's my client—says, 'didn't know you were a dog person,' and Kyle tells him, 'they weren't my dogs.'"

"Dogs," I said. "He said 'dogs.' Meaning more than one."

"You got it." Larry paused. "The night you nabbed that pit bull—you said that even dogs that are trained to fight don't generally bite people."

"That's right," I said. "Unless someone's dumb enough to get between a couple of them when they go for each other."

"Kyle," Larry said, "is definitely dumb enough."

"So whose dogs were they? Did he say?"

"Nope. I told him, 'Kyle, I sure hope you reported that, that's no joke, a dog that does something like that.' And he just laughs again and says something about the dog belongs to a buddy of his and is worth a bundle."

"Worth a bundle." I took a sip of wine. "And we can rule out

Westminster, I'm guessing."

"I thought you might find this interesting."

I set my glass back down, thinking it over. "This guy Kyle, I sort of pictured a businessman type."

"Yeah. He wears suits, if that's what you mean."

"Good suits?"

He laughed. "Not Italian tailored, if that's what you mean."

"Joseph A. Bank?"

"Yeah, he'd do Joseph A. Bank."

"Larry, dog fighting—it's street. Why would this guy be hanging with people who fight pit bulls?"

"That's the question."

"He do drugs?"

"Couldn't rule it out. My client, Dom, doesn't think so, though."

"Would Dom know?"

"They were business partners for almost seven years. Can't rule it out, of course, but Dom's pretty savvy about stuff like that."

"Well," I said. "I'm not sure it really tells us much."

"Yeah. There's one other thing that is bugging me about this guy."

"What's that?"

"He was broke, supposedly, when he first sued Dom. But he sure isn't living like he's broke."

"How so?"

"Guy's driving a new Lexus IS C convertible."

"Maybe it's his girlfriend's."

"Naw, I checked," Larry said. "It's in his name."

"Credit's a wonderful thing."

"There's no lien on it, that I could find."

"Really? You said the whole reason he was trying to force that building sale was that he needed the money."

"Well, that's the other thing. He's dropping the suit. We show up at the courthouse and all of a sudden he wants to cut a deal. Buy Dom out."

"So that's why you got all chummy about his sore arm."

"Sore is an understatement. We're talking hamburger."

I wrinkled my nose.

"So what do you think?" Larry said. "Interesting coincidence, isn't it?"

I nodded. "But devil's advocate," I said. "What's to say Kyle didn't catch a break somewhere? Maybe he won the Take Five. Maybe his rich aunt died. Maybe some business venture he had going has started to make some money."

Larry shrugged. "We can rule out possibility number three. No business venture Kyle Warren ever got involved in ever made any money."

"Well, I admit the dog bite thing is weird. But to me, all it says is that he's hanging out with the wrong friends."

I heard a burst of laughter from the living room and gave a little start.

Gil.

I'd been so absorbed I'd completely forgotten about Gil . . .

I shuffled my feet nervously. "We'd better get back to the others."

Then I caught the look on Larry's face.

Something about it made the hair on my neck stand up again.

"What," I said. "Don't—"

"Look," he interrupted me. "This thing with Kyle. It's probably nothing. But there's something weird going on. I thought maybe drugs, too. And maybe that's what it is. But if it is, Kyle's not in it to buy. He's in it to sell."

"Explain."

"Nothing much to explain. But he's acting . . . I dunno. Cocky. Like he's pulling a big one over on someone. I thought at first it was us—that he had figured out some way to get the upper hand in this property deal. But I've looked it all over fifteen times since then, and the deal he wants, it looks like it's legit. He's got something else going on."

"It could be anything," I said, but I knew where Larry was going.

"How much money did you say is in this dog fighting business, Paige? You said tens of thousands, potentially, right?"

"Yes. If it's organized. If they bring in out-of-towners."

Larry nodded.

"But you realize this is all speculation," I said. "There's nothing to go on. Guy with a dog bite buys a Lexus."

"Convertible."

"Whatever."

"It's just hinkey, that's all."

I knew what he meant. The back of my neck still felt funny. And I was getting this stuff all second hand.

Another burst of laughter from the other room.

"Larry?" I said.

"Yuh huh?"

"This Kyle, does he own other properties?"

"Yup."

"So, as part of the, you know, lawsuit that you had going there . . ."

"Mmmm."

". . . you probably obtained some information about them, right? What properties he owns?"

"It's all public information. But I can email the info, if you want."

"Thanks."

"On one condition."

I was about to take a sip of wine but now I lowered my glass. "What's that?"

"Don't do anything stupid. This is a Rochester police department deal if you find out he's breaking any laws, right?"

"Right."

"I mean it, Paige."

"Uh huh," I said.

He gave me an I'm-not-convinced-you're-telling-the-truth look. I shrugged.

"Paige—" he said, but at that moment Char and Marguerite breezed through the kitchen door and I kind of started, like I'd been caught doing something I shouldn't, and Char said, "hey, we're gonna walk Lady, okay? Larry, want to come with us?"

Oh Gawd. Char was speaking to me in code—I needed to get back to Gil and *fast*.

"Actually," Larry said, "I have to get going." And then he turned back to me. "You okay?" he said.

"I'm fine," I said and became aware of how close I was

standing to him.

I side-stepped away.

"Take it easy, Paige," he said, giving me that charming smile of his. "I only bite other dogs. Not their handlers."

How did he always manage to get a rise out of me? Now my face was all hot again.

He knew it, too—he laughed. "I'm just gonna get my coat, okay?"

And then I felt a twinge of something else. Like I'd read Larry wrong. Or, you know, like maybe I was a bit disappointed that he hadn't made a pass at me. Pride, I suppose.

I followed him to the door.

"Hey, Larry."

"Yeah." He slipped into his coat.

"Thanks for, you know. Doing this."

He shrugged. "It's a diversion. Although—"

I felt a bit alarmed again. "Yeah?"

His eyes met mine and he opened his mouth to talk, but he must have changed his mind because he just shrugged again.

"You're doing great," he said. "Your ex-boyfriend or boyfriend or whoever he is—he's got his eye on you."

"Really?" I felt a tickle in my gut.

"He'd jump you right now if you'd let him," Larry said.

But he didn't smile.

And that was that—he left, and I smoothed my hair and gripped my wine and fixed a smile onto my face.

And slipped back into the living room.

30

My first priority was to position myself near Gil, but without being overly obvious. So I pretended to check the bowls of munchies and quietly circled the room. Destination: the far side, near the window, a spot that would put three people—Stash, Candace, and Donna—between us.

Perfect. Just close enough to join the conversation, not too close . . .

"So Stash," I said as I took my spot. "How's work going these days?"

He didn't answer. He hadn't even heard me.

A second later I realized why. It was Donna. He was transfixed by her. She was chattering with Candace, and Stash was trying to break into the conversation but couldn't. He kept opening his mouth to say something then clamping it shut again, a look of amazement on his face as he struggled with his bedazzlement.

Donna, meanwhile, was oblivious. I caught a bit of what she saying to Candace. From what I could tell it was about breaking up with Walter. But then all at once she turned away from Candace and toward Gil and said, "So! Are you taking a puppy?"

Stash's mouth snapped shut again.

"I probably should," Gil answered. "I hear they're great chick bait."

His voice was a hair too loud.

"Definite chick bait." Zach came over to re-join Candace, grinning at her to show he was teasing. "Tie one to a piece of string and drag it down Park Ave., you'll have enough phone numbers to keep you busy for six months at least."

Candace rolled her eyes at Donna. "Listen to them."

Donna giggled.

"I had a dog once," Stash said. "He was blind in his left eye. Girl come up to me one time, she gives me hell for walking him with the good eye toward me. Said he couldn't see if a car was coming. Like I was going to walk my dog into the road."

Donna didn't seem to hear him, but Candace cranked her head around to give a sympathetic nod. I was feeling sorrier and sorrier for Stash.

"So Gil," Donna spoke up again. "What do you do?"

Now this, I wanted to hear. But he didn't get to answer, because Candace broke in. "Oh, don't you know? Gil's an artist. A sculptor. He had a huge show in Syracuse a few years ago."

I could only see Gil in profile but I could tell his smile was tight.

"An ARTIST?" Donna was practically squealing. "This is so amazing! I've just gone back to school—at RIT—for fine art!"

Damn cashmere was way too warm.

Donna was fairly bursting from her sweater, she was so excited.

Stash, completely overcome, made a gurgling noise. He half ran, half fell, toward the kitchen and his Budweiser.

Cripes, that Donna sure took up a lot of space.

I heard the front door just then, and a moment later in came Lady, dragging Marguerite, and then Char followed a minute later, but she was looking over her shoulder as she came into the room. I guessed why. She'd seen Stash in the kitchen. I could picture the scene, him standing in front of the open fridge, pouring beer down his throat with both hands.

Marguerite unsnapped the leash from Lady's collar and Lady bounded into the living room, tongue out, to make the rounds, shoving her muzzle at anyone who made eye contact with her. Char, on the other hand, headed straight to me and leaned her head toward my ear. "What's going on with Stash?" she said in a low voice. "He's—uh—standing by himself in the kitchen and doesn't look so good."

I tilted my head toward Donna.

Char's eyes widened slightly. "Really?"

"Yep."

"Hey, Paige."

Whoops. That was Donna speaking now.

I bit my lip.

"Is there any more Chardonnay?" she asked.

"In the kitchen," I said.

I realized my mistake a beat too late.

"Oh!" She "I'll go get—"

"No!" I said.

"No!" Char said at the exact same time.

But it was too late. Donna, carried by the momentum of her offer to fetch the Chardonnay, was already halfway across the room.

Char and I didn't even look at each other—we didn't need to. In an instant we were after her.

Anything to protect poor Stash from taking a direct hit.

But we were too late. There stood Stash, in the middle of the kitchen floor, swaying slightly, with Donna before him, giggling. "Oooh," she said, "You're kinda cute when you're smashed!"

"Stashy," said Char, "C'mon, lemme take you home."

"Wanna beer?" Stash held out a Bud to Donna like an offering to a Goddess.

Donna giggled again, saying something about being a wine and martini girl.

Would this evening never end?

"C'mon Stashy," Char said again, and this time she took Stash by the arm and he let himself be led to the door.

I followed them and handed them their coats.

"You're a good friend, Char," I said and Stash nodded and repeated my words, "You're a good friend, Char."

I watched Char guide him down the sidewalk toward her car— and then I noticed something else.

Gil's car wasn't parked on the street—at least, not anywhere I could see it.

My heart nearly stopped.

I flew back indoors and into the living room.

But I already knew what I'd find. I already knew he wouldn't be there.

He'd slipped away.
He was gone.

31

We were hanging out at the Johnson Museum, Cornell's fine art museum.

The building (which, if you care about such things, is also the first museum designed by I.M. Pei) is a boxy mid-century concrete structure that juts out toward the lake valley like a slab of rock from a cliff face. The view you want to check out, if you ever get there, is on the fifth floor—it overlooks the city and the north end of Cayuga Lake.

It's breathtaking on a normal day, but that day—I've never seen the lake look the way it did. A sharp sunny day in early February, and somehow the lake was more than reflecting the blue of the sky, it was capturing it and condensing it into the most intense shade of blue imaginable. It was like a gleaming inlay of lapis lazuli. I didn't have a camera with me, but even if I had, I wouldn't have bothered taking a picture. Nobody would have believed it. That color. The photo would have looked fake.

"Look at the lake," I said and a moment later felt Gil at my side. "Is that blue, or is it blue?"

"Essence of blue," he said, and touched me, his hand first on my waist and then dropping down, stroking me, and I became completely motionless with the thrill of it.

Immobilized.

He could have yanked my jeans off and had me right there and I would have let him . . .

His hand fell away.

I refocused my attention to the scene through the window . . . it made me feel distant and above everything, like I imagine I'd feel if I were royalty, because we were so high, looking down on the valley that way.

I took a breath.

I'd been waiting for an opportunity to bring up the whole "after we graduate" topic again.

Now was as good a time as any.

"Gil," I said, in my most natural-sounding voice. "You know what I said, about taking some time off before vet school?"

"Yeah."

"I'd probably better start looking for a new job. Something full time. I was thinking. And—" I drew a breath. "We could also look for a new apartment. Something a little quieter. We could find something with room for a gallery—"

For his art. So he could display his art.

I waited.

He didn't say anything.

I felt him move away.

Something's wrong.

"Gil?"

"You mean, this summer," he said.

"Well. Yes."

He didn't say anything. Again.

I stepped toward him. "What?"

"I got a letter."

"A letter?"

"From this lady. Marla. She's in Seattle."

Lady?

"I met her when I was out there."

And then he told me. That this Marla person wanted Gil to go out and do a series of sculptures for her. She was offering "real money," he said. As opposed to fake money, I guess. Like the kind of money they'd paid him last summer to teach kiddie art classes at the Y—the only job he'd managed to find around Ithaca that had anything to do with being an artist—after nine months of looking.

I turned and went back to the window, fixed my eyes again on the gleaming blue surface of the lake.

He can't mean he's moving out there. He means he'll fly out for a week or two, meet her. Then come back here. Do the work here.

"I dunno how long it will take," he said. "Six months, maybe."

Steady, Paige. Steady. This wasn't a break-up. This was just Gil, being Gil . . . People have to do their own thing. Especially young people like us, people in their twenties.

"I see," I said. "Six months. So . . . what about your senior year?"

"No point in getting a degree, really, now that I have a commission."

I swallowed. "I see. That makes . . . sense." I forced myself to say the words, to keep my tone steady.

"Six months," he repeated, but then he said "Maybe a little more. Maybe a year or so."

A year or so.

Some gals might think I should have protested. I should have tried to talk him out of it.

Or I should have followed him.

Or I should have issued an ultimatum—fine. Go, then. But you and I are over.

Believe me, all those options crossed my mind, as I stood there, fighting to keep myself under control.

But I controlled myself. It's like when your dog gets loose somehow—your kid leaves the front gate open and your dog gets out and dashes down the sidewalk. Your first impulse isn't necessarily the most sound, because your first impulse is to chase him. Run down the street, hollering his name, COME HERE FLUFFY.

And sometimes you have no choice—sometimes you need to close a little distance between you and your four-legged escapee.

But there's another tactic that you should keep in mind—that often works much better.

Run *away* from the dog.

It works. It works because dogs are social animals. You call to Fluffy in a happy voice, like you're setting out on this most marvelous amazing adventure filled with whatever Fluffy most loves about life. Squeaky toys and liver treats. You make Fluffy think that if he doesn't spin around and follow you he's going to miss out on the best fun EVER.

So instead of resisting the things Gil said to me that day, I got myself under control and then I turned to him and said, "Well, cool. You want to get something to eat?"

And he said he did, and as we headed out I reminded myself that this wasn't new ground. He'd taken off before—and he'd come back.

I just needed to keep my cool.

32

I wondered who this Marla was.

"She's old," Gil told me.

Old.

I Googled her. There was an article in the Seattle Times about a charity fundraiser and there she was.

Marla Fritze.

Her hair was piled on top of her head and she was wearing what looked like a beaded dress over a pair of jeans.

She wasn't *old* old . . .

I would have loved to asks him more about her, of course, but it would have made me sound worried or even jealous so I didn't.

We were out browsing the area antique stores, and had stopped at one of our favorites. It was more like a flea market, really. Chaotic, stuff piled in the corners that looked like it hadn't been moved since the Nixon administration, mildewy dusty smell . . .

Gil loved to shop in places like that. He'd find weird stuff he could use in his sculptures.

I mostly just poked around and marveled at how much stuff we people accumulate. And wondered what stories all that junk would tell if it could talk . . . who had it belonged to? Why had they bought it? Had they loved this junk? Had they believed it to be beautiful?

I wandered back toward the front of the shop, and it was then I noticed the ring.

It wasn't an engagement ring. It was a cocktail ring. Two enormous white rhinestones side by side like a crystal infinity sign, with two smaller ones snuggled up next to them.

The price tag was a little rectangle of paper attached to the ring by a tiny string, and the tag was turned face down so I couldn't see the price.

It couldn't possibly cost very much.

"Would you like to try it on?"

I looked up at the shopkeeper, a gray-bearded man with reading glasses sliding down his nose. "It's adjustable," he said, and unlocked the case and handed me the ring, and I slipped it on and held my hand straight out. The rhinestones caught the light coming through the storefront windows.

I thought about how I'd look wearing the ring that night—waving it at Gil's artsy friends—what a pisser it would be, that flashy ring! Lookit the size of my rock, I'd say, and what a laugh we'd all have. And they'd say "are you really engaged" and we'd just laugh.

I caught the price tag in my hand and checked the price—thirty-five dollars.

Perfect . . . a thirty five dollar postmodern engagement trinket, a ring that cost little and meant even less . . . and yet. And yet . . . it would bridge the separation, wouldn't it. An engagement ring . . . it would bridge the separation between Ithaca and Seattle—

"What's that?"

I started.

Gil, back to the front of the shop.

I did okay. I laughed and held out my hand again, back of my hand facing me again and said aloud the words I'd imagined in my head. "Would ya lookit the size of this *rock!*"

"Blinding," he said.

It was a bit of a cringe-worthy moment, to be honest. It's not like we'd ever talked marriage. It was dangerous, to make him feel like I was pushing for it.

So I dropped my hand.

He was carrying a ceramic planter shaped like a duck. "Ooh, nice find," I said—plenty glad to be able to change the subject.

I pulled the ring off.

But then he surprised me. As he set the planter on the counter, he said, "I thought it was supposed to be a diamond."

It's one of the nicest things he'd ever said to me, too, if you think about it.

He'd made it sound like marriage was actually on the table.

So I laughed again, and said, "It's not like we could afford a diamond"—as if marriage was on the table—and handed the ring back to the shopkeeper.

"It's the thought that counts," said the shopkeeper in his shopkeeper's jovial voice, and then, "Just the planter then, right?"

I followed Gil out of the door and to the car, and when we got in I said, "Good price on that duck."

He handed me the plastic bag with the planter inside and stuck the key in the ignition, and pulled the car out onto the highway and I glanced over. Gil's got a Roman nose which gives him a regal look in profile. He'd started wearing his hair short by then, it was thick and dark blond and curled out at his collar . . .

When you love a man and you know he belongs to you—there's nothing like it. And it's nothing you can explain—it's a private thing, a thing only the two of you know, or maybe not even the two of you, maybe you are the only one in the world who knows. But that's okay. Some secrets are okay.

"I'm hungry," he said. "Let's go get a beer."

33

Before I'd met Gil, I'd built my identity around my career.

So naturally, when he'd packed his stuff and moved out of the apartment I thought okay, I'll just do it. I'll go back to what I was before.

I'll become a vet.

But I couldn't do it.

I still wanted to work with animals. That never went away. But the thought of grinding through a doctorate and with Gil gone— all that work and for what?

For what?

So I could pretend to be in control of things I couldn't control?

My friends freaked out. My dad—oh, I don't even want to go there. He went totally livid and totally frantic by turns.

He's the one who helped me get my dog catcher job by the way. After he'd calmed down and accepted everything.

Not that I didn't go through the proper channels and everything. But he knew somebody who knew somebody, and I expect he made a few phone calls.

I suppose he thought I was having a breakdown of some kind, and that having a steady job would help me get through it.

So I left Ithaca, set up in a new city.

And then Charlene moved to Rochester, too . . .

And turns out this job suited me. And Gil seemed to be making decent money from the work he was doing for that Marla person. Anyway, he could afford to fly back to see me often enough . . .

PART II

34

It has to be hormones.

There has to be a reason that puppies are so irresistible—and no, it's not enough to say "they're so cute!" It's deeper than that, it's bone deep, it's blood deep. So it's got to be hormones.

Puppy breath, for instance. Puppy breath is intoxicating—there's no other word for it.

I hated to leave them. I'd get up in the morning and—because it was time now to start weaning them—I'd warm some milk and put it in a big stainless steel dish and add some puppy chow. And then I'd walk Lady, and by the time I was back the chow would be softened, and I'd put the dish on the floor and the puppies would crowd around it.

And I'd change the newspapers in their pen, and then I'd sit down with them and they'd crowd into me, and tumble around me, and climb into my lap and lick my chin.

And I'd breathe that puppy breath . . .

I hated to leave for work.

But work was busy. The job is like that. Quiet for weeks, and then all of a sudden it gets busy.

I started getting wild animal calls that week, for instance. It started a bunch of calls about skunks. Like four calls, all within a couple of hours one morning. Yeah. Because when the weather breaks in the spring, skunks become active—they're hungry, so they emerge from their winter hidey holes and wander around looking for food. But this is during the day, so people who see them freak out, they think omg the skunk is walking through my yard in broad daylight, doesn't that mean he has rabies? So I'm calming them down, no no, it doesn't mean the skunk has rabies, it just means he's hungry.

Then a woman phoned me about a squirrel in her attic. At first, she sounded matter-of-fact, so I figured it wasn't that big a deal. But she called back about fifteen minutes later, and was a little creeped out. Then came a third call and she sounded out-and-out frantic.

I was probably not sympathetic enough, to tell the truth.

I'd take a squirrel in the attic over the squirrels in my head any day of the week.

Anyway, when we got to frantic, I told her I'd be out within the hour. Hung up, then realized that, dammit, that wouldn't leave me time to help Char at lunchtime like I'd promised, so now I needed to call her to reschedule.

She was at the spa.

Donna answered the phone.

Donna. Ugh. Just the person to remind me all over again about the puppy party debacle. "Paige!" she cooed, and before I could even ask for Char she started telling me how much fun my party had been and that "we have to get together again soon—girl's night out!"

"Yeah," I mumbled, "that would be great," or something to that effect, and finally finally finally she put me on hold and got Char.

"We're going to have pick up your plywood after work," I said. "Got a woman with a squirrel problem who's going to burn her house down or something if I don't take care of it."

Char said okay. Char is very cool about last minute changes of plan.

I asked her whether she thought the party had gone okay.

"Paige, I thought it went GREAT."

I floated a comment about Larry. "You don't think he was too much of a problem, do you?"

"Nope, I don't. In fact, I noticed that Gil was looking at you—a lot."

Exactly what Larry had said. "You think?"

"Uh huh. And you looked great."

"I was sweating like a pig."

"No, that's 'glowing.' You were 'glowing.' Like an angel."

I forced a little laugh.

"Hang on, Donna's talking to me."

I held the receiver, irritated, and after a second, Char came back on to tell me Donna wanted us to get together for a girl's night out. "Yeah," I said. "She mentioned that."

"You have anything going on this weekend?"

Argh. "No," I admitted. "Not really. Hey, my other line's ringing."

"Okay, I'll set something up with Donna and let you know."

I hung up my cell and picked up the office phone.

Mistake.

My buddy Skip Wendt.

"No, Mr. Wendt, I can't have her arrested for feeding your cat. Like I said, I will stop by and speak to her again. Yes, I understand."

It was really getting tiresome. In fact, I was tempted to blurt out something completely ridiculous—along the lines of "damn it, Skip, ask the woman on a DATE!"

But of course, that would be a dumb thing to say. It would only aggravate the man more than he was already aggravated, and even worse, what if against all odds Char was right, and Skip actually took up my suggestion and asked Maddie out? Was I really in the mood to see someone else fall in love and be all happy?

Most certainly not.

I was actually in the mood to take a swing through Ellison Park and bust people for not keeping their dogs on leash.

But I couldn't, because I had to do the squirrel in the attic call.

35

I pulled up to the house, a nicely kept-up farmhouse next to a field of newer, expensive homes that looked cheesy by comparison, and that had stripped the farmhouse of its pastoral landscape, which made its lines all the more modest and quaint next to the garrets and arched-window pretense of its McMansion neighbors.

There was a realtor's SOLD sign thrust into the middle of the front yard.

The woman who answered the door was slight and much more timid in person than she sounded over the phone, at least when she was in frantic mode. She led me to the attic.

Although arguably more charming than McMansions, old farmhouses also share their space a bit more readily with the local critters. For the same reason they're also draftier, I suppose. They've settled, they've been weather-worn, they've got little cracks and crevices that invite company.

Of course, on the face of it, squirrels are one whole heck of a lot nicer than, say, raccoons. Or skunks, or bats. But for some people, squirrels are, apparently, sort of furry Godzillas. Only smaller. I figured my client fell into that category. Probably because she grabbed a broom propped up near the attic door and held it at the ready while we ascended the stairs.

"I don't think you'll need that," I said. "There are two of us."

She nodded but didn't put down the broom.

My flashlight beam probed the eaves and cast rubbery shadows as it passed over the piles of stacked boxes. I couldn't see any evidence of squirrels. "Do you know how they're getting in?"

"No."

Sigh. "If you don't block where they're getting in, you'll just end up with more."

She sucked in her breath.

"Do you ever hear them in the walls or anything?"

"No. I don't think so."

"I don't see anything here, really. I'll look at the house from the outside."

It didn't take long. There was a baseball-sized hole in the end of a soffit on the south side of the house. I showed it to her. She was doubtful. "It's so tiny," she said. But I assured her they'd be able to fit. Big enough for a squirrel's head, big enough for a squirrel.

I got my trap, a jar of peanut butter and a packet of hulled sunflower seeds from the truck. She watched as I set the trap and scattered a few sunflower seeds on the attic floor around it. Chum. She'd picked up the broom again.

"Leave the light on," I told her. "You're around during the day?"

She nodded.

"When we catch one," I said when I'd finished, "you'll probably know it. It'll make a nice racket. Call me right away. If there is more than one coming in, we don't want them learning to avoid the trap, so we need to get it out as soon as we can."

"What about the hole?"

"You'll have to leave it open until we're sure we've trapped any of them who know about it. Then you can block it. Staple hardware cloth over it to start. Then after a couple of weeks, when we're sure no squirrels are trying to get in any more, you can have it repaired. Oh, and you should do a thorough check for other holes, too. There might be more than one. They'll chew holes in soffit vents, too."

She was married. There were wedding photos and kid photos hanging stylishly from wires on the stairwell.

But I was careful not to suggest it would be her husband, and not her, up there on the ladder.

Grrl power.

She walked me to the door, then asked me if she should get

rabies vaccines for her kids.

"Not if they haven't come in contact with the squirrels, no. But don't let them near the trap once we catch one. Leave it alone. Call me and I'll deal with it."

I pulled my Kevlar gloves out of my jacket pocket and waved them at her, and for the first time, she smiled.

That's it, sister. They're only squirrels.

Squirrels are easy.

I drove the truck around Brighton for an hour or so.

Did not bust anyone for breaking leash laws.

Went back to the office, and at long last got the promised email from Larry. Subject line: Here's your Warren properties, sweetheart.

Sweetheart. Gah.

I checked the time. It was nearly five by then. My Warren property research would have to wait.

I texted Char. *Pick you up at 5:30.*

Yeah. Squirrels are easy.

36

By the time I finally got home, walked Lady, and replaced the puppy pee-soaked newspapers it was past eight.

There was still some wine from the party, so I poured myself a glass. Then I logged back online and looked at Larry's email again.

Five properties.

I keyed the addresses into Mapquest. Some appeared to be commercial. Some were in more residential areas.

I sat back and took a sip of wine while the maps were printing.

Lady wandered over and nosed my hand, asking to be petted.

I looked at my cell.

I could call Gil . . .

I could dial his cell . . . maybe he had the night off tonight . . . he'd pick up and I'd finally hear his voice. And maybe get a read on his mood. Because maybe seeing Larry at my house again hadn't been a big deal—maybe the only reason he hadn't called me for going-on-three days now is that he was busy, too busy, getting settled into his job, maybe an apartment, he'd come down with a head cold—something.

But of course I couldn't phone him. Because if he wasn't upset, phoning him would make me look needy and desperate. And if he was upset, phoning him would remind him of why—and the last thing I needed to do was poke a stick into the bee's nest and rile it up.

I needed to give it some time.

I went upstairs and wandered over to my dresser, and opened my jewelry box and looked at the ring.

When had Gil bought it, I wondered. It had to have been before he left Ithaca for Seattle, right?

No way had the ring sat in that antique shop ever since that day I'd first tried it on . . . he had to have bought it before he left.

I slipped the ring back onto the fourth finger of my left hand. Such a gaudy thing! Such a laugh it would have been to wear it in Ithaca . . .

I twisted the ring back off and held it up close to look at it again.

Then I returned it to the box, and shut the lid.

It would be fine. It would work out.

I just had to sit tight.

But at the same time, I had to be rational. Because like so many guys, Gil is a "man of few words." And while men of few words *seem* romantic, what's really going on is that we women fill in between those few words with all the crap we wish we were hearing. So suppose some guy you were in love with once brings something up that you'd done together, and you ask him why he brought it up, and he says, "oh, nothing." You don't hear that. Admit it. What you hear is: "I was thinking about that time we were walking with Trixie on the railroad bed behind our place, that time, and she found that skunk. Remember? We'd been invited to a party at Professor Heinbeck's place that night, remember? But there we were, instead, our clothes stinking of skunk from carrying Trixie home—she wouldn't walk herself, she was so freaked all she'd do was squirm herself against the ground—so we spent the evening at home, instead, holding Trixie in the tub and dousing her with tomato juice and downing the Sutter Home White Zinfandel we'd bought to take to the party—we finally gave up on the tomato juice, whoever says tomato juice gets skunk smell out has never actually tried it—and by then we were both too sloshed to drive, so we put on Little Feat 'Dixie Chicken' and climbed into bed and rocked and rolled instead. Remember? Remember how I set Roll Um Easy on repeat so it would play over and over, 'roll me easy, so slow and easy'? Remember how you kissed me that night, remember, like you knew it would never be enough?"

Admit it, ladies. Man of few words, he's like a blank canvas. And we fall for it every time, and get all sappy-eyed, and next thing you know, we're helping him pass his few-words genes onto the next generation. I mean, think about it, that explains a lot, doesn't it? Think about it. Those jokes about cavemen grunting, what they don't show is what their girlfriends were filling in between the grunts.

What the Caveman says: "Grunt."

What the Cavegirlfriend hears: "When the firelight flickers, your face, your face becomes Mystery itself, I see in it my past, my future, my comfort, my fortune, and I long to mingle myself with you forever and ever."

And next thing you know, Cavegirlfriend is spreading her furs out on the floor for some guy whose vocabulary doesn't even include verbs.

I'm sorry. Do I sound bitter? But you see, there's a kind of certainty when you work with animals, what old-fashioned writers used to call the "poor dumb animals"— dumb meaning unable to speak, not stupid, of course—and there's another kind of certainty when you are sitting across the table from your cousin or your girlfriend or your sister, if you're lucky enough to have a mom or sister, and you can talk, really really talk, really really get to the crux of things, get to the crux of the biscuit, as I once heard someone say. It's the in-between place where the trouble starts, where there's a sprinkling of words, but never enough, and you're left always hanging, hanging on the little bits you've gathered . . .

Argh. And then the worst of it is, sometimes you find out that they really were thinking, if not exactly what you thought they were thinking, something damn close to it. And then, you just want to throw yourself down and die for them.

37

I emptied the squirrel lady's Havahart trap three times over the next couple of days.

I figured that would be it, for her fine furry friends. But I reset it, just in case. And then—because I was feeling a little guilty about feeling impatient with my buddy Skip Wendt—I figured I'd take a preemptive swing by Maddie's place.

She didn't act nervous, this time, about seeing me. Far from it. She asked me in for a cup of coffee.

I declined.

"Oh, he won't mind," she said, waving a hand dismissively toward Mr. Wendt's house.

I gave her my professional frown. "Ms. Ingersoll, you don't have his cat here now, do you?"

"Oh no, dear, he went home earlier. About 10:30, I'd say."

"You know, if you just fed him outside, on your deck, maybe Sk—Mr. Wendt wouldn't get so irritated."

"It isn't the same, you know. He begs to come in. He knows what he wants."

"We can't always just let animals do what they want," I said with professional primness. "I'm helping someone right now who's got squirrels in the attic. Squirrels love to live in attics. But the smell of their droppings is just awful, and they can chew through insulation. Or electrical wires."

"Bruce is clean."

She calls Fred "Bruce." It's unfortunate—two one-syllable men's names—it's getting hard for me to keep them straight.

And I don't think Wendt would have liked it much if I

accidentally called his cat the wrong name.

I climbed back into my truck, and because I couldn't tell if he was watching or not, I drove slowly as I passed Wendt's house and gave two short honks on my horn and waved at his windows.

Next stop was my apartment. It's important to get puppies used to being handled. I'd picked up a couple of buckle collars, so now twice a day—once at lunch, once in the evening—after I replaced their soggy newspapers I strapped a collar onto one of the puppies' necks, hand-feeding bits of kibble as I did so, so he'd think it all a fun game complete with snacks. Then I'd snap on the leash and take the puppy for a little walk around the apartment, clucking as I walked so he'd follow me.

Then I went back to the kitchen and did the same with the next puppy.

It filled my time.

It kept me from thinking so much about Gil.

Oh, and the other thing I did to fill my time was to take a look at Kyle Warren's properties . . .

38

Dogs don't make a lot of noise when they're fighting. Well, they do, but it's not high-volume noise. The spectators, on the other hand, can get really loud. Especially if it's an organized fight. Meaning, not just a couple of guys who meet on a street corner or in a back yard, pony up $50 and unleash their dogs. But an event. Advance ads in *Blood Sport* or *Dog Fighting*. Out-of-towners bringing in their winning dogs—their "champions." And a couple dozen or more other guys, some who have dogs they want to try, some who just come to bet on dogs. That's where the noise is going to come from. Plus there's usually alcohol.

So if you want to escape notice, you have to either hold the fight someplace with no neighbors or figure out some way to contain the racket. A lot of dog fights happen in rural areas for this reason. In cities, abandoned buildings in industrial areas are a good choice, since there are no residential neighbors nearby to notice if a bunch of guys suddenly start hollering on a Saturday night.

For that reason, I didn't even bother looking at the Parsons building. The High Falls District had become too much of a clubbing spot. Too many lights on after sunset for the real low lifes.

Instead I started with the second property on the list, an empty standalone storefront just inside the city's northeast line.

I drove by, peering out of my windshield.

Its nearest neighbor to the east was separated from it by a side street, and beyond that a short block of shops—drycleaner, a florist, a vacuum cleaner repair and parts dealer.

All 9-5 type businesses—meaning that after hours, they would be mostly empty.

I flipped a u-ey and swung into the wide blacktop driveway flanking the west side of the building, taking a good look at the house on the other side of the drive as I pulled in. The house had been converted to commercial. Its bottom floor appeared to be a nail salon and tattoo parlor, and there was a "for rent" sign in the front yard which presumably referred to the second floor apartment.

I pulled the rest of the way into the drive and came to a big crumbling parking lot, ragweed and dock sprouting up through the cracks. It took up the entire back of the property, and was bounded by a rusty and dilapidated chain link fence with several large holes. Beyond the fence, a brushy hedgerow that blocked the building visually from the homes the next street over.

I pulled up into the northeast corner of the lot, shut off my engine, and got out of the car, leaving my door open. The building had a few low windows, all in the basement level, covered with dust and grime and framed by scraggly weeds that had pushed up between the blacktop and the building's concrete foundation.

I had to crouch down to look in, and cup my hands around my eyes to cut the glare.

I didn't see evidence of much activity at all, let alone dog fights. A couple of silvery canisters—propane tanks, I expect—were propped over against one wall. There was a sheet of plywood on the floor with a notch cut from one corner. Some other lumber scraps. A couple cardboard cases from Budweiser 12-packs. Some empty beer bottles.

For a dog fight, basements are the first choice because of the noise factor. But if they were fighting here, you'd also expect the windows to be blocked. And there was no pit. The plywood and other lumber—that could mean anything.

I went back to my car and looked at my MapQuest map, and then headed north to look at the other properties.

They were all rentals. I'd suspected as much, based on the addresses. Lower middle class neighborhoods.

It took me almost an hour to check them all out.

They all appeared to be occupied.

I got as good a look as I could at the backyards.

The only dog I saw was a skinny terrier mix tethered to a dog house at the last address I checked. He raised his head off his paws and looked at me when I pulled over to the curb and rolled my window down. There were a couple of dishes on the bare ground in front of his house . . . it's automatic for me, of course, to note whether they have water. And it looked like he probably did.

I got back into my car and thought it over. The empty storefront was the only one that really had any possibilities, although I couldn't really rule out the residences. They were rental properties after all, and neighbors will tolerate stuff from renters that would raise eyebrows otherwise.

What I needed to do was to come back and have a look later in the evening to see if I could catch anything going on. Either that or talk to somebody.

I'll admit, I felt pretty frustrated. Although I suppose it was unrealistic to think I'd get a real lead that easily.

And Gil still hadn't called, and we were doing that stupid girl's night out that Donna had arranged, and Char had been begging me to help her paint her booth . . .

I didn't want to. I didn't want to be around people. And knowing what Char was thinking—that being alone was the worst thing for me right now—that only made it worse.

I thought about lying to get out of it—all of it. I've got a headache, I've got a stomach ache, I've got the stomach flu—but if I had, Char would have probably come over and force fed me herbs or something.

I was stuck.

39

She was building the booth at Stash's place.

Yeah, Stash owns a house. How's that for bizarre. This scrappy little guy with the tattoos, doesn't own a pair of jeans without blown-out knees, high school education—and he's the one with the house. With an actual mortgage.

It's a little house, mind you. Seven hundred square feet or so—little post-WWII house plunked down on the edge of a tiny lot not far from Kodak's manufacturing complex. But it's a house, all the same, and Stash takes care of it, too. No garage, but he'd built a little lean-to against the back and that's where we were working. The lean-to was for firewood—he heats with a woodstove—but that time of year it was mostly empty, leaving enough room for Char's booth to be out of the rain if need be.

Better than trying to assemble and paint the thing in her apartment, anyway.

Stash wasn't home. He was out hooking up an air conditioner somewhere. But Char had a key to his place—Char's the sort of person who ends up with keys to peoples' places—not that we needed to go inside. She had all the paint and brushes stored in the lean-to.

I'd brought along a puppy—the biggest of the three females—so when I got there I tethered the pup to an ash sapling at the edge of Stash's lawn where of course she immediately got tangled in the nearby honeysuckle bushes.

Oh, and the booth wasn't going to be mauve after all. Char had ultimately decided on indigo. With gold Zodiac signs stenciled all over the outside.

"I like it," I said, standing back to look. And I really did. Strangely enough.

"Mmmmm. You should let me read the cards for you, Paige. You really should."

"I don't need the cards," I said. "I need for him to call me. Or better yet, just stop by."

"Maybe he's been busy. Maybe he's doing art again."

I sighed. "I just wish Larry hadn't shown up at the party."

"Cards," she answered.

I rolled my eyes and went to untangle the puppy again, then came back and picked up my brush. "Oops. I think we're short one Virgo on this side."

"No big deal. Nobody will notice."

"Except the Virgos. Have you finished the curtains?" I know she had the material picked out. She'd found some velvet drapes at the Salvation Army to use for the material.

"Oh yes, they've been done for a week, now."

"So you're almost ready to open up shop."

"Yup."

"Any idea where you're going to put it?"

"In front of Rundel Library, I'm thinking. I've tested it, and there's a nice vortex there. Should be perfect."

I nodded. Of course.

"Somebody sees your puppy," Char said. And I looked up, and sure enough, there were two women, overweight, wide faces. They looked like sisters. They were standing at the end of Stash's driveway looking at the puppy.

"Hi," I said.

"He's so cute!" the older woman said.

"She," I corrected her. "And she needs a home, if you're interested. Do you want to say hello?"

One of them lived three houses down, it turned out, and no, she wasn't really looking for a puppy, but she'd be sure to tell Stash if they changed their minds.

She kept stroking that little puppy and letting her jump up and leave little puppy kisses on her chin.

She may not have been looking for a puppy, but she'd found one.

I gave her my number.

"Anyway," said Char a minute later, "Gil *has* to call you."

I dipped a brush back into the gold paint. "Not sure what you mean by 'has to,'" I said.

"Didn't you say he'd found a home for one of the puppies?"

I stopped mid-brush stroke and our eyes met.

"Damn," I said softly. "You're right. Unless . . ."

She shook her head. "No—he can't change his mind. It's for a kid, right? The boss's daughter?"

My heart was pounding all of a sudden and I felt my face break into a stupid grin. "I can't believe I didn't think of this. Char, you're a genius."

Char tapped the side of her forehead with an index finger. "Psychic powers, baby," she said. Then she looked more closely at my face. "Paige," she said. "What are you thinking?"

I shook my head. "Nothing," I said. "Only—"

"Only what?"

"I need to fix this whole Larry situation."

Char shook her head. "Leave it alone, Paige. It'll sort itself out."

I dipped my brush back into the paint. "I know what you're thinking," I said. "You're thinking that I screwed up, bringing Larry into the picture in the first place—"

"What's done is done, Paige."

I knelt to work on an Aries sign ram's head near the bottom of the booth wall. "It was a good plan, though. It just got a little out of hand, is all." I squinted and touched up the edge of the ram's twirly horns. "All I need," I said, "is a way to smooth things over. Just a little tweak."

"Just . . . be careful," she said.

She couldn't resist, I suppose. Not that I blame her. And she was only trying to look out for me—I get that.

But I'd learned my lesson. I was not going to make the same mistake twice.

I stepped back to survey my work. "I think this side's all done, now."

"Cool," said Char. "So we have just enough time to clean up before dinner."

Ah. Dinner.

I was feeling much better about things, I almost didn't mind that I'd be spending the evening with The Donna.

40

Donna had picked the restaurant, of course—she was the organizer. A place on Park Avenue. We took a table in the nook formed by the recessed entryway. Char and I slid into the booth seat, which was against the wall, while Donna and Marguerite pulled out the two chairs opposite.

I took my second look around. Hammered copper table tops. Eight foot palm trees. Techno jazz. The lamp shades on the windowsill next to our table were sprays of upturned blown glass tulips.

"Whoa," I said to Char, "this is almost too hip for Rochester."

"Très New York," she agreed.

Donna had settled into her chair. "Walter and I used to come here." She pulled out a compact and checked her face.

The server dropped our menus on the table.

"Remember," Donna said as she tucked her compact back into her purse. "We have to drink martinis."

"Donna!" Marguerite protested. She was wearing a peasant blouse and had a scarf tied over her hair. A few bits of hair had started to fall back out around her face, though, so it looked a little better, softer.

"Marguerite's not dressed for martinis, Donna," I suggested. "She looks like she's in the mood for . . . I dunno, a Dos Equis, maybe."

Donna giggled.

Marguerite nodded in solemn agreement.

"And Char," I said, "is dressed for green tea." She was wearing a calf-length blue jean jumper with the zodiac signs embroidered on it—they formed an ellipsis that ringed the dress from her left shoulder to her right hip, like a sash. She'd embroidered them herself, of course.

Donna giggled again. "Paige, you're too funny. But it's martinis—you all promised, and I'm the one who chose what we were going to do, remember?"

"Marguerite." I was looking at the drink menu. "There's a chocolate one."

That brightened her up a bit.

"I want strawberry," Char said. "It'll be good, right?"

"You'll looooove it."

"Hot pepper for me," I decided. "I may as well make the agony complete."

"Walter," Donna said, "drinks pork martinis."

"Pork!" Char made a face. She's a vegetarian. Well, she's usually a vegetarian. She goes off the wagon once every three or four months.

Donna smirked and settled back into her chair. "Yeah. He makes his own. He puts a hunk of sausage in some vodka and lets it sit for a couple of weeks. Then drinks it."

"Eww!"

The server came back and took our order, and Donna and Char started talking about the massage parlor.

I looked out the window at the bright red CVS store lights across the street, then turned to Marguerite. "So," I said, "I heard you quit the massage business. What happened?"

Donna and Marguerite exchanged solemn glances. "She was accused of harassment," Donna said.

"No kidding!"

"Tell her, Mar."

"Oh. It was nothing, really. A guy wouldn't stop grabbing me, and when I complained, he said it was me who'd been after him."

"Old guy?" That was from Char.

"Uh huh. I guess."

"Fat," I say.

"Not so much."

"Just enough," I said. "I can picture him perfectly. Mid-to-late fifties. Still has his hair. Bit of a paunch, arms full because he played sports in the dim distant past, but no muscle definition any more, of course. Married. Considered good-looking at one time, but he's long since given up the abs machine in favor of a few reps of 'sit up quick and grab the masseuse's breasts.'"

Which actually got Marguerite to crack a smile. "How'd you do that?" she said. "Only I don't think he's married."

"I'm surprised David didn't back you up," Char said. David is the owner-manager.

"David is a pig," Donna said.

Sounded like there was a story there, I thought.

"So speaking of work, Char," Marguerite said. "How's your booth working out?"

"Well, there's this sausage guy."

Donna giggled.

I looked at Char. "Sausage guy?"

Char nodded. "Yeah. He sells sausage sandwiches. Hotdogs, that sort of thing. Anyway, he seems to think the sidewalk by the library belongs to him."

"Well," I said, "in a way it does, if he, you know, has a permit."

Char shrugged. "He's lowering the vibration."

"Which can't be good for your business," said Marguerite.

"Well, yes and no. People who detect the disturbance he gives off tend to be drawn to me."

"How many readings are you doing a day?" I asked.

"Five or six."

At 10 bucks a pop. Not a living wage, although it was under the table, which would help some.

Then the server was back. She handed Donna her martini first, and Donna picked it up and held it in the air, waiting for the rest of us to get ours. "A toast."

We raised our glasses.

"To men. The ones who aren't pigs."

I hid my sigh and took a swallow of martini. The vodka was pretty smooth, but then the hot pepper oil hit. I could see it, red, floating on top of the vodka in tiny blobs, reminding me of those novelty desk ornaments you used to see in mall gift shops in the 80s.

"Another toast," said Char, and I knew what she was thinking.

Cancel it out. Char pays a lot of attention to—not karma exactly, but vibrations, which kind of operate like karma if you aren't careful. "To true love, because you know, it really does happen."

We clinked our glasses again.

"This is really pretty good," Marguerite said cautiously. "I can't really taste the vodka."

"Exactly," Donna smiled. "See? I told you they were DEElicious." Then she turned back to Char and I, gave a big smile and said, "So, speaking of true love. Tell me all about this Gil."

The food menus were still on the table and I picked mine up. "Are we going to get any food?"

"You'll have to ask Paige," Char said. "Gil's her guy, ya know."

"Oh!" Donna looked at me. Her eyes were wide like she was surprised but something about them was also blank, unreadable. "I didn't realize—lucky you, Paigey!"

"Thanks," I said.

She giggled. Again. "Too funny—that Larry—he's a lawyer, right? I thought you and he—"

"No." I shook my head. "He's just a friend."

"You have huuunky friends. Char, you never told me your cousin had such hunky friends!"

I could see Char out of the corner of my eye. She was motionless as a bodhisattva. As a statue of a bodhisattva.

Donna, meanwhile, had segued somehow back to Gil. "I can't believe he's an artist! And just when I decided to go back to school for art myself. I mean, I've known I had talent, of course. Everyone always told me. I won a blue ribbon at the county fair one time for an oil I did, did I ever tell you that, Char? Back in high school. And he's so gorgeous!" She kind of caught herself then and said, "And Larry—Paige, you have such hunky friends!"

"Here's our server!" Char said, waving her hand in the air.

I looked down at my menu. I was going to have to do something to cut through the taste of that hot pepper oil.

Then suddenly it hit me—an idea.

I looked back up at Donna.

"You know," I said, "Larry's single."

Her eyes flew open in utter amazement again. "Ooooh," she

said. "Do you think——?"

I felt Char, under the table, nudge my shin with her foot, but I ignored her.

"Could be," I said, smiling warmly. "I'll see what I can do."

"Oooooh," Donna repeated and kind of wriggled in her seat.

41

My kitchen had turned into a puppy playground.

It was the only option, really. They were outgrowing the pen. I couldn't let them have the run of my apartment.

They'd have torn it to shreds.

So instead, I bought a second-hand baby gate at a garage sale and used it to confine them to the kitchen.

It wasn't a perfect solution. They quickly discovered a spot near the table where the wallpaper was starting to pull away from the wall, and turns out, that makes a wonderful toy. I tried taping it back down, hoping maybe they'd move onto some other diversion. But one of them apparently considered it a challenge and soon had the tape worked loose.

I think I know who it was, too. One of those little males was so smart—too smart to forget something as interesting as flapping wall paper.

Plan B: I tried spraying the wall with some stuff I got at Petsmart that makes things taste bad, supposedly.

That didn't work, either. Maybe my puppies had no taste buds.

Then I came home one day, and about a square foot of the paper had been turned into confetti, and the next batch of puppy poop had gold and black fleur-de-lis accents. So I gave up and yanked off that entire panel, leaving a layer of dried yellowing wallpaper paste behind.

Oh well, I didn't really like the wallpaper anyway.

And painting my kitchen would give me something to take my mind off . . . other things.

The puppies were almost five weeks old now by that point.

Which meant I really needed to get going to find them homes. My little puppies, all grown up.

I didn't know if I'd be able to stand it . . .

Just keep busy, Paige.

I drove to the hardware store and bought some of that gel you can put on wall paper that dissolves the paste, so you can pull it off a wall without using a steamer. And some paint.

I called Char from the store to discuss colors. She suggested robin's egg blue. It would be a good color for me, she said, as I needed to open up to the cosmos, and a room in that color would evoke "the heavenly vault."

I went with cream instead. Or, to use the official name of the color, Pineapple Fizz.

Nod to my landlord's sensibilities. He's a very nice man, after all, I would hate to give him apoplexy.

Landlord (croaking, from where he lies on the floor in a heap): "Paige, I said it was okay to paint. Not violate the laws of nature!"

Painting with a roomful of puppies is an interesting experience, by the way. At first, I tried giving them the run of the kitchen while I was working. Dumb idea, I know. That same little male who I suspect led the wallpaper brigade managed to rub a just-painted section of wall, so now instead of all black he was piebald. It was a good look for him, really—unusual for a lab mix.

"Maybe it will make you more adoptable," I told him as I did my best to wipe the paint off his fur with a damp rag.

He licked my fingers and tried to play tug-of-war with the cloth.

I also liked the Pineapple Fizz-paw-prints effect on the linoleum.

Anyway, once that experiment had come to its inevitable conclusion, I switched strategies. Corralled them into their exercise pen while I painted. They didn't like that much—they barked piteously with their piercing little puppy voices and generally made a racket. Promising that, if I just let them out, they'll be good.

They were so loud, in fact, that I almost couldn't hear my phone ring.

I clambered down from my ladder as fast as I could and

grabbed it—and at long last!

It was Gil. Calling about a puppy.

42

The puppies were still barking—it was hard to hear—but I caught that the boss's name was "Dan," and I was supposed to pick a puppy from the litter and take it to Dan's house. For Dan's daughter.

Gil.

His name sounding over and over in my head.

But I kept a grip. Because it didn't matter that the guy I loved was on the other end of the line. Placing the puppies isn't something I'd ever do lightly—no matter the circumstances.

So I took a deep breath. "It sounds good, I said, "but they'll give the dog a good home, right? Proper vet care—"

"I don't think they eat dog, if that's your question."

Teasing me. A good sign.

"Gil," I said. "You know the line of work I'm in. I see an awful lot of neglected and abused animals—"

"Take it easy, Paige. He's actually my boss's boss. House in Victor, wife, 12-year old daughter who's been saving up her allowance for, like, five years so she can buy a dog."

"Buy a dog?"

"I think she wanted a collie."

"Ah, so we just paint one of the puppies tricolor, name her Lassie and teach her to pull small children out of mine shafts. In fact, one of the pups is already almost there—I'm painting the kitchen and he's managed to get into it."

"Well, the collie part is negotiable, apparently."

"You're sure about that—"

"You need to do a background check, let me know."

I laughed.

"Shall I swipe his coffee mug at work so you can get his prints?"

"Knock it off."

But he didn't sound at all upset.

Gil.

"So what do you say?"

I forced myself to focus. "What's the daughter's name?"

"Taylor."

"Ow."

"What?"

"Puppy teeth." I'd let the puppies out of the pen while we were talking, and was sitting on the floor. A couple of the pups were clambering over my legs, and a third had decided that my unoccupied hand would make a nice chew toy. I tucked it under my right armpit and turned my body away slightly to show that his mouthing wasn't my idea of fun.

I took a deep breath. "So you'll go with me, right? To take the puppy to Taylor."

"Sure. Week from Saturday work?"

I did some quick mental math. The puppies would be just old enough. . . I had a vet appointment next week so they'd be wormed and vaccinated . . . "Yeah, that should work." Another deep breath. "But Gil, you know me. Just to be clear—if we get out there, and I decide it's not right—it's not the right situation for the puppy—I get to change my mind."

"It'll be fine, Paige."

"I know. I just—this will be the first one. So it's going to be a little . . . hard."

And it would be. I was crazy about these puppies. Despite the wallpaper. And the growing volume of pee and poop.

"Well. You have to do it sooner or later, I guess."

"Yeah."

I felt, all of a sudden, like I might start to cry. But I kept my grip. "I appreciate you doing this, Gil."

"No problem," he said, and then the words I most wanted to hear. "You around later?"

You better believe it, Gil Rudman.

"Yes," I breathed. "Yes."

And that's how things worked out again, for me and Gil.

Didn't I tell you they would?

43

When I finished painting, I decided to take a drive out past the Warren properties.

No change—nothing that struck me as hinkey, anyway. These were relatively decrepit neighborhoods, of course, so there was plenty of local color. Derelicts pushing shopping carts, prowling hip hoppers, cars crawling by to the thudding rhythm of their base speakers. But other than the random mutt on a leash, I didn't see anything that suggested dog fights.

Frustrating.

Was it possible that I was missing something?

And then I thought of Trish Whitehead.

Trish and I were never what you'd call friends. She was two years ahead of me, and by the time she'd transferred to Cornell I was with Gil, and socializing with him and his buddies pretty much exclusively.

But we had something in common: she'd ended up abandoning vet school, too. She'd decided that instead, she wanted to focus on dog rescue, and I was pretty sure the breed she picked was pit bulls.

It took me a while to find her number, but I did, finally, and left a message and a half hour later or so she called me back.

We chitchatted for a bit, catching up, and then I told her I wanted to know more about dog fighting.

"It might be gangs," she said, and then ticked off what to watch for. The fights are held in garages, basements, warehouses, abandoned lots, parks. Ask people if they've seen people—kids— congregate with their dogs. Look for dogs with spiked collars.

Look for blood.

"I knew about the spiked collar thing," I said. "That's what my pit was wearing when I saw him last."

I was thinking, as well, about his injuries. Yeah. Look for blood. I'd seen blood . . .

"Well. No question he's been used to fight."

"Trish? Tell me this—is there anything I can do, you know, to kind of help the Rochester Animal Services guys?"

I waited while she thought this over. "That's a tough one. The people who fight dogs, they get caught one of two ways, usually. Either someone—you know, a neighbor—notices what's going on and calls the police. Or else one of them gets busted for something and cuts a deal, becomes an informant."

I sighed. "In other words, there's not a damn thing I can do."

"It's awful, isn't it."

"I should have just kept the dog."

"Well, you can't save them all." She was just saying that to make me feel better. Or make herself feel better—about all the dogs she can't save.

"When I saw him the second time, I really couldn't grab him," I said. "But the first time, I could have."

"They don't always make good companion dogs. Not if they've been trained to do go after other dogs."

"I know."

I promised to keep in touch and I promised to let her know if I got anywhere with my pit bull.

"My" pit bull.

When exactly had that crept in?

I knew the answer to that question.

The first night I saw him.

But that's what happens, I guess. You start thinking of them like you have some kind of claim on them.

44

"Uh, I don't think we're in Kansas anymore," I murmured to Gil.

We were walking from the parking lot toward the entrance of the Memorial Art Gallery and I'd just spotted the third evening dress. "I think we should go back to my place—I think I need to change."

"You look fine."

"Well thanks, but it's not a question of looking fine. I am seriously underdressed, Gil."

"It'll be fine. Relax."

Easy for him to say. We were at the entrance now, and had caught up with several other couples, and I was able to get a better look at the men. They were all in sports jackets. So was Gil. He had jeans on, not dress slacks, but even so . . .

I, on the other hand, was in capris and loafers. I wasn't just one category away from black backless floor length dresses and strappy high-heeled sandals. I was off by about a four.

Too late now. There were people behind us in line now, too, cutting off our escape. One of the men in the group ahead of us ceded door-holding responsibilities to Gil. I straightened up and walked past him to the fellow taking tickets inside the door.

A moment later, Gil and I stood together with our heads bent over the program.

"What do you want to do first?" I said.

Gil shrugged. "I dunno. Let's wander."

The exhibition itself was contemporary Russian and American screen prints. But tonight there were other things to see also. A jazz trio, a dance orchestra, a soprano singing Russian folk songs, a couple other vocalists doing Russian popular music. We started by checking out the ballroom, where the dance orchestra was playing. It looked like a wedding reception. Like a wedding reception kind of late in the evening. White linen-covered round tables, a temporary bar, a few people dancing, a few other people seated, making small talk. And a lot of empty space.

"How about later on this one," Gil said.

"I think we should go look at the prints."

We walked back past the sunken pavilion in the center of the gallery, where the jazz trio was beginning its nine o'clock set. "I figured out where I made my mistake," I said suddenly.

"Mistake?"

"In picking my clothes. I was back in student mode."

"You look fine, Paige."

"Yeah. I feel like a freaking teenager."

"Is that a bad thing?"

"Only if I get caught with alcohol."

The gallery was better. Smaller space, so it felt like we were part of the crowd. I stopped thinking about how I was dressed and started paying attention to the prints—and to Gil. This was his element, and you could feel it. Some of the prints he ignored, some of them he didn't. He stopped longest in front of the political ones—the ones where the artist was trying to make some sort of political statement. Then, when he was ready to move on, he would touch my shoulder or arm—but he was completely unconscious that he was doing it, completely unaware that it made me tingle, the assumed intimacy of it. We'd fallen into boyfriend-girlfriend mode. This was how we used to walk through exhibitions. Him looking at the art, me with half my eye on the art, half my eye on Gil.

It's not that I don't like art—I do. But it's his enjoyment of it that I get off on the most.

It was crowded enough that we couldn't get close to all the prints on the first pass, so we circled the room a second time to catch the ones we'd missed.

"Seen enough?" he said to me finally.

"Have you?"

He nodded.

"Let's go check out the folk singer."

She was upstairs, where the pre-Twentieth Century art is displayed. In a huge vaulted room with a marble baptismal font in the center. The music had already started, and the rows of folding chairs set up in the room were mostly already filled, so Gil and I stood in one of the doorways.

Gil touched my shoulder again, and when I looked at him, he bent down and whispered in my ear.

"Let's get out of here."

I nodded and we walked through Ancient Greece and Rome to the staircase.

45

"Well, that was interesting," I said when we were back in Gil's car.

"How so?"

"For one thing, I didn't realize Russian folk singers were classically trained."

He laughed.

"Anyway," I said, "if I ever win the lottery, I'm going to buy up all the advance tickets to the museum's upcoming preview shows. And give them away to college students."

"Uh huh, bankrupt the museum with the added insurance premiums."

"Why not? I, for one, think it would be worth it. And the spectacular drunken damage they do will get the museum lots of press, too. Don't forget that."

He started his car. The muffler was starting to fail so he had to raise his voice when he spoke next. "So where to, now?"

"A club somewhere?" I suggested. "You choose."

"Okay," He said. "I've got an idea."

◊ ◊ ◊ ◊ ◊

I read the posters on the way into the club. Glenn Tilbrook. Formerly of Squeeze.

Gil grinned at me some more, the same devilment in his eye. "Too late to change your mind now," he said.

"No, no, this is perfect!"

"And you're dressed right, this time."

We pressed into the club.

It was standing room only.

Which meant we had to stand awfully close to each other.

I didn't want it to be over. Ever.

But of course it couldn't last. Two sets, and he was driving me home.

The Rochester streets are pretty quiet that time of night.

We sat, waiting for the light to change, where Monroe Avenue crosses the expressway in the South Wedge. And, typical me, I was realizing that, because we'd been in a club, with music, we really hadn't talked all that much, and how many questions I had. Even besides the obvious. Like, for instance, why he'd given it up—his sculpture.

You'd think it would be easy to ask. But it wasn't. I knew him. Chances were better than 50/50 that he wouldn't like the question—he had never really liked being asked, directly, about anything having to do with his art—and I didn't want to spoil the evening by having him go moody on me.

So it was him, Mr. Taciturn, who broke the silence, right as the light turned green. "Good show, didn't you think?" He meant Tilbrook.

"Yeah." I said. "And the MAG exhibit, too—where did you get the tickets for that?"

"Oh. Friend of Marla's."

Marla.

"Ah," I said casually. "How is Marla, anyway?"

"Fine."

I hesitated. I was treading on dangerous ground, and I knew it. But I had to try. "Everything work out like you'd hoped, with her? The work you did for her and everything?"

"Yeah, fine."

I swallowed. It's not like he doesn't open up. He does, sometimes. But it's not on any timetable but his own. Whatever had happened to him in the past six years, Paige Newbury wasn't going to find out about it. Not tonight, anyway.

"Well," I said. "I'm glad it worked out for you." Then, bravely, "it's what you deserve, you know—to be recognized by people for your talent."

He made a sound. It could have been a snort, but it was too faint to tell for sure.

I looked at him.

That profile, lit by the streetlights as we drove . . .

And then we got back to my apartment.

And he followed me in, and I walked Lady and the puppies, and then he followed me upstairs to my bed.

46

I started taking puppies out with me on my rounds—because what better way to find homes for them than let people meet them?

Only that Friday I fudged it a bit—instead of taking one of the pups who needed a home, I took the one who was already spoken for.

The one that Gil and I were going to take to Taylor, his boss's daughter.

"C'mon, Kid," I said to her as I buckled the beensy little collar onto her neck.

I'd started calling each of them "Kid." I didn't want to name them. I was trying hard not to think of them that way.

Then after I'd finished circling Brighton I decided to swing by Rundel Library, to give Char a little moral support.

She was easy to spot.

I have to admit, even just driving by: the booth was pretty spectacular. She'd added some trim after we'd painted it—strips of gold in rows along the corners of the frame, and more gold in scrolly patterns on the top of the front, over the window.

I honked my horn and waved as I passed, and then finally found a spot to park.

It was a cool day, and cloudy, so I cracked the windows open and left the puppy in the truck.

I had to cross Court Street to get to her, and as I waited for the light to change, I saw a woman pull up the stool to the booth window for a reading. So I didn't go right to the booth, instead I climbed to the top steps in front of the library entrance to wait.

It was 5:45 and the sidewalks were crowded, by Rochester standards. There is a bus stop in front of the library, of course, and the Bausch & Lomb building is nearby, so people were rushing from it to the parking garage.

I saw the sausage guy Char had mentioned. He was doing a brisk business too, I noticed. Pedestrians were stopping, and also people in their cars, who would pull over to the curb and jump out to order a sandwich. I wondered idly if they ever got ticketed for that.

After ten minutes or so, the reading was apparently over. The woman got up off her stool and pushed it back in next to the booth. A little cluster of students—high school students probably—had paused now in front of the booth so I took the library steps two at a time—I wanted to get down there before Charlene started another reading.

"Hey, Char. Your booth looks great."

"Thanks." She grinned at me. She was done up to play the part. No turban, but hoop earrings and real glittery eye shadow, and a huge clump of beaded necklaces. And her top had Gypsy sleeves, of course.

"So what are you doing? Tarot?"

"Some. Mostly spirit guides."

The students had moved off. I tipped my head at them. "They didn't leave because of me, I hope."

"Nah."

I pulled up the stool. "Hey, fake that you're giving me a reading," I suggested. "It's always good if businesses look like they're popular. I can be your shill."

She gave me a look. "You and your ideas. How about I just give you a real reading?"

"No point, my guides are on an extended vacation." I swatted around above my head as if chasing off a mosquito. "See? Nothing."

"They are laughing at you, now," said Char.

"Nice. Supportive bunch of guides, I've got."

"It's very loving laughter."

"I see."

"So has Gil calmed down about the whole Larry at the party

thing?"

It wasn't a question I could easily answer. Things seemed to be back on track for us. Our date had been marvelous. Magical.

And yet . . .

I guess it's a bit like when you break a dish. You can glue it back together. Do a good enough job, and you might not even be able to see the crack. But it's still there. Always. Always, in the back of your mind, you're thinking there's a place now that's a bit weaker than it should be . . . that might break again.

I could see the sausage vendor from where I sat. He had just handed a white hot loaded with condiments to a customer.

He seemed to be giving me dirty looks.

"Speaking of calming people down, I see you haven't made peace with Sausage Guy," I said.

Char laughed. "That stuff he sells—it's like, ten paces back on the reincarnational wheel, every bite of that garbage you put into your body."

"You should team up with him. Half price readings with the purchase of a sausage sandwich. Only, I suppose peoples' guides would be yelling 'spit that out! spit that out!'"

"Exactly."

"You don't get hot in there?"

"No. The top is open." She pointed up.

"Well, I think the booth looks fabulous," I said. "Hey, want me to help you break down for the night?"

"Sure." She stood up and pushed aside the back panel so she could step out.

"Guess what," I said while we lifted the booth walls off their hinges. "I think I found a home for another one of the puppies."

"You mean, besides the one Gil found a home for?"

"Yeah."

"Who with?"

"Lady who saw me out today in the truck," I said. "I've started taking them out with me on my rounds."

"Good idea." Char nodded. "So—when are you and Gil taking the other one to that little girl?"

"Tomorrow," I said. "Hey, here comes a customer, I think."

I could see Char out of the corner of my eye, looking at my

face.

"It's nothing," I said. "It's just gonna be hard—watching the puppies go to new homes and everything."

"You still planning to find a home for Lady, too?"

"Yes," I said quietly, and when she didn't answer I added, "Don't worry, Char. I'll get a dog myself someday. It's just . . . not the right time, yet."

47

"So. Which one are you going to keep?"

Why does everyone keep bugging me about keeping a dog?

"I'm never home," I said, not looking at him. "It wouldn't be fair."

The puppies had eaten and now they were chewing on each others' ears and taking turns being bossed and bossy. Gil and I were finishing mugs of coffee behind the safety of the baby gate that blocked the doorway to the kitchen.

"Looks like they've started on your linoleum," he pointed out.

"Yeah." Where they'd pulled up a chunk of linoleum, over next to the fridge, you could now see a piece of filthy plywood subfloor. The spot, I noticed, was shaped kind of like Texas. Forty-seven more states to go, and then they could work on doing an Alaska by the sink and a Hawaii under the kitchen table.

"Won't it make them sick?"

"Probably. But they survived the wall paper. And they haven't really been swallowing it. I've sprayed it with some stuff that makes it taste bad."

"You mean, taste worse than linoleum?"

"Apparently, linoleum is quite flavorful to dogs."

"Maybe it's actually manufactured from beef byproducts."

"Yeah. They need to do something with all the really, really cruddy stuff they can't use to make dog food." I glanced at my watch. "I suppose it's time to get going."

He stepped over the child gate easily and took my mug from my hand, which just about did me in. I'm a huge sucker for that sort of unconscious chivalry. Plus he was wearing a white pocket tee. Which didn't help. That 50s look.

I knelt down into the pile of puppies and started talking to them to stop myself from paying any more attention to Gil. "Here Kid, here you go." Buckling the collar back onto the little female.

Then one of the other puppies now grabbed the leash in his teeth, and I turned to pry it loose, and when I turned back Gil had stooped down and gathered the little girl pup to his chest. "How about I carry her for the drive," he said.

"Sounds good," I said, trying not to stare . . . that little black puppy, wriggling happily against Gil's white tee shirt, kissing his chin with her red tongue. "Let's get out of here."

We headed east out of the city. It had been pouring rain a little while ago. Now the wet air was shot through with sun. The glare on the wet pavement was painfully brilliant, but finally we got to Route 65 and turned south. The sun wasn't shining straight in the windshield any more, and I relaxed a bit.

"How's she doing?" I glanced over.

"Just threw up," Gil said.

"Oh."

"You don't need to worry about your car, though, it's mostly on me. Make that, all on me."

"Any linoleum?"

"No. Puppy chow."

"There are napkins in the glove compartment. We could have used the crate."

"Nah. I get a discount on jeans anyway."

I watched him from the corner of my eye as he gathered the little pile of wet puppy chow from his lap and wrapped it up in a napkin. "Just set it on the floor in the back seat," I said when he was done. "I'll get it later." He had to twist around to do that, and I could smell him, and feel the warmth of him as he reached back between the seats.

He straightened back out again and stroked the puppy. She'd become subdued and solemn on his lap, as if grasping that something momentous was happening in her baby life, or maybe emptying her stomach didn't do enough to relieve her carsickness.

"Turn here," he said, and I did, he pulled a slip of paper from his back jeans pocket. "Right on Oak Briar," he muttered and then, "I think this is it, coming up, slow down. Yeah. Turn right here."

Our destination, it seemed, was somewhere within an enclave of newer homes. We threaded our way through a series of irregular intersections, and finally arrived at a cul-de-sac and he said, "this is it, then, that house there," and pointed.

I pulled into the driveway.

"I'd like to carry her now, okay?" I said.

We made our way over the pavered walkway to the front door.

I set the puppy down on a patch of grass a few feet from the front stoop.

Might as well let her empty herself before moving in.

And then the front door flew open and a girl's voice squealed, "Moooooooooooom! Daaaaaaaaaaaaaaaaaad! They're here! It's my PUPPY!"

◊ ◊ ◊ ◊ ◊

"Well," I said as we circled back around the cul-de-sac. "One down."

He didn't answer.

I glanced over at him. He had his head turned from me like there was something interesting to watch out the passenger side window.

I maneuvered back toward Oak Briar, collecting my thoughts.

This was my chance, and I knew it. It was now or never . . .

So I chuckled.

And then I said, "Poor Larry."

Gil snorted quietly and from the corner of my eye I could see his body stiffen slightly.

If I needed any proof that the Larry thing was a problem that still needed fixing, I now had it.

But I pretended to be oblivious to Gil's reaction, of course. I chuckled again and shook my head. "He's been trying to work up the nerve to ask Donna out—"

Oh Gawd. The second I heard the words I realized how utterly implausible this sounded. Larry? Nervous around a woman? Not in this lifetime.

I had that same nervous feeling in the pit of my stomach that I'd had when I first suggested to Larry that he pose as a sort-of rival.

Paige. You just don't learn.

And now it was too late. I'd put it out there. I had to see it through.

So I kept going.

"You know he dropped in the night of the puppy party—he found out she was going to be there—that's why he was skulking around in the kitchen that way!"

We were at a stop light.

I waited until the light turned green.

Gil still didn't say anything.

Good sign.

Keep going, Paige.

"Yeah," I said. "He wants me to fix them up. The poor guy."

"So fix them up already."

"Mmmm." I nodded. "Right. It's kind of a . . . delicate thing. She's not really over her ex, you know, she was dating this other guy Walter for quite a few years, now—"

From my peripheral vision I could see that Gil was looking directly at me now. I glanced over.

Not good. The expression in his eyes—not good.

"Larry," he said, "doesn't strike me as the kind of guy who needs help getting fixed up with women."

Ugh. Press forward, Paige, press forward. "Not usually, no!" I said. "But Donna—I'm telling you, the man's smitten."

"Smitten?"

"Yeah. He's . . . he's got it, bad."

"For Donna."

"Yeah."

"The one in the sweater."

The memory of Donna at the puppy party, in her skintight jeans and skintight glittery sweater rose up in front of my eyes, and I felt my cheeks color slightly. *Press forward, Paige. The only way out is straight through.* "He says she's, like, his dream girl or something."

Gil snorted again. "Well. For someone who thinks he's met the girl of his dreams, the guy sure seems to spend a lot of time around you."

"Oh, he can be a bit of a flirt," I said. "But—" I fumbled a bit through my mind. Somehow, somehow, to show Gil that Larry wasn't—and then the words popped out. "In fact, you know what would work? We should double date."

"Double date."

I snapped my fingers. "That's it, really. Gil. It would be perfect—a way to, you know, fix them up, break the ice—"

And also make it loud and clear to her Donna-ness that Gil is 100 percent already taken . . .

I was watching Gil surreptitiously out of the corner of my eye. "What do you think?" I said.

He shrugged. "I think," he said, "that all women are pretty much nuts."

But then he reached over and dropped a hand on my thigh.

"I'll set it up," I said, relaxing back into my seat and feeling his hand stroke my jeans, and thinking to myself that he probably had at least a couple of hours free before he had to go to work . . .

48

It was only later—after Gil had left me warm and soft and tangled up in my bed sheets—that I started thinking through the other piece of my plan.

Well, two other pieces, technically.

Donna—I wasn't worried about her. She'd jump at a chance to bag a handsome, unattached attorney.

So that left Larry.

To be honest, if I'd come up with this idea a couple months ago, I'd have figured it for a no-brainer. Larry as I knew him then, guy who enjoys the ladies, the eternal player—I'd have figured it would be easy—I'd have figured he'd be a shoo-in for a double date with any woman with ample breastage and a tendency to throw her eyelashes wide open in a picture of surprised innocence.

Rawr.

Right?

But on the other hand, the man had proven more difficult to manage than I'd expected.

I thought about the story he'd told me way back when, about the two women: the one that chased him, the one who didn't.

About which one he wanted more.

I kicked my legs loose from the sheets.

Maybe I should, you know, coach Donna a bit. Make sure she knew not to throw herself at the guy . . .

I sighed.

Not sure ol' Donna is the coachable type.

No. I had no choice, really. I had to rely on Larry—one more time. I had to be completely up front with him and get him to promise—promise!—to act the part.

That is, the part of being one hundred percent hot for Donna. My cell was on the bedside stand.

I picked it up, then remembered again where I was—in bed, and was that my panties still entwined around my left ankle?

Urgh.

Better to shower and dress, Paige my girl, before you make this next phone call . . .

And wow, was I ever glad I took my own advice that time.

49

"Lar," I said, tightening the belt of my bath robe as I spoke. "Got a second?"

"Sure do."

"I, uh . . . need another little favor."

"Ah," he said. "You're in luck, beautiful. It so happens I am in my car and can be there in less than ten."

AGAIN?

"No!" I said. "Wait!"

Too late.

He'd hung up.

I stared at my phone.

I couldn't freaking BELIEVE it.

I hit redial.

He didn't pick up.

I can make a dash for it. I can make a dash for it—

I looked down at my cell again.

6:30.

Gil's at work.

His shift started an hour ago.

So—for once—there was pretty much zero chance of him showing up and finding Larry here. . .

So just relax, Paige . . . oh Gawd, I'm in my bathrobe!

I took the steps up to my bedroom two at a time, let my robe fall as I yanked open my dresser drawer—and was just zipping my jeans when I heard Larry's SUV pull up out front.

Phew.

I gave myself a mental shake. Told myself to just be cool. Yes,

I would have preferred to handle this over the phone. But the fact was, I needed Larry's help to pull of this double-date idea of mine. And what was the big deal, anyway, with seeing him in person?

I gave myself another little shake and went downstairs to let him in.

"Hey, Larry." I opened the door.

"Hey, babe," he answered, before I could dodge he'd given me a quick peck on the top of the head.

He walked past me toward the kitchen.

I saw he was carrying a paper bag. A wine bottle-shaped paper bag.

He stepped over the child gate and the puppies swarmed him.

"Hey, puppies," he said, and then, called over his shoulder to me, "Glasses over the sink?"

"Sure, yeah. But Larry—"

"I know, Paige. You were just on your way out. Corkscrew?"

"Drawer next to the stove."

He opened the wine and poured two glasses and handed one to me while he stepped back over the child gate. And yeah, I took it. What was I going to do? He was here. And it was a Saturday night, after all.

I followed him into the living room.

"Siddown," he said, patting the couch cushion next to his. "You look kinda stressed. Good thing I had the wine, eh?"

"I'm not stressed," I said. "As a matter of fact, Gil and I—"

"Did you smell it?" he asked, gesturing with his glass.

I put my nose down into the wine glass and whoa. Flowers. Flowers and strawberries and smoke and spices.

"What is it?" I asked, and took a sip.

It tasted even more delicious than it smelled.

"A Santa Barbara Pinot," said Larry. "Like it?"

I forgot myself a bit and slid, without thinking, onto the couch next to him. "It's amazing."

"See?" He grinned at me. "You're more relaxed already. Now lemme have it."

I took a deep breath. "I'm gonna be up front with you, Larry. I need your help—one more time. Gil . . . still seems a bit upset about you being at my house that night."

Larry set his glass down. "Paige, you're too worked up about this. C'mon." And he patted his lap. "Feet up here," he said. "I give marvelous foot rubs, you know. Marvelous backrubs, too—all you have to do is ask."

"Larry, you have to admit—it looked pretty bad. You and me, holding a private conference in the kitchen like that. You know he walked out later that night without speaking a word to me."

He frowned. "But you've seen him again since, right?"

"Well, yeah."

He shrugged. "Eh, Paige, you gotta learn to relax about these things." He bent toward me and picked up my legs and swiveled me so he could rest my feet on his lap. "Chances are he's totally over it."

I pulled my feet away and put them back on the floor. "Pretty much," I said. "But—"

He picked my legs back up. "It's just a foot rub," he said. "If your boy walks in, I'll tell him you're helping me study to be a reflexologist."

I sighed. "He's working," I said. "Because believe me, if there was any chance of him walking in on us again I would not have let you come over. Ya know, Larry—"

"Just give it to me straight, Paige," he interrupted. "What do need me to do this time?"

He'd started digging into the pads of my feet with is thumbs.

"Ouch," I said. "Wow."

"Feels good, eh?"

I jerked my foot back. "Ow. No, actually, it tickles."

"Well *now* it does, because you've tensed all up again. It only tickles if you're tense." He pointed at my foot. "C'mere."

I sighed again and put my foot back on his lap and tried to relax. And sure enough, his fingers in the muscles of my feet were like—

"Well?" He looked at me. "Out with it."

"Okay." I paused a second, then plunged into it. "Larry, I need you to go on a double date. With me and Gil and Donna—that woman at the party."

He nodded. "Ah. The one in the sweater."

That sweater again.

Funny how men all notice the same things about a woman.

"Yeah. The tight sweater over the enormous boobs. That's the one."

He nodded thoughtfully and started pulling gently at my toes, which cracked—rather deliciously to tell the truth. "So this is to throw Gil off the scent," he said. "He'll see me in the willing arms of the luscious Donna, and he'll know that you are most certainly *not* the true object of my desire."

I felt the inevitable blush crawl up my face. "Look," I said. "If you don't want to . . ."

"Oh, no, it's a good plan. And I'm happy to help. There, is that better?"

I nodded and he swiveled my legs back around so I could drop them to the floor.

"You're a good friend, Larry." I said, feeling suddenly . . . I dunno. Sad or something. I guess that the foot rub was over. Not that I'd asked for a foot rub.

"You get tired of chasing this Gil character, you can always trade up, you know."

I covered my reaction with a light laugh. "Yes. You've mentioned that option."

Before he could say more, his cell phone went off.

I listened in, of course. Not that I could pick up much. Whoever was on the other end was doing most of the talking.

Larry smiled and winked at me every once in a while.

It didn't sound like the sort of conversation he'd be having with a client. Or the plumber.

"Lady friend?" I said when the call ended.

"Would it matter to you if it wasn't?"

I rolled my eyes.

"Anyhow, Paige, as I was saying, I think it's a good plan. We double date, he spends the whole night watching me make love to another woman—he'll get the picture."

I took a sip of wine. "No need to lay it on so thick, Larry."

"Hey, I'm being serious. I don't mean sex, you know."

"Sure, you don't."

"There's more than one way to drive the point home."

He grinned at me devilishly.

But I was having none of it. I rolled my eyes. "Really, Larry," I said. "Knock it off."

"Hey, you hired a lawyer. It's my job to screw people."

"Stop it! Geez. I'd rather work with dogs."

"Yeah, all day long dealing with man's best friend."

"Well, they aren't always my friends. They get scared sometimes."

"Ah, so you're not a dog idealist."

"Being a realist can sometimes save me getting bitten."

"Like with men, eh?"

I laughed in spite of myself. "You never quit, do you?"

"Actually, I was thinking about your ex, there, but I'll let you talk about me instead if you want."

"Gil? The problem with Gil isn't getting bitten. The problem with Gil is . . ."

I paused.

What was the problem with Gil, exactly?

Larry was watching me, expectant.

"I dunno, exactly," I mumbled.

What am I even talking about? There's no problem with Gil . . .

Larry had brought the wine bottle into the living room and set it on the floor next to the couch. He picked it up now, and leaned over to refill my glass.

"So," he said as he set the bottle back down. "Shall we get to terms?"

Terms?

"What do you mean?"

My heart was suddenly hammering. He couldn't *possibly* mean—

"Well, I do you this favor—I should get something in return, right?"

I started to stand up, but he reached over and touched my shoulder—it wasn't that he held me down, not at all, but like a little shock went through me that made me almost limp.

"Larry," I whispered. "Don't."

His eyes caught mine.

I looked away.

And he laughed.

"Paige," he said. "Don't worry. All I want is what you'd already promised. You know. Our make-up date."

"I can't—"

"Paige."

I looked over, and he was leaning slightly toward me and his eyes were . . . gentle? Or was it just that super charm of his, that he could turn on like normal people flick a light switch?

"Paige," he said again. "We're friends. It's just—two people going out for dinner. As friends."

I nodded slowly. "But if Gil—"

"He'll never know about it," he said. "And we'll do it after the double date. After he's seen how crazy I am for Donna."

He stood up. "I've got to meet someone in a couple of minutes."

"Oh," I said. "But the wine?"

"Enjoy," he said. "Share it with Phil." Then he put out his hand. "So we have a deal, right?"

I hesitated for a split second, trying to clear my head. "The double date comes first," I said.

He nodded.

"And you promise—promise—to behave yourself. No funny stuff. No . . ." I tried to think of how Larry might subvert the whole experiment. "I mean, you'll turn all your charm on Donna, none on me."

"Of course."

"And if you don't behave, the make-up date is off."

He grinned. "Of course."

So I took his hand and shook it. "Okay. It's a deal."

I stood by the living room window a minute later, watching his SUV pull away.

Forward, Paige.

He hadn't finished his glass of wine. Kind of irritating, that he'd jumped up and run off so abruptly that way. To meet the person who'd called him, of course. The lady friend.

50

"I told you, Char. No cards."

I'd come home from work and walked into my apartment, and there was Char.

Like I said, she's has a way of getting ahold of peoples' keys.

She was sitting at my kitchen table with her Tarot deck spread out all over.

"This isn't for you," she said without turning her head. "It's for her."

She tilted her head toward Lady, who was standing next to Char with her head in Char's lap.

"Oh," I said, and knelt to greet the puppies crowding around my feet. They were getting so big! "You can read Tarot cards for a dog?"

I tumbled one of the pups onto his back and gave him a tummy rub.

"Uh huh," she said absently.

"How is she going to pay you?" I asked. "Kibble?" I stood up and went over to the spot near the fridge where I'd spread out newspapers—they pretty much all did their business there, in the same spot, which was nice.

"Look where the Five of Cups is." Char said as I passed her again, carrying the day's soggy newspapers to the garbage can. She pointed to a card on the table. "Poor Lady."

"Okay. Why 'poor Lady'?"

"Oh, having her people throw her away like that."

"Mmmm," I said, stepping out of the pen. "You walked her, right?"

"Yeah, sure. See, she has the Nine of Wands and the Queen of Wands right here, and here."

"And that means?"

She didn't answer. Which made me start to feel a tad suspicious.

"Char?"

She made a slight shrug with her shoulders.

"Okay, you can't do this," I said. "What's it mean, the two wandy things?"

"Well, you understand that this is partly what I'm picking up intuitively," she said slowly.

"Yeah, sure. Out with it, Char."

"Well, you know the sort of dog she is, and how people just immediately like her. I just think, you know . . ."

"Cha-ar!"

"Maybe this is the best situation for her, is all."

"Oh, no! Don't you start on that, Char!"

"Hey, I'm just telling you what the cards said."

I laughed but I knew I sounded nervous. "Char, those cards did not say, 'Paige should keep the dog.'"

She smiled at me indulgently. "They didn't need to, Paige."

"I'm starved," I said. "Let's get some pizza or something, okay? Could you please put those things away?"

I drove. Our destination: an upscale pizza place. At Twelve Corners. So-called because it's an intersection of three major streets, except instead of meeting at a single point, they form three sides of a little triangular park. So there's the three corners of the park, each of which faces another three corners—two acute and one obtuse, ha ha ha, bet you didn't think you'd have to remember your geometry to hear my story. For a total of twelve. I once Googled an aerial view, and it's pretty striking, the symmetry suggesting a carefully crafted symbol of some kind, like those geoglyphs in Peru—the huge animals and geometrical figures that look like nothing from the ground, but from the air you can see that they were built to some intention. They were meant to communicate something.

Not that I think Twelve Corners is signaling UFOs. But it does look pretty cool from above. From the ground, on the other hand, the intersection is a bit disorienting—there's not much in the way of stand-out visual cues to help you tell one junction from another. I'd lived nearby for a good two years before I didn't have to do mental calculations to figure out which way to turn, to get where I wanted to go, as I approached the place.

The pizza you can buy there, on the other hand, is perfectly fine at ground level. I picked a slice with fresh mozzarella, sliced tomatoes and basil. Char's was ravioli. That's right, ravioli pizza. Kind of in the same league as a potato chip sandwich. Nouveau comfort food.

We ordered, and paid, and got our number from the counter guy. Then we drew our drinks from the self-serve soda machine and sat down.

"So guess what I did for about two hours yesterday," I said.

"What?"

"Found out some more stuff on dog fighting."

"From Larry?"

I started. Larry? Why on Earth would she mention— "No!" I said. "Online." I freed my straw from its paper sheath and jabbed it through the plastic X in the lid of my soda cup.

"So what did you find out?"

"That people who organize these things—if they want to make real money, they can't just do a fight or two. It has to be a regular event that they keep going for a period of time."

"What do they do? Sell tickets?"

"Well, it's gambling. So they get the house cut."

"Oh."

I sighed. "Of course, with my—I mean, with that pit bull, there's no way of knowing if he was used by an organized gang. His injuries—it could be a couple of guys fighting their dogs."

"You realize that you let yourself get involved with that dog. I'm just sayin.'"

The counter guy brought our pizza to our table.

"Yeah. I know," I said when he'd left.

"Have you talked to the Rochester animal people anymore?"

"No. There's no point. They can't just drop everything and start hunting for a dog fighting ring without knowing whether it even exists. Just because some bleeding heart feels bad about some pit bull."

"Well, what are you going to do?"

"Let it go, I guess."

What choice did I have, when I'd hit a complete dead end?

51

I was responding to about the seven thousandth "barking dog" complaint so far that month.

It's one of the commonest complaints under any circumstances, but for some reason, either the dogs or the people were even more nuts than usual.

Usually I don't actually hear the barking myself—most barking complaints come in at night and are routed through the Brighton Police Department. I get involved later, following up. But this time the call came in from a retired couple so they were around during the day. And the dog was one very lonely Malamute.

If you've never seen a Malamute, think an oversized husky. And like huskies, they aren't so much barkers as howlers. That's what this fellow was doing. His people had put him in the garage, presumably before they left for work that day, and he was pacing around the concrete howling like his doggy heart would break.

"We just moved in," the wife explained as I peered through the garage window at the dog.

"Is he out here doing this every day?"

"No." Now the husband took over. "We didn't even know they had a dog until today."

"Well," I said. "If you can stand it for a few more hours, I'll plan to come back by this evening and talk to them."

"That all you can do?"

"If they haven't left the dog out here like this before, they may not realize how stressed he'd get," I explained. "So I'll talk to them, they'll make different arrangements for the dog during the day, and you'll have your peace and quiet."

"That's ridiculous," the husband said. "Listen to him. Why should we have to put up with that?"

I looked in again through the garage door window. There was a water dispenser over in the corner. No apparent cruelty violation. I tapped the window and the dog froze and looked at me, ears pricked. "Hey fella," I said in a soothing voice. "Are your people gone, honey?"

I turned to the couple. "The noise ordinance isn't as stringent during the day as during the night," I explained. "There really aren't any laws being broken here. But I'm sure your neighbors wouldn't want you to have to listen to this all day. I'll talk to them, okay?"

The husband made a face like he had a turd in his mouth. But he didn't really have a choice.

I was back in my truck when my cell rang. It was Charlene.

"Hey, I need to ask you a favor."

"What's up?"

"Well, I have to move my booth."

"What happened?"

"There's a police officer here. He says I need to move."

I sucked in my breath. "Okay. Give me five minutes."

A little crowd had assembled by the time I showed up—about twenty people ringed around the booth. I pulled up next to the curb and flicked on my flashers. The booth had been partially disassembled and Char, standing nearby, face flushed, was gripping a ticket in her hand. A uniformed cop was standing near her, not talking, just kind of presiding. About fifteen feet away, a mounted policeman sat on his horse. I suppressed a smile. Char, busted. And they'd called in back-up.

I nodded at the officer standing by the pile o' booth. "Afternoon."

He nodded back and introduced himself. "She needs to get this off the sidewalk."

"I understand."

Looks like, for the second time, I'd be transporting Char's personal property in the town's truck.

"C'mon Char."

"Let's put the flat pieces in first."

"Yup."

"Out of the way, folks," the cop said and Char and I hoisted the sections of her booth and carried them to my truck.

"How much is the ticket?" I asked.

"I dunno. Twenty-five dollars, I think."

The two pieces that were stuck together were pretty heavy, but we managed. As we walked back to collect both stools—the one she'd left outside for customers and the one she sat on inside the booth—I noticed the sausage guy. Smirking. He'd probably called in the complaint. Not that I hadn't seen it coming.

"Where shall I meet you?" I asked Char after we'd put the stools in the back seat of her car.

"Might as well take it to my place," she answered.

52

By the time I left Char's it was late. I still needed to swing by the Malamute house, but first things first—I needed something for dinner, and was running low on puppy chow. So I went by Pittsford Wegman's, and something pretty interesting happened. I was wandering around in their prepared foods department when I ran into one of the staffers from Lollypop Farm at Wegman's. We said "hi" and were going our separate ways—me toward the Chinese food buffet and her toward the bakery—when she called my name and walked back over.

"Hey, Paige, it just occurred to me. We had someone stop this week, looking for a dog that went missing in Brighton."

"Oh, yeah?"

"Black lab. Female."

"Thanks. I'll keep my eyes open."

"Okay. Probably a long shot, though," she said. "Apparently the dog's been missing for a couple of months."

Now I was paying attention. "Oh, really? Two months?"

"Yeah. She said the dog may have been pregnant, too, when it disappeared."

May have been. Ha. "I don't suppose the dog's name was 'Lady.'"

"Yes! Lady! Did you pick her up?"

I shook my head. "No. Sorry. But I got a call about the dog, too. About two months ago, in fact. Maybe a bit more. Two and a half."

"Oh. She said she hadn't reported it."

"She didn't exactly. She was pretty upset. She hung up without giving me a name or call-back number."

Which wasn't a lie.

"Oh. Well. Too bad."

"Yeah, too bad."

Not. I stood looking at the Kung Pau Chicken.

But I was thinking about Lady while I looked. Wondering if that woman missed her dog.

Wondering what was right, ethically speaking, in that particular situation.

Return the dog to her family?

I shook my head.

No.

No way was Lady going to the animal shelter if there was any chance she might end up back with that woman who'd abandoned her .

Malamute place next. As I expected, the people were apologetic—horrified that their dog had been any trouble. Or maybe horrified that The Law had found out about it. Hard to tell the difference, sometimes. But their story was plausible. Their youngest had turned 10 this year, and now the wife had gone back to work—they didn't realize the dog would freak out if he was left in the garage. Etcetera etcetera.

My gut said I wouldn't be getting another call about this dog.

Because that's the thing. It's about consequences. And consequences is knowing that if you keep on a certain path, things are going to get bad. Or, at least, uncomfortable.

Kirsten Mortensen

53

Gil was late.

Okay, so. The guy's an artist. You have to cut him some slack. He's not a clock watcher.

But to be honest, I'd been looking forward to some alone time with him—no, more than that. I *needed* some alone time with him. But instead it was now less than 20 minutes to the starting bell of the infamous Double Date, and here I was pacing my apartment—nervous. Yeah. Despite telling myself I had no reason to be. Despite telling myself, over and over and over, that I could trust Larry to behave. That I'd struck a good bargain, really—he *had* to behave or no make-up date.

But what if he didn't?

It's a game to him. That's the problem. A game. And Gil—Gil's gonna be the other guy in the room. The one Larry will naturally want to beat.

Ugh.

I flashed back, again, on my idea of coaching Donna. Too late for that, now. Sure, I'd tried to drop some hints when I phoned her to set things up. She'd reacted pretty much how I'd expected when I told her that Larry wanted to get to know her better, she was all oh-my-Gawd and how-can-I-ever-thank-you and you-are-my-bff-forever, yeah, Donna, double forever best friends, that's us.

Or is it best friends forever squared?

I can't keep track.

Then she gave me a perfect opening. She asked me if I had any advice. "You're pretty good friends with him, right? Any advice for me? What does he like?"

"Sports," I muttered. "And, uh, you know—women who play it kind of cool."

"Kind of cool." She repeated my words like she had no idea what they meant.

"You know how some men are who kind of enjoy . . . you know. The sense of making a conquest."

"Ah," she said.

But I have no idea if she really got it, and I had no stomach to try again.

And so now here I was, and if only Gil had come earlier like he'd said—oh! To have had even a half hour of skin-to-skin time before—

The doorbell rang.

I flung the door open and it was all three of them, arrived at once, and oh—all it took was a glance to know that this was going to be one hell of an evening, the look on Gil's face—why did he have to get there at the same time—

"Come on in!" I said in my chirpiest voice, and stood aside and Donna oozed by and then Larry stood back and said "after you" to Gil, and Gil's face flashed something very close to a sneer as he stepped inside and past me.

"Anybody want a drink?" I called out as I darted after them.

I got a better look at her in the kitchen—she was dressed in these pimento-red capris and pimento-red scoop neck tank top. Her belt was a wide gold chain that would be totally fetish if it were silver. And her nails and lipstick were an exact match to the rest of her red.

Oh, and before her glass was half empty she'd already started out giggling ferociously at anything either of them said. Larry or Gil.

Like a demented squeeze doll.

And me? I felt like a perfect slug. I briefly considered spilling wine on myself, in fact, so I'd have an excuse to change before we left for the restaurant, swap my dull clay-colored top for something else—only there was a fatal flaw to that plan. I had nothing in my wardrobe that could out-peacock Donna's getup.

And even if I did—that wasn't me. To feel all discombobulated like that, and over what?

Over how another woman presents herself . . .

So instead I gulped from my glass and kicked myself for ignoring the advice of my cousin and best friend. Or what would have been her advice if I'd let her speak her mind. It might not have been very useful advice, in a lot of ways, but it would have spared me this spectacle.

And Larry and Gil—the both of them were already fully caught in her orbit. Circling helplessly, like a couple of brainless moons. Making me the knobby, pitted asteroid whose only hope was a direct hit and ensuing catastrophe.

"More wine?" I said, waving the bottle, and the three of them smiled blankly and waved me off. Donna was telling a story about getting hit on by some Buffalo Bills player at a hotel in Philadelphia. Larry, to his credit, was acting boyfriendish, opening the wine and sitting next to her on the couch. And of course, he's a sports person, and hadn't I given her this very advice, to talk about sports? So pretty soon he was leaning into her and stealing glances at her valley o' goodness—and Gil! Gil watched her like a dog who's been given a biscuit for no reason. The look on his face is a cross between ecstasy and "huh?"

"So you were in the lobby?" Larry asked.

"Yes! And it was the same guy we'd seen in the hall, checking us out."

I poured myself another glass of wine.

Gil had just gotten out of the shower. His hair was damp and his neck was pink from razor burn, and when I stepped past him I could smell him, his skin and his soap. But he'd seated himself on the chair next to the window, which meant I couldn't sit next to him, and Donna kept smiling at him as she talked.

Thank God, it seemed like she was almost at the end of her story. The punch line was that the player wanted both Donna and some other girl to come up to his room. A double dip. Donna turned him down. Giggle giggle, she was, into, you know, more traditional relationships.

Well, except for when the picture of her Flaming Redness in a three-way might burn itself into the brains of any nearby single males.

"Hey, guys?" I said. "Suppose we should head out? If we want to make our reservation."

Maybe it was my saying that or maybe it was just coincidence but Larry shook off the spell a bit and stood up. "How about I drive?" he said.

So we all got into his SUV. Me telling myself to relax, just be natural, it will be fine.

◊ ◊ ◊ ◊ ◊

The destination was Mario's Via Abruzzi, an haute Italian restaurant that seemed, at the time I made the reservations, to be the right mix of pricey and casual. But the thing about drinking a bunch of wine on an empty stomach, by the way, is that afterward things either make a whole lot more sense than they did before, or a whole lot less. Chalk this one to the "whole lot less" category. The faux classical decor framed Donna like a hyper-real goddess in a Maxfield Parrish painting. I was reduced to blurting "Pinot Grigio" to the fellow who filled our water glasses, and for the first time Larry actually looked at me, and said, "hold off for a sec, there, Paige, maybe we'll order a bottle—and have our server bring us a couple orders of the bruschetta, will you?" And then he beamed some kind of lawyer beams at the water pourer guy, which made him go away.

"Sure! A bottle!" I said. "Donna, what would you like? White or *red?*"

She tossed her hair a bit and looked up at Larry all doe-eyed. "Oh, I don't know! Larry, will you pick something?"

"How about we'll let Gil pick," said Larry, and Donna handed Gil the wine list.

Our server came and set the bruschetta on the table and Larry nodded at me. "Paige," he said, then caught himself. "Ladies, a little something to hold you until the wine gets here."

"I don't care for any, thanks," I said grimly.

"Me either!" Donna said, smiling at Larry. "I'm watching my carbs."

"On second thought," I muttered, and reached in front of her to grab a hunk of the bruschetta. "Is there butter?"

"Would you like some bruschetta, Gil?" Donna asked and

when Gil said "sure," she handed the plate to him and he accepted it with just the slightest of nods, like he was some god and the bread a routine offering from a devotee, and I had to fight to keep my jaw from dropping.

And my damn jeans. They fit fine when I bought them but they'd been shrinking ever since and I realized all of a sudden they were way too tight in the waist. "Where's our waiter, waitress person?" I said to nobody in particular, and Larry murmured "easy," to me under his breath, and I thought how amusing this must all be to him.

"So Gil," I said sweetly, "what did you pick?"

He'd just taken a huge bite of the bread and had to chew and swallow quickly to answer. "California Zin," he said.

Larry knocked his leg against mine under the table before I could make another reference to the color red, and flagged the water pourer—he was seating another party two tables away. "We're ready to order our wine," he said and the pourer told us he'd get our server.

"So Gil," Larry said, "Did you follow the Seahawks when you were on the west coast?"

"Nah. I'm not much of a sports fan, really."

"Unless it involves threesomes," I interjected brightly.

"Before I started taking art," Donna said, looking first at Larry and then at Gil, "I was, like, huge into football, and also ice hockey, you know we have an ice hockey team right here in Rochester, the Amerks, but now it doesn't seem as important anymore."

"Yes," I said, "Sometimes it can be hard to pay attention to more than one thing at once."

Donna giggled. "Oh, it's not that. But you know, art is so much more refined."

Gil once did a disintegrating sculpture titled Tackle. The idea was that the figures—football players diving onto a prone figure on the ground—would start out looking graceful and human, but as the sculpture collapsed they'd end up in the shape of a bomb crater. He'd always planned to do Tackle II, that would be rigged with sacks of red paint, so there'd be blood all over at the end.

But I wasn't about to bring this all up to be subjected to

Donna's treacley adoration.

Instead I said, "Well, I don't know, athletics can be very beautiful. I've heard football players sometimes train in ballet."

Donna giggled again. "Well, I didn't mean that!"

"Mean what?"

"Here's our wine," Larry said. "Just in time, right, Paige?"

That was an understatement.

Our server listed the specials pertly while she poured the wine, and we listened and looked at our menus.

Then she was gone and Larry lifted his glass. "Cheers."

We clinked our glasses.

Donna clinked hers to Larry's last and smiled and took a sip.

"So Donna," I said, "what are you having? They used to serve rabbit here." I laughed to show how fun this was. "Too bad they took it off the menu. It's really the perfect combination. Cute on the outside, meaty on the inside."

Donna wrinkled her nose. "Chicken Portobello for me. What are you having, Gil?"

"Pasta." And she asked him which one, and then leaned into him when he pointed at one of the dishes on the menu and said, "mmmm, I was thinking about that one, too."

"Yeah, pasta has no carbs," I muttered, and then in a bright voice, "Well, since there's no bunny, I'm leaning toward the calamari. You know, squid. Lower life form, slimy in its natural habitat."

Larry was kicking me under the table again. "The steak here is excellent," he said without looking up.

"Calamari," I answered darkly.

I noticed Gil was looking at me.

"What?" I said but he didn't answer.

"Oooh, we have to leave room for dessert!" Donna squealed suddenly, pointing to a dessert cart that's just rounded a corner into sight. "Larry, you just have to split one of those with me! Look at the cannolis! And that chocolate cake!"

"Sure, sounds good," Larry said and Larry kicked me yet again, before I could recycle my "carbs" comment.

The server was back.

"Calamari for me!" I told her, and then Donna ordered her

chicken and leaned into Larry again as she passed her menu to the server.

54

"So, just exactly how drunk did you get?"

I shifted the receiver to my left hand and adjusted the ice pack on my forehead. "Char, it was awful. And I think she went home with him."

"Who? Donna, you mean? With Larry?"

"With Larry, yeah, but Gil—"

"Well geez, Paige, isn't that kinda what you wanted to have happen?"

I suppressed a moan. "Yeah. I guess. But—Char, don't take this the wrong way—what is it you see in her, exactly?"

"She is actually a very sweet person. But you put her into a . . . volatile situation. Her break-up with Walter hit her really hard."

"Oh my god, I feel like crap. The calamari—that's what did it. I *hate* calamari."

"Uh, Paige, I believe it was the four glasses of wine on an empty stomach."

"My stomach wasn't completely empty. Larry made me eat some bruschetta."

Silence.

"Char?"

"Yeah. You know. I think I'm changing my mind about Larry," Char said slowly.

I moved the ice pack to my forehead. "I'm never going to drink again."

"You may have to start listening more to the guy. Within reason, of course."

"I don't know what you're talking about." I moaned aloud this time. "I have to go back to bed."

"Anyway, I still don't see why you care whether Larry took her home. It's Gil you care about, right?"

Gil.

"Gil had the time of his life," I said. "Char, I completely lost it. I completely lost control of it—of everything."

"It'll be okay—the important thing is, Paige, you did what you set out to do. You proved to Gil that there's nothing whatsoever between you and Larry."

"Yeah. I guess."

"So, everything's okay, right? Except the hangover, of course."

I groaned.

"If they get married," I said, "I'm wearing red to their wedding. And I'm getting a boob job, too. I'm going to have cleavage deep and wide enough to lose a basketball in."

"Perfect," Char says. "Then you could use your cleavage to catch the bouquet."

"Ouch. Don't. It hurts my head when I laugh."

Somehow I managed to walk Lady and the puppies.

Then I crawled back into bed.

And laid there with my head pounding and my stomach in knots.

Damn it.

Because yes. I'd accomplished what I meant to accomplish.

But for some reason it bothered me.

I rolled over and groaned, and then said the words out loud into my pillow.

"I wouldn't care if it was anybody else," I said. "But Donna? *Donna?*"

And then I burst into tears.

Because I felt so sick.

That's why I was so upset.

The hangover.

55

I finally got back to sleep, and when I woke again the pounding pain in my head had subsided to more of an annoying ache.

I was able, finally, to keep a little food down.

Mentally—that was another story. Mentally, my main goal was to put last night completely out of my mind. I didn't want any highlight clips running through my head. And I sure as hell didn't want to try to figure any of it out.

I did my best.

I played with the puppies.

I taught Lady to roll over.

I made myself a cup of tea with honey, and noticed that my head hardly hurt at all anymore, and wow, did the tea ever taste good.

I let the puppies out of the kitchen and settled into my couch with my mug nestled between my hands, and watched the puppies explore and play fight with each other.

But images from the previous night kept popping back up. Donna flirting with Larry. Donna flirting with Gil. The annoyed looks on the faces of the people the next table over—I was talking too loud! Disturbing them . . . the wobbly walk to the parking lot, to Larry's SUV, the back of Donna's head . . . Gil acting distant . . . I moved away from him to the other side of the seat, leaned my head against the window, so cool on my cheek, ugh, my stomach, need to puke, need to . . .

Kyle Warren.

I sat up straight.

Larry had said something about Kyle Warren?

Gah! Why had I drunk so much freaking wine?

I gulped a swallow of tea.

Kyle Warren.

It started to come back. Yes.

It was in front of my apartment . . . Larry had parked by the curb. . . Gil was helping me out of the car . . . Larry was asking if he needed any help . . . Donna said something I couldn't hear. And then Gil was on one side of me with his arm under mine, guiding me to the door, and Larry had my purse . . . he found the keys, he opened the door, he was holding the door while Gil guided me over the threshold—

"Oh, Paige. I almost forgot to mention—I've got a date with a judge to settle that case with Kyle Warren. Cash offer. How he got his hands on thirty grand in cash . . ."

And for that moment it was as if I wasn't drunk. My eyes seemed to focus again—but Gil, Gil, stop! I need to—

". . . beats the hell out of me where he gets it, but I sure wish—"

I could hear him, but it was too late, it was like listening through the wrong end of a telescope, and then the door was swinging closed, Gil was saying something now, too, of all the stupid things, he'd never seen me do anything quite this stupid before—ugh, get me to the bathroom!

Get me to the bathroom, now!

My tea was nearly gone, lukewarm.

I took another swallow.

His arm looked like hamburger.

"Yeah. My pit poodle."

I set down my mug and collected the puppies and put them back in the kitchen.

Frustrating. Frustrating. Two big DOTS staring at me. One being Kyle Warren's improbable involvement with a badly socialized dog. The other being Kyle Warren's improbable thirty thousand dollars in cash.

They had to be connected, but how?

How?

I turned on my computer and logged onto the county clerk's website and started poking around in the records database.

There were a gazillion "Kyle Warren" files. Property records, of course—the same five properties I'd been watching. Plus a bunch of lawsuits, counter suits, counter-counter suits. Two divorce filings. A pistol permit.

I clicked on a few of the records.

He had a lot of liens against those properties . . .

I got up and put the kettle back on the stove and then for kicks I searched again, only this time I didn't use Kyle. I searched on "Warren" alone, and just on property records.

Warren's a common name. The search gave me pages and pages of records.

The kettle whistled.

I made myself another cup of tea and sat down to scan the results again.

And all at once the skin on the back of my neck started prickling again—just like it had at the puppy party, when Larry was first telling me about Kyle . . .

I keyed a couple of the addresses into Mapquest.

I picked up my cell.

The last thing I needed that afternoon was another conversation with Larry Crawford. But I had to bounce this off him—if I was onto something important, I trusted him to know it.

I took a deep breath.

Keep it light, Paige.

And I dialed his number.

"Hey, beautiful. Feeling better?"

Keep it light. Ignore the flirting.

"Yeah, Larry, I'm fine. Got a sec?"

"For you, I've got hours."

Bet you had hours for Donna last night too.

Gah!

Get a grip, Paige.

I cleared my throat. "It's about your buddy Kyle."

"No buddy of mine. But go on."

I cradled my phone on my left shoulder so I could switch back from Mapquest to the results of my last county records search. "I've found some other properties and it's odd—they're owned by a Warren, but not a Kyle Warren. And they look to be purchased as foreclosure properties, from the city. Cheap."

"You're online," he said. "I can hear you clicking keys."

"And you are in a restaurant. I can hear people talking."

"Good one, Paige. Although we're sitting in the bar."

Donna.

I kept my voice light. "Ah, so you're talking to me with your date sitting there?"

"Date? I'm here on business, my dear. And he'd wandered off somewhere when you called, only here he is, back. Want to say 'hi'?"

"Mmmmm. Not really."

But Larry didn't take that for a "no," and a second later, another male voice was talking. "Hi, is this Paige?"

"Yeah."

"Tim Bartlett. I'm the guy Larry's scared shitless to meet in court."

Then Larry had the phone back. "Bart's full of crap, Paige, he's never won a case from me in his life."

"Okay, Lar, I'll ignore him."

"So are you calling about our make-up date? Because I can ditch Bart right now if you want."

My stomach had been feeling so much better. Now I suddenly wished I hadn't drunk that second cup of tea.

"Larry—"

"It's our deal, Paige."

"Can we get back to the Warren thing please? Is there any way he'd be going by 'Peter'?"

"Peter."

"Your friend Kyle."

"Kyle. Hmmm. Middle initial P. His middle name is . . . Peter. Interesting."

"Yeah," I said. "And maybe it's nothing. But I cross-checked the purchase dates of the Peter Warren properties and it looks like he was filling his shopping cart at the same time Kyle was."

"You don't say. Paige, would it be sexist of me to start calling you Nancy Drew?"

"Depends on your tone of voice."

"Okay, I'll be very respectful. Ms. Drew. How's that?"

"It's a start."

"You've got a lot on the cap, Ms. Drew, you know it?"

"You say the nicest things, Larry."

"I would do some nice things too, if you'd let me." He paused. "Hey, it would be sweet, if you've stumbled on some assets the SOB has hidden away."

"I dunno about assets," I said. "These are probably pretty rundown properties. But if he's running a dog fighting ring, I'll see him go to jail for it."

"Go get 'em, Nance. Hang on, Bart's asking me if I want anything to eat. Hang on, yeah, Bart, I'll do a burger or something . . . okay, Nance, I'm back. So, did you have a good time last night?"

Ugh. Like he didn't know. "Sure, Larry," I said in my driest one of voice. "Time of my life."

"Well, you did what you set out to do, right? Showed your boy Phil—"

"Not now, please, Larry," I said.

Or I'll start to cry.

"Paige." His voice was gentle all of a sudden. "You okay?"

"I gotta go, Larry. But I'll email these addresses to you, okay? Let me know if you can—"

"Sure, Paige," he said. "I'll check them out."

56

My strategy of taking puppies out with me on my rounds paid off when I met a newly married couple while I was gassing up my truck.

They'd just bought a house with a big yard and were looking for a puppy.

That's not all I did, of course. I put up fliers around town, and put an ad on Craiglist. So pretty soon I was down to four puppies—and I knew they wouldn't last much longer, either.

I kept an eye on Lady as her brood dwindled but honestly, she didn't seem to mind. I admired her for that. Nothing seemed to bother Lady.

Me, on the other hand—I admit it, I really struggled. It didn't help that Bizarro World stuff started hitting me from every angle. Like the day I was out patrolling and got a call about a missing ferret that happened to be in Skip Wendt's neighborhood. The ferret was missing because apparently it was allowed to have the run of the house, as are a couple of teenagers, who, being teenagers, are about as good at remembering to close doors as a ferret would be, if a ferret could reach the doorknob. "This has happened before," the mother told me as we looked out across the backyard. "But this time, we think Basil has been gone since last night."

"Basil?"

"He's the male. The female is Brenda. You know, like Brenda Starr. But she didn't get out. Only Basil did."

I could have said something about maybe he'd gone looking for the black orchid serum but I didn't. "Nobody missed Basil until today?"

"I wasn't home." She was apologetic. "I usually feed them. When he didn't come when I called this morning, that's when I figured out he wasn't in the house."

The neighborhood's yards weren't exactly thick with places for a ferret to hide. On the other hand, a ferret who wants to hide doesn't take up a lot of room. We walked the perimeter of her yard, but I didn't have the feeling that Basil was going to pop up that easily.

"The best I can say," I told her, "is to put some food out on the back step and call him at his regular feeding times. If he hasn't wandered too far off, or if he manages to get back into earshot, you might get lucky."

"Poor Basil," she said sadly.

Poor Brenda, I thought to myself.

It had been awhile since Skip had called about Maddie stealing his cat—well over a week, which was kind of odd—and I wasn't far away, so I decided I'd swing by that neighborhood too—only since Skip hadn't called I'd go to Maddie's house instead of his.

I parked and went to her door and rang the bell.

Nothing.

I could see her car in the garage, so she was home.

"Maddie," I said in a loud voice against the door, "you're avoiding me, and that can only mean one thing."

I pushed the doorbell again, twice this time. After another minute or so, I heard a "clunk" from somewhere inside and heavy footsteps, which is kind of weird since Maddie is only about 4 foot 9. But before I have a chance for this to even really sink in, the door opened.

And there stood Skip.

For a split second, I thought I'd mixed up their houses. I'd been back and forth between both places so many times. "Mr. Wendt?"

He just nodded at me. Then yelled, "Maddie! Dog catcher's here."

Fred rounded a corner into the foyer, sat, curled his tail around his haunches so it overlapped his front paws, and blinked at me.

Wendt was wearing a bathrobe.

"Uh, look, sorry to have bothered you." I stepped back away from the door. I could hear Maddie coming down the stairs now. She stuck her orange-coifed head around the corner and smiled and waved. "Hi, Paige, dear! How nice of you to drop by. Would you like to come in?"

"No, no, I—I was just—I just came by to say 'hi.' Sorry to have bothered you when you have company."

"Some people call first," Wendt said.

No answer to that. I made a break for my truck.

Now I'm sorry, but that was just too much.

I didn't even try to sit and collect my thoughts.

I was living in Bizarro World.

57

Maple trees always drop a lot of seeds in late spring. But that year was ridiculous. And the way they land—you know maple seeds, those little helicopters as people call them, and when they land, the seed part hits first, and the little dry brown blade sticks straight up. So the lawns with maple trees—and they are all over the place around here, Norways mostly and Silver Maples—Silvers are a fast-growing tree so municipalities have put in tons of them—were porcupined with these dry brown seed wings. And the roads, and people's driveways, the edges of the driveways where the asphalt meets the lawn turf, are just heaped with them. It's ridiculous.

What was that a sign of? I don't know. But it was peculiar. Don't you think?

The weather turned hot, too. Broiling hot, upper 80s hot—heck, lower 90s, hot, if you believe what peoples' actual thermometers read, instead of what they report from the airport.

It's the kind of hot that we usually get in August, or maybe early September. The lawn outside my apartment was actually turning brown—and it wasn't even summer yet, for God's sake.

I didn't have AC in my apartment, so I bought a floor fan and put it in my kitchen. Then started schlepping the puppies, one by one, up to my bathroom, and putting them in the tub to wet them down. Lady, too, of course. Not that I really thought they were in danger or anything. But phew. They just sat and panted. And Lady. She kept giving me these looks like, hey, you're the human, fix it, c'mon!

So of course my apartment reeked of wet dog. Because it was

so humid anything that was normally odorless smelled, and anything that normally smelled stank enough to raise the dead.

And then . . . I knew I should have stopped myself. But Gil and I . . . we used to let Trixie sleep in our room. It's the hot dog thing that reminded me of it. I can remember the hot nights, lying awake, listening to her pant, listening to her pad into the bathroom where we kept a pan of water for her. The backyard of that house was bordered by a hedge of mock orange and this time of year the fragrance would fill our bedroom and mix with Trixie's doggy smell. And then Gil would wake up early—he was a morning person—and if he didn't have to work he'd take Trixie out and then come back to bed and keep me there, with him, for hours . . .

58

With the P. Warren properties added to my list, I now had almost a dozen properties to watch.

I paid special attention to the new ones. Drove by them after work sometimes, sometimes my lunch hour.

I never used the truck, though.

I didn't want anyone to know someone from animal control was paying attention.

I tried to be smart, as well, about the routes I took—on the outside chance someone might notice me—I'd thread new routes through those old streets, with their classic early Twentieth Century homes, spacious and worn, many with little gardens, people sitting on lawn chairs out front, kids dashing about.

That's what I was doing when I got my pittie.

I can still hardly believe it happened. I was at a four-way stop, waiting for a big white van that had the right of way. The van crawled out into the intersection and turned, and I pulled out to follow it. It was blocking a good deal of my field of vision, so I didn't see the dog until I was almost abreast of it.

Brindle male pit bull.

I thought, "it can't be my dog."

But lookie at who was walking it.

Mr. Stocky Guy. That heavy-set Hispanic I'd met outside the city grocery store.

And this time he was alone.

I pulled over to the curb and got out of my car.

If he recognized me, he pretended not to.

The dog was wearing a chain choke collar this time.

And he was limping.

Stocky Guy paused to let the dog sniff the ground at the corner of a driveway and the sidewalk.

I must have known what I would do if I ever got into this situation. Because I didn't even stop then to think. I just walked right up to the guy.

"Doesn't look like he's been winning," I said.

He didn't answer me.

He smelled like beer again.

"I'll give you ten dollars for him."

The man grunted dismissively. The dog crouched to relieve himself.

I didn't see any evidence that Stocky Guy was going to pick up afterward, but I wasn't about to point that out. It's not like I was on duty. And I had more important injustices on my mind.

I don't carry a purse. I keep my money and debit card in the back pocket of my jeans. Now I pulled out all my cash. "Look," I said. "I know you fight this dog. But he's not a winner. He's worth nothing to you. I have . . . twenty . . . twenty two dollars cash here. That's all I have on me. Look, here's some change. Take twenty two dollars, and change, for the dog. You can keep the collar."

"Twenty two dollars." It was a statement.

"You keep the collar. Just let him off the collar into the back seat of my car."

"I don't fight him." His words slurred slightly. "The neighbor's dog, he jumped the fence and went at him."

"Whatever. I don't care, okay? I like the dog. I don't have a dog, I want him, for a pet. Twenty two bucks."

He walked the dog over to my car and I held the door open while he let him loose into the back seat.

"His name's Mojo," the guy said.

Like I was going to call that dog by the name that jerk used when he was urging him to tear up other dogs.

But I didn't say anything, of course. I got into my car and drove off.

Best twenty bucks I ever spent.

The dog stood on the back seat.

The passenger-side window was open a crack.

He whuffed happily at the air as we drove.

◊ ◊ ◊ ◊ ◊

"I need a rope."

Char wasn't the sort of person who misses a beat in situations like that.

She just said, "Fresh out of rope. Will a bathrobe sash work?"

"Yep."

With Lady at my place, there was no way I could take the dog there. So I'd driven straight to Char's.

"C'mon," I said happily. "Wait 'til you see what I've got."

So she followed me down to my car.

She knew instantly who it was. "Oh, Paige! You got him! How did you get him?"

"Bought him." My grin split my face. I opened the car door, watching him, but he was fine. Just as relaxed as could be. I got in next to him and stroked his head. His tail thudded the seat. "Look at this fellow, Char. He's a complete sweetheart."

"He's safe to be around?"

"He sure seems to be. Around people, anyway."

I tied the end of the bathrobe sash around his neck and led him up into her apartment.

Char went straight to the sink and filled a bowl with water, and brought it over and set it on the floor.

I was already on my cell phone.

"Trish?" Char asked when I hung up. You're gonna take him to that pit bull sanctuary?"

I nodded. "She didn't pick up, so I left a message. Okay if I keep him here until I hear from her?"

"Sure."

"You'll need to close him into your bedroom if you have company. He's probably okay but—to be on the safe side. Especially around kids."

"No problem."

He'd finished drinking and was nosing around on the kitchen floor in search of crumbs.

"Making himself right at home," I observed happily.

"That mess on his front leg, is that from fighting?"

I nodded. "See how the cuts circle his leg?"

"Shall I take him to a vet?"

"Better not." The dog was done exploring the kitchen. Now he sat in front of me and looked up, giving me a doggy grin. "He's a lucky guy he didn't get put down the last time. You're a lucky guy," I said to the dog and stroked his head.

His tail thumped the floor.

"Where's the sanctuary?"

"Ohio."

And then we had some tea and I told her the whole story of how I'd found the dog. And when I was done she said, "you know, you were meant to save this dog. You knew it from the first time you saw him."

"I guess."

"C'mon, Paige, you think it's just coincidence that you stumbled across this dog three times? Three times?"

"I don't know, Char. It could be just luck."

She smiled. "You know it's more than that."

I felt too fine to argue. "He needs a new name."

He'd come back into the kitchen and was sitting next to me with his head on my thigh while I gave the base of his ears a good scratch. "Would you look at that face! What a face. Look at his big eyes! Golden eyes, Char!"

Char agreed he was gorgeous.

"Pick a name for him Char, okay?"

"Okay. I'll channel it."

"To signify his new life," I suggested.

"Yes, exactly."

I got up. "Okay. You work on that. I'm gonna go get some dog food, I'll be back in a half hour, okay?"

"Sounds good."

59

I slid into my seat and stuck my keys into the ignition.

Hesitated.

But I had to do it—I pulled my cell out of my purse and scrolled to Larry's number and hit the call button.

"Larry," I said. "I got the dog."

"The dog. You don't mean—"

"Yep. Our pit bull. I just brought him over to Char's place— he's thin and beat up, but as beautiful as ever."

My eyes suddenly filled with tears.

Happy tears.

"Well," he said. "Congratulations. How'd you do it?"

"Pure luck," I said, and then I told him the rest of it. "Twenty bucks," I said. "Oh, here's Char, hang on."

She'd come out to where I was still parked.

I rolled down the window.

"Tor," she said. "It came through right away," she said. "Loud and clear."

"Tor. I like it."

"I looked it up in the dictionary. It means 'rocky peak.'"

"Perfect. I'm talking to Larry. Larry," I said into the phone, "his name's Tor."

"So what's next?" he said.

"Well, assuming I can get Doug to fill in for me, I'm gonna take tomorrow off and drive him to a rescue sanctuary in Ohio."

"Day off, huh? So how about we get together when you're back—this calls for a celebration, don't you think?"

"Oh! Well, I dunno know what time I'll be back—"

"C'mon, Paige. This is a big deal. And you still owe me that make-up date."

Tomorrow night . . . Gil would be working . . . and you know what? This was a big deal. I did want to celebrate. "Okay," I said. "Sure."

And then we hung up. And then I called Gil's cell and left a message for him, and then I called Doug and sure enough he'd be happy to fill in for me tomorrow.

Gil called me back after he got home from work that night. He congratulated me too, although to be honest he didn't get excited about it as Larry had. Not that he would. He'd never met the dog. It didn't mean as much to him—to him it was like work talk, me and dogs, me and rescuing dogs.

Whereas with Larry—you know. There was some history.

60

We left at four in the morning.

From Rochester to Cleveland, the drive, along Interstate 90, skirts Lake Ontario first, then Lake Erie. The sun had come up by the time we hit the stretch west of Buffalo where you can see Lake Erie from the highway. Tor was in the front seat with me this time. He'd stand up every so often, but when I said "sit" he would sit back down. Even sitting, though, his muzzle could reach the windshield of my Civic. The glass was soon smeared with nose prints.

We rolled into Trish's place mid-morning. I could hear dogs barking. I leashed Tor and took him out onto the lawn to relieve himself, and then saw Trish walking up the driveway from her barn.

She was dressed in overalls and a black PETA baseball cap, and her hair was done in two braids. It had been cut short while she was at Cornell.

I was smiling pretty hard. It was good to be there.

"Hey!"

"Hey!"

She got down on one knee to greet Tor. "So this is your fella, huh?"

"This is the one."

"Aw, look at your leg, sweetie!" she murmured sympathetically. "Yeah, he's been fought, alright." She touched the scabs. "Look at him. He's got one high pain threshold. So you bought him, huh?"

I'd told her the story on the phone. "Yup."

"Twenty bucks?

"Twenty two dollars and fifty seven cents."

"Gotta do what you gotta do. C'mon, I'll show you his new home. Tor, right?"

I nodded and we headed toward the barn.

Tor knew there were other dogs about, of course, and his tail was stiff. And I could feel how tense he was through the leash.

"It was a horse barn once," Trish said as we went inside. "We've converted the stalls so they work for dogs. We call them cubbies. We use them for sick or injured dogs, or for when we get pregnant ones."

"The rest stay outside?"

"Yeah. We have 42 dogs now, counting Tor, here. We couldn't fit them all inside."

"Anybody in here now?"

"Only Derrick. He's got cancer and had to have a leg taken off." We walked over to one of the cubbies. Derrick, a white Bull Terrier, was curled up on a blanket in the corner, asleep. "He's deaf, he doesn't know we're here. Watch this." Trish banged on the wall of the stable box with her fist, and Derrick lifted his head, looked at us, pulled his lips back in a doggy grin and pulled himself up off the floor to limp over. Trish pulled a dog biscuit out of her overall pockets and fed it to him through the chain link on the front of the cubbie while she scratched the side of his head.

Tor's hackles were at full mast now, so I didn't get too close to Derrick's cubbie. When dogs are fought, they learn to be on high alert any time another dog is around . . .

"The vet gives Derrick maybe six weeks. But he's 11. He's had a pretty good life."

"How long has he been here?"

"About three months. His owners brought him when he got sick. They couldn't afford the vet bills."

"How many permanent residents do you have?"

"We have about 25 who we probably can't place. We get a few like Derrick, who are sick or something. But most of them that we keep on have aggression problems. We can't really place dogs who might bite someone, or another dog. Our insurance is already ridiculous. All it would take would be one mistake . . . and . . . phew. I don't know. We could be done for."

"Better to err on the side of caution."

"Yeah. We sometimes get someone who is knowledgeable enough about dogs, and who, you know, doesn't have kids or any other animals. The right situation, and you can place one, even if it's a dog with problems. That's the difference between us and a municipal shelter."

We decided to leave Tor in one of the cubbies while we went outside. He was already keyed up—best to get him used to the place slowly. So we settled him in with some water and a handful of kibble, then headed out a side door and around to the back of the barn where the outdoor runs were.

Dozens of pairs of pit bull eyes were watching us. Several of the dogs were barking pretty insistently, and a few were jumping up excitedly against their chain link walls, but some just looked at us silently—sizing us up.

Each of the outdoor runs was on gravel and outfitted with a molded plastic, insulated dog house. About half of the enclosures were standalones—they didn't share any walls with other runs, and had sheets of plywood between them and their neighbors.

Trish saw me looking at them. "We set those up that way to minimize fence-fighting," she explained. "Especially when we bring in new dogs, we don't want them making each other crazy through the fence."

"Makes sense," I said. "But you let them socialize, right?"

"Yeah, we have a play yard over there." She pointed to a fenced-in enclosure I hadn't noticed before, off to our left. It was maybe a quarter of an acre in size and had some battered agility equipment set up inside. "What we try to do is pair each resident dog with a buddy. It takes a while sometimes to find two who won't push each other's buttons but if we're patient we can usually manage."

"So you do agility with them?"

"Yeah, a couple of the volunteers are into it. And it's great exercise for the dogs."

"So, speaking of volunteers, you're going to let me pitch in for a bit before I leave, right?"

She laughed and pointed to some tools leaning up against the back of the barn. "If you don't mind starting with poo pick-up in the play yard, and then you can supervise some play time while I clean kennels."

"Sounds good."

◊ ◊ ◊ ◊ ◊

I stayed around until after lunch.

It was hard saying good-bye to Tor. "You never know," Trish said. "We may find out he's fine with other dogs. He sure seems laid back. Maybe he is placeable."

"I hope so," I said.

I gave her a check for $50 before I left. It wasn't much but it would help pay for Tor's dog food for a while. And I made her promise to call me after his vet check-up, so I could pay for his neutering. And shots.

My car felt pretty empty on the way home.

Tor—what a gorgeous animal. What a sweetheart . . .

I turned on the radio and found some pop music station on FM.

But I didn't really hear the music.

I'd fallen for that dog that first night, when I'd said "sit" and he'd dropped into that perfect tucked sit, and I'd tossed him the bits of salmon . . . he'd trusted me.

A dog like that, abused like he'd been abused. And yet he'd trusted me . . .

I switched the radio back off, and glanced at the clock on the dash.

I'd be home in plenty of time for that date with Larry.

Crap.

I couldn't postpone the thing forever.

Might as well get it over with.

61

I wish I could say it was awful.

I wish I could say I was miserable the entire evening.

But it's Larry. And Larry—he knows how to show a gal a nice time.

◊ ◊ ◊ ◊ ◊

It was one of those fresh warm evenings, my apartment windows were open and a sweet breeze was wafting in, and I could hear a robin singing in the Norway maple by the street and a grackle in the hedge making his squeaky door hinge noises.

I toweled my hair dry and then flicked through the clothes in my closet.

It was plenty warm enough to wear a dress.

And I had a new one. I'd picked up at a discount at Marshall's—and it was such a pretty dress and fit me so well. An off-the-shoulder, silk tank dress with an empire waist. One of those kind of dresses you buy and get home and think, "now when am I going to have any reason to wear THIS?"—whatever weird fantasy had possessed you, when you were in the store, being, by then, long gone.

So there I stood today, holding it at arm's length like a potential dance partner and thinking I should really wear something that says we're-just-friends, but oh. I was in such a mood . . .

I put the dress on.

I looked at myself in the mirror.

Big risk here—risk that I'd give Larry the wrong idea.

But he'd said, himself, that we'd be going out as friends. And the silk felt so good on my skin, so cool in the warm summer air . . .

I heard the deep husky growl of an SUV engine, and peeked out the window.

"Liking this weather?" he said to me a bit later.

"Yeah," I said, climbing into his truck. "It's days like this that make it worth it, living through the winters up here. Like the joke where the one guy is hitting himself on the head with a hammer, and the other guy says, 'why are you doing that,' and the first guy says 'because it feels so good when I stop'—a day like this, it's stopped."

He laughed and turned toward the city.

"Where we headed?"

"Someplace nice. I see you're dressed for it, this time."

I felt a little blush creep onto my cheeks. And of course he noticed—of course he said something.

"You're a knock-out when you want to be, know that, Paige?"

My blush deepened. "Knock it off, Lar. We're doing this as friends, remember?"

He laughed. "Friends can still pay each other compliments, Paige. Anyway, admit it—it's nice having an admirer, isn't it?"

I started to laugh, then bit my lip.

He eased the SUV onto the expressway. "Plus we both have something to celebrate. You saved your pit bull. I just won a big case."

My opening—I asked him to tell me about it, and not only was it fairly interesting—he'd defended a fellow lawyer, a criminal defense attorney, against a bunch of fraud and money-laundering charges—it also distracted him from the flirting.

And pretty soon we were at the restaurant. 2 Vine, a tony spot in the East End.

Linen-table-cloth tony.

"I told them a table away from the windows," Larry murmured into my ear as we follow the maitre'd.

He ordered some wine, and since we'd pretty much exhausted the topic of his recent case win—and since by the look in his eye I could tell he was about to go on another charm assault—I cast about for other safe subjects. "So what else is going on? You get that case with Kyle Warren settled?"

"Oh, that." He jerked his chin slightly. "Hit a bit of a snag on that one."

The server poured our wine. "What happened?" I asked.

"Just a temporary setback. Dom and I had some bad luck on the judge."

"Is he a bad judge?"

He shrugged. "Let's just say he's not my biggest fan."

I smiled. "Has a doable wife, does he?"

"Hey, it's not my fault she's bored at home." He laughed, but then he stopped short and looked at me. "You do realize, Paige, that my reputation is worse than my actual behavior."

"Mmmmm."

"You think I'm off screwing around every night?"

"I wouldn't know," I said. The question made me feel uncomfortable, to be honest.

I set my wine glass down and reached for my water.

"The fact is, Paige, most nights, I'm at home. By myself."

"What's 'most nights'? Three out of five?"

"And how about Gil?" Larry said. "What does he do with himself when he's on the other side of the country. Have you considered that he might—"

"I wouldn't know," I said.

"You know how you can tell?" He picked up the wine bottle and refreshed my glass. "I'll tell you. If a guy is paying attention to you—then you're the woman who's on his mind. If he's not—"

"I'd rather not discuss Gil."

Larry leaned forward. "Fine, Paige. We'll talk about us. Because I could get serious about you. You know that, right?"

I set my glass back down and tried to laugh but then I saw the look in his eyes again and the laugh died back down my throat . . . and into my belly . . .

Where it exploded into a case of queasy butterflies . . .

"Larry, cut it out." I tried, again to make it sound like we were both joking, but my voice came out so peculiar. "This is a fake date, remember?"

His eyes held mine.

How does he *do* that?

And then he laughed, and picked up the wine bottle, and poured a bit more into both of our glasses. "Of course I remember, beautiful," he said. "So onto some safe fake date conversation, right? Anything going on in dogcatcher land?"

I took another swallow of wine. It was a good wine, a 1989 Bordeaux, the sort I can't really afford, and the buzz from it was somehow subtle and intense at the same time. I knew I'd need to start eating soon, though, before "intense" degenerated into trouble. "Not much," I said. "Let's order, okay?"

"Sure." He flagged the server, then raised his eyebrow at me when I ordered a steak.

"Hey, I eat steak sometimes."

He laughed. "You're all woman, Paige."

I rolled my eyes and he grinned. There was no stopping that guy, there really wasn't. But my belly was warm with wine and I'll be honest. It didn't feel half bad, him flirting with me the way he did. Nope. In fact, sometimes . . .

I shook the thought away.

The server brought our food. My steak was delicious, and Larry kept leaning over the table to pour another splash of that wine into my glass, and about half-way through my meal I noticed there were three women at the table next to us who kept looking at him. I mean, they couldn't keep their eyes off him.

Have I mentioned how good-looking the guy is? And he was wearing one of his custom-made Oxford shirts that fit him so well . . .

By the time we were on dessert, I confess, I'd pretty much put that pit bull out of my mind.

◊ ◊ ◊ ◊ ◊

"Let me walk you to your door."

If that isn't the oldest line in the book, it has to be in the top three, but did I argue?

No, I did not.

I let him walk me to the door.

And I let him take the key from me and put it in the lock and turn it.

"You liked that wine."

"Uh huh."

"You drank practically the whole bottle, you know." He grinned at me.

"Did not."

"Better watch out, you'll get a reputation."

My cheeks felt hot. "Be good, Larry," I said.

I thought then that he was going to turn and walk down the sidewalk toward his car.

But he didn't. He just stood there, looking at me—and I knew what was coming next wasn't going to be fun. I knew it. But it was like I couldn't move—like I had to stand there and face it, take it—take the worst he could dish out.

"Tell me, Paige," he said. "What do you want with that guy?"

I should have been ready. I should have had an answer on the tip of my tongue. Always. Anything.

"I'm serious," Larry said.

"It's—it's just that—"

He leaned in and spoke again, his voice low this time. "You have history," he said. "I get that. But Paige, men aren't dogs."

"Dogs!"

"I've been paying attention, Paige. To what you're doing—to what you've been trying to do. Pull him in, without him knowing it exactly—it's a game to you, it's like when you want to catch a loose dog—"

"No." I'd found my voice. "No—I love him, Larry."

"You're right, Paige, about one thing at least. Men—real men—have a lot of animal in them. We are like dogs, in a way. But not quite as simple, Paige—"

"I never said—"

"We deserve to be treated better."

And then he pulled me in and he kissed me.

A real kiss.

A breach the wall kiss.

I guess I should have seen it coming. But even if I had, what I couldn't have seen was that I'd like it. A lot. So much so, that I not only took the kiss, I almost asked for more. A lot more. I mean, I came that close to throwing everything else away—Gil, the ring, my dreams—and just losing myself in Larry's kiss, and his arms around me, and the way he was pressing his hips hungrily against mine.

But thank God, I recovered my senses, and pushed him back and said, "Okay, Lar, that's . . . enough."

I sucked in air, tried to catch my breath—

Larry shrugged his shoulders to straighten his jacket. "You're something special, Paige Newbury," he said. "You know that? One of a kind."

"Stop. Stop it."

He looked at me for a moment, then said, "Okay. I'm stopping."

"Thank you."

"For now."

"Because it isn't what we want."

"No. Because you've had too much to drink."

"Right, Larry." I smiled triumphantly. "I see what you did right there."

He cocked his head slightly to the side. "I don't know what you're talking about."

"If I agree with you, it means it'll be okay for you to kiss me some other time—some time when I haven't had too much to drink."

He didn't answer right away. He just studied me—and the smile on my face started to feel awkward and die away.

"All right, Paige," he said. "I quit."

"Good!"

"No." His eyes were dead serious. "I've been thinking it over. I was really looking forward to this night, you know—"

I opened my mouth to say something but he reached out and put two fingers on my lips to stop me.

"Enough banter," he said. "Because I've got something to say and, for once, I want you to hear it. You think you're pretty smart, with your schemes—no! Not a word!—but you get so caught up in them that you don't even notice what's going on in front of you. And Paige."

231

He leaned toward me so that his face was nearly touching mine.

"When you don't notice what's going on in front of you—you lose it."

He straightened back up. "Good bye, Paige," he said. "Don't forget your key's in the lock."

And he turned around and walked to his SUV.

And I leaned back on my door. I must have had too much to drink . . . my head . . .

The SUV pulled away.

Good bye?

I stepped inside and closed the door and stood for a minute in the foyer, wondering what the hell had just happened to me.

62

I was down to the last puppy.

I started taking him and Lady for walks in Ellison Park. I figured it would be a great way to find a home for the last puppy—he was the little male with the star on his chest.

Just like his mom's.

But a funny thing happened. I was standing on this arched bridge that spans Ellison Creek, near where people go to let their dogs swim, and a middle aged woman stopped to pet Lady and her pup. The pup was all distracted by the other dogs he could see and smell around the park, but not Lady. Lady was all for being petted. She was practically in the woman's lap.

The woman was thin, fit, with white hair—but prematurely white, her face was still youngish. Wearing a Columbia sweatshirt and Birkenstock sandals. I told her the puppy needed a home, and she smiled kind of absently like people do when they are being polite but really, really don't want you to pressure them to take in a dog. And then she stood up and said, "I just lost a dog."

"Oh. I'm sorry."

"Cancer. She was 16."

"That's a good old age. What kind of dog was she?"

"Oh, she was a mutt. Mixed breed."

Every time the woman stopped petting her, Lady pushed her nose into the woman's hand again, and every time Lady pushed her nose into that hand, the woman petted her some more.

I took a deep breath. "Lady, here, needs a home, too. A good home . . . as soon she's back from the vet. She's getting spayed."

"She needs a home? Really?"

And I could tell by the way that woman's face changed, at that moment, that I was going to be saying good-bye to Lady pretty soon . . .

63

I was on my way—again—to case Kyle Warren's properties.

Only this time, for the first time, something crossed my mind.

Wasn't it a bit odd to see Stocky Guy up on that side of the city, when the last time he'd had the dog, it was in the South Wedge?

Not that there's any law against people showing up in completely different corners of Rochester . . .

I turned down the street where I'd picked up Tor.

I pulled over to the curb and opened my glove compartment and pulled out the Mapquest maps that I'd printed out the night I'd first looked at the P. Warren properties.

He owned three houses on this street.

All three were obviously vacant. The lawns were scruffy and the first floor windows were boarded up to keep vagrants out. So were the basement windows.

The westernmost house had graffiti spray painted on the side.

But then I noticed something I'd missed—somehow—every other time I'd driving by.

They were all in a row.

It's not that you don't see vacant houses in Rochester. But for a number of years, now, the city's housing council started a program to get vacant houses either occupied or torn down. So seeing three in a row like that was a little odd.

I got out of my car. Two of the houses had faded neon orange "For Rent" signs stapled onto the front doors. The middle one didn't.

Across the street, a white-haired woman in baggy shorts and a print top was poking at a little flower garden with a stick.

I got out of my car and went over to say hello.

She looked at me. "I'm killing weeds," she said.

I nodded, like it was perfectly normal to kill weeds by jabbing them.

"I can't really bend over any more. But if you poke them back into the ground, they go away."

"It's warm out today," I said. "Make sure you're drinking lots of water." She looked flushed.

"The nurse tells me that, too. I don't care for water, really."

"Lemonade, then."

"That's what I say, but she says, 'no, no, no, Abigail, it's all sugar, sugar's bad for you. Everything is bad for you, you know."

I nodded sympathetically. "Of course," I said, "sugar is bad for people if they are diabetic."

"I am perfectly healthy," she said primly.

"Then I say, drink all the lemonade you want. At your age, you should be able to have lemonade if you want lemonade."

So then we were friends.

"Are you here visiting?" She leaned the stick against her porch steps.

"No," I said. I gestured at the three vacant homes across the street. It had crossed my mind to make up a little fib—claim I was looking for a house to rent, or an investment property, but it didn't really seem there was much need. "I am curious about those three houses."

She gave me a dark look. "I don't like the people who moved in."

"Oh. Aren't they empty?"

"Someone lives in the middle one. And he has too many dogs."

My stomach tightened. "How awful. Do they bark a lot?"

"Dogs, dogs, dogs. Coming and going, coming and going."

I paused. On the one hand, if I hung out and questioned her awhile, I might eventually get something useful. On the other hand, the less of an impression I made on her, the less likely she'd mention our conversation to anyone else.

I had a lead. That was enough.

"Well," I said, "some people just like dogs, I guess."

236

"I had a Yorkshire Terrier once," she told me, brightening.

"Ah, a Yorkie. Was he a sweetheart?"

"He used to dance on his hind legs at mealtimes. I never taught him to do it. He taught it to himself, all by himself."

I listened to her tell more Yorkie stories for a couple minutes. Then made my excuses and left her to finishing poking her weeds.

64

"Your kitchen looked so much better after you painted it," Char said.

She wanted me to help her paint hers.

And I really, really didn't want to get roped into it. For starters, her color ideas were enough to drive anyone nuts. Assuming she could even decide on a color. She'd been painting and repainting blocks of paint samples on her walls practically since time immemorial. Her technique was to tune into the sample of the month to see if it was right. One time I'd stopped by to get some money from her that she owed me, and there she was, sitting cross-legged on a bar stool in front of her latest color sample (chartreuse that time) to feel its vibration.

Apparently the chartreuse hadn't passed, or the tangerine, or the magenta. Instead she'd chosen lilac. With yellow trim. I privately wondered if it wasn't going to look like the inside of a giant Easter Egg when we were done but she'd said something about a glue gun and purple sequins so I figured I'd better reserve judgment until I could see the final effect.

"Char," I said. "This isn't a good time. I'm really busy right now."

"You don't have any more puppies," she said. "It'll be fun. Please?"

"It will *not* be fun."

"I'll cook dinner after."

I sighed. "I can only stay until 4. No later."

I don't actually know why I agreed to go at all. But I did, and a little while later, there I was, rolling her ceiling.

Also in lilac, by the way. Good grief.

And we had only one long-handled roller. So she had me working from a step ladder with a short-handled one.

She could tell I was grumpy.

"Are you sure you can't stay to eat something?" she said.

"No. I've got plans."

"Date with Gil?"

"He's closing the store tonight," I said. "So yeah, he's stopping by when he's done—it'll be 11 or so probably. But what I meant was I may have a lead on a dog fighting ring—it's connected to those people who had Tor."

"Oh, really!" She smushed her roller around in the paint pan. "What do you mean?"

"I think I know where they are fighting. So I'm going to stake the place out."

"When, tonight?"

"Yeah." She'd started spreading paint overhead but now she lowered the roller.

"What?" I said finally.

"You should wait a bit."

"Huh?"

"Don't bother with those houses tonight."

I considered the uneasy feeling that touched the pit of my stomach. Then pushed it away. "There's probably nothing going on with them," I said, maybe to myself as much as to Char. "There's really no danger to me or anything."

She didn't answer.

"Stop looking at me like that, Char," I said. "You're giving me the creeps."

"Look, Paige," she said finally. "There's something I have to tell you."

The uneasy feeling in my stomach suddenly pitched up and transmogrified into a bit of genuine willies. "Char," I said.

"Listen to me. I'm sorry. But you know how I keep saying you should let me do the cards for you?"

I nodded. "But you know I don't—"

"Yeah. You don't believe in any of that stuff. But I—I love you, Paige. And Paige—"

"Geez, Char." I knew, in that instant, what she'd been up to. "You've been doing Tarot readings on me anyway? Behind my back?"

"Well . . .yes."

"Gee whiz, Char—"

"The Death card keeps coming up."

"Oh CHAR." I burst out laughing. "You know it doesn't mean anything! And even if it did—you've told me yourself. What the Death card signifies is *change*. Out with the old, in with the new, blah blah blah—it doesn't mean anybody is going to actually *die*."

Her brow was pursed.

Stop being a doofus, Char.

"And look at my life, lately!" I went on. "Tor to the sanctuary. Lady and the puppies to their new homes—"

And I've lost Larry . . .

But I didn't say that aloud. Aloud, I said, "Char, *if* the cards mean anything—and I don't believe for a second they do—it's that you've picked up on *that*."

She looked away from me, and dipped her roller back into the paint pan. "Well," she said, "Anyway, I was thinking of renting a movie. The Notebook."

We'd seen it, together, when it was out in the theaters. We'd both loved it.

"Okay," I said, "let me think about it, okay? And Char, don't ever do that again with the cards. Honestly. You really had me creeped out for a minute."

65

It was about 8:00 when I headed back out. A half hour before sunset.

My plan was to drive by a couple of times and look. That's all. Then call Char, and if she was still interested we'd watch that movie.

I didn't want it to be obvious that I was looking at anything. So I drove a normal street speed, glancing casually at the vacant houses.

They looked the same as ever.

About the only thing that caught my attention, in fact, was an Accord with gold hubcaps, parked at the curb a few doors down. The sun happened to be slanting into it, so despite the window tint I could see that a guy sat in the driver's seat. Sleeping, apparently. A black baseball cap was pulled down over his face. The letters BP were appliquéd on the front of the cap. It wasn't a logo I recognized, but then, I don't do the hip hop thing.

I got to the end of the street. I had hours, still, before Gil got off work, so I decided to circle the block and have a look at the properties from the backside, from the next street over.

It was dusk now, and the neighborhood had turned quiet.

I parked my car, locked it, took a deep breath to quiet my heart a bit, crossed the street, and walked up the driveway of the house I judged would back up to about where the Warren houses were.

Nobody saw me.

A moment later I was looking into the backyard of the westernmost house. A couple of cars passed, then another, this one with its base thudding so loud the air vibrated.

There was no fence, just some trees and brush. I skirted them, keeping in the shadows, until I was across from the middle house.

It had a little shed in back that cast a shadow as well.

All I intended to do was look. That's all.

But when I got to the house, I found the back door unlocked.

66

You know what?

I hesitated.

I hesitated.

It crossed my mind, Paige, leave it be. Get to your car, call the RPD, call the city animal services.

But then I remembered, again, the way Tor's front leg looked the day I bought him.

Like hell was I going to just back off now. Do more of nothing while meanwhile more dogs were forced to suffer unfathomable pain and cruelty.

So I opened the door and listened.

Nothing. The place was empty. Had to be.

I stepped inside, closed the door behind me, waited for my eyes to adjust.

I headed straight to the basement.

And there it was: what I'd been looking for.

The pit.

Plywood. About 8 feet square, four feet high. One section was removed, leaning against a wall.

I walked around, looking. On the other side of the room stood an old dinette table with four scanners set up on it, side by side— they'd use them to monitor police radio broadcasts during fights— and some crinkled ointment tubes and a few rolls of gauze. Stuff they kept on hand to dress wounds.

The windows were stuffed with insulation and tattered blankets.

I forced myself to breathe deeply.

This was it. What I needed to know.

The cops could take it from here.

I turned around and headed back upstairs. The basement steps led into the kitchen, which was filthy, stacked with empty pizza boxes. A couple of roaches skittered across the counter.

I poked my head through the door into the hallway that led to the front door.

And then I heard footsteps.

Heavy, scuffy footsteps.

Somebody was walking up the driveway.

I held my breath.

Was my mind playing tricks on me?

Then I heard the rattley doorknob on the back door moving.

I didn't have time to think. I slipped off my shoes and tiptoed quickly into the front hallway, and then onto the first landing of the stairs so I would be out of sight.

Whoever it was, he was indoors now, clumping toward the basement.

I stepped down from the landing and tried the front door.

Locked.

The only way out was the door I'd used to come in.

Clumping footsteps coming back up from the basement.

The kitchen light flickered on.

I was trapped.

somewhere to hide somewhere to hide

I darted up the stairs, my mind churning, ticking off my options. Whoever it was in the house with me—he might well do a complete walk-through to make sure nobody was here, that nothing was amiss.

My only hope was to find a decent hiding spot—and hope he did a piss poor inspection.

The stairs creaked slightly under my feet but the noise now coming from the kitchen—sounded like somebody unloading bottles into the refrigerator—masked it.

I looked around at the top of the stairs. A bathroom. No shower curtain, even if the tub was a smart choice. The attic. But if I got up there and it was empty—I didn't let myself think what would happen. That left the bedrooms . . . in the weak light from

the streetlights outside, I could see the first one was full of junk—
boxes, piles of filthy clothes, a filthy old window air conditioner. I
considered burying myself in a pile of clothes. I checked the other
bedroom. It had a mattress, but the mattress was on the floor, no
bed frame to slide under.

I fought to keep from panicking.

Then, back out in the hallway, I noticed a narrow, built-in linen
closet, floor to ceiling, next to a laundry chute.

I opened the closet door—and finally caught a break.

Not only was it empty of junk, it had been gutted at some
point. No shelves.

I set my shoes on the floor, climbed into the closet and
managed to pull the door shut—not easy to do, as there was no
latch from the inside.

It was cramped but I managed to pull my Visa card and my
Wegman's Shopper's Club card and all my cash out of my back
pocket, and feeling my way in the dark, I sandwiched the bills
between the cards and wedged the whole thing between the closet
door and the doorframe to jam the door.

I'd just finished when the clumpy footsteps came up the stairs.

I heard lights switch on and switch off. The bedrooms. The
bathroom. Then up the attic stairs. Footsteps overhead. Back
down the attic stairs.

The sound of pissing coming from the bathroom.

Back past me again.

He didn't check the closet.

I wiped my hands on the legs of my jeans as I heard him go
back down to the first floor.

I realized how much I was shaking.

Because it seemed maybe I had pulled it off.

My hope now was that the person downstairs—whoever he
was—wouldn't be staying very long. So I could get the hell out of
there.

◊ ◊ ◊ ◊ ◊

But he didn't leave.

Instead, he got company.

Lots of company.

I know, because as it turns out, sound from a basement travels rather well up a laundry chute.

Meaning that I suddenly found myself with a front row seat to the dog fights that were about to begin two floors below.

67

Not that the activity was restricted to the basement. The second floor was busy also, especially at first. The bedrooms were, apparently, a good place for drug transactions. Which was more bad news for me. My hand was closed over my cell phone in my front jeans pocket. My worthless cell phone. Because, you know, I couldn't exactly chitchat with a 911 dispatcher with those people in the next room.

I could dial and hang up. And they might call back . . . I wouldn't be able to answer . . .

They'd send a patrol car to check on me, right?

A single patrol car?

I wondered how many people were in the house . . .

How many guns . . .

An argument broke out below. Somebody owed somebody else some money. The angry one was mollified when he was promised he'd get paid, because "Devil, he a winner."

Those two sounded like they might be African Americans. But not everyone in the house did. Dog fighting, you see, cuts across ethnic lines.

I said the sound traveled pretty well up the chute. But it wasn't crystal clear. These old houses are lathe and mortar, so the sound was deadened by the walls. I couldn't hear low noise, but as the activity increased, voices started to rise, and I could pick out snatches of conversation. Dog's names. "Devil" got mentioned a lot. Also "Rock" and "M-Dog."

And then all at once the sound died down. And then exploded again, and through it, I could heard the faint noises of dogs, snarling.

It had started.

Tears sprang suddenly to my eyes. *This wasn't what was supposed to happen.* I was supposed to be able to stop them. I wasn't supposed to be stuck, trapped, powerless to do a thing.

Gil.

I'll text Gil. I'll tell him where I am, what's going on. And he'll call 911, and . . .

Gil was at work.

He wouldn't have his cell with him now.

I'd have to tough it out until the end of his shift . . .

A surge of noise welled up from the basement. Yelling—cheering . . .

Gil.

And it wasn't the time nor the place, right there in that closet, to be thinking about Gil—no. Not about Gil.

About our relationship.

But that's exactly what happened. And I couldn't stop it. As if there, trapped in that stupid closet, for the first time I couldn't escape it—it was like I was trapped also inside that thought, the thought I most didn't want to face.

How ever since the day I met Gil, I'd never known for sure if he was going to be there for me—

It doesn't matter.

But it did matter.

It mattered tremendously.

With Gil, I'm alone.

I touched the keypad of my cell again.

The screen lit up.

"need you, no joke," I tapped onto my phone. "trapped @pwarren house. dog fight. plz call cops!!!!"

I hit Send and gripped my phone.

Nothing to do now but wait . . .

Be there Larry, be there . . .

And please. Don't be too angry with me. I'm sorry . . . I'm sorry for how I treated Gil . . . how I treated you . . .

Please don't be angry. Not now . . .

The noise below me surged again. They were probably starting to get drunk and goodness knows what else . . . it was hard to tell exactly what was going on. I could make out cursing. I could tell when the dogs had locked, because the spectators would start bellowing at the handlers in the pit to break them up so they would attack some more. With a dog fight, you see, the object is for the dogs to damage each other. If they clamp down on each other and just hang on—it's like two spent boxers hugging each other to buy some time, to rest.

Can't have that.

I tapped a key on my phone to make the screen light up again. Nothing.

He'd said "good bye."

Maybe he's ignoring me . . .

Maybe he blocked my number . . .

Someone bellowed "chickenshit!" and a few minutes later a door slammed . . . so a fight had ended . . . the owner of the losing dog was leaving, humiliated.

They often just kill the dogs who lose.

I started to feel sick. Lightheaded. Partly from fear, I supposed. Partly because there wasn't a hell of a lot of fresh air getting into that little closet.

I wondered how much longer this was going to go on.

I shut my eyes.

And then I did my stupidest thing yet.

I dropped my damn phone.

68

They shouldn't have heard it.

But in an utterly perverse twist, that phone hit the closet floor just as the noise in the basement suddenly abated. Maybe another fight was about to begin, and the bets were all in and so they'd suddenly fallen quiet in anticipation of what was about to happen. Or maybe it was just one of the moments like you might have noticed at a party, where the rhythms of the conversations suddenly synch out and a pause hits at once across an entire roomful of people, and some joker says "oh, somebody musta just died."

Only that's not what they said this time. Because the phone didn't just thunk. It bounced. And the closet floor was wood—the phone actually clattered.

And I heard someone say "what the fuck was that?" and somebody else said "nothin' man" and then the first voice said "yeah" and then told someone named Jeremy to get his ass the fuck upstairs and check it out.

I held my breath, listening.

It was clunky footsteps guy again.

The noise downstairs quickly picked up, but I could hear him all the same.

He was walking through the first floor rooms again.

Then I heard him come up the stairs.

And now that he was closer I heard something else. He wasn't alone, this time. That was dog nails clicking on the steps.

Past me. Into the bedrooms. Back to the hallway.

He was standing outside the closet door. I could hear him

breathing. I could hear the dog pant.

And then I heard the dog snuffing at the crack at the bottom of the door.

The closet door rattled.

He was tugging on the latch.

But I had that door wedged pretty tight.

He cursed, and the tugging stopped, and I heard him go up the attic stairs again. Then back down.

And again, the footsteps stopped next to the closet.

Again, the dog snuffed.

He pushed on the door, then tried yanking on the latch again. More cursing. And I'd started talking to him with my mind. Ordering him. *Give up. Give up. Give up. Go away.*

He didn't give up.

He gave another hard yank.

And the door popped open.

My credit cards and cash hit the floor.

And I was looking into the face of the guy in the baseball cap who had been napping in the Accord a few hours ago.

Jeremy glanced down at the scattered bills, and then looked back up at me.

His face was expressionless.

His left hand was holding a choke chain that was around the neck of a dog—a pit bull.

A brindle pit bull.

Tor!

But it wasn't Tor, of course—and this dog's hackles were raised and its eyes, fixed on me, were tense.

Not good.

But for all that, it wasn't the dog that had me really worried.

It was the gun.

69

First things first, right?

Jeremy knelt down, set the gun on the floor—he knew I wasn't going anywhere, with that dog straining at me—picked up my cash and credit card, and stuffed them into his jeans pocket.

Then he picked up the gun again and—his eyes still blank as a zombie's—gestured at me to step out of the closet.

Which I did.

"You a cop," he said. It wasn't a question.

I shook my head no.

"You a cop," he said again.

"No," I said.

"What the fuck you doin' in the closet."

I didn't really have an answer to that question that I felt like sharing.

"I ask you a question, bitch."

Indeed he had.

I opened my mouth to say "laundry." I'd always been a bit of a smart aleck. Might as well die one.

But before I got a chance to say it, all hell broke loose two floors down. A huge crashing noise. Yelling.

Jeremy turned his head toward the stairs, listening.

The dog stood on tiptoe, eyes fixed on my face. I avoided eye contact. Force of habit. Don't stare at a potentially aggressive dog.

Then Jeremy and I both heard it. Someone yelling "cops!" Thundering footsteps as people ran up from the basement. Doors slamming open, doors slamming shut. More footsteps outside the house.

Larry! I thought, and then *the place is going down and the rats are jumping ship.*

But then Jeremy turned and looked at me again. And the expression in his eyes had changed—it was an expression I still see now, in my nightmares—an expression that was beyond hatred, a crazed hatred.

He dropped the leash and raised his gun.

It's funny how my attention switched, at that second, to the thing I could do something about.

The dog.

We animal control folks, not being superheroes, don't do well at fending off bullets. But when an aggressive dog jumps at us, we know exactly what do to. Protect the face. Protect the throat.

I never heard the shot.

But I felt the dog. All 85 pounds of him, on top of me, as I hit the floor.

Then Jeremy's footsteps pounding down the stairs as he made his getaway.

The shouting was all outside now. I could see flashing lights, blue and red, playing on the ceiling.

I rolled the dog off me.

I may not have heard the shot, but I knew what had happened.

There wasn't much blood.

I looked for the entrance hole. Found it in the dog's right haunch.

I was sitting there, on the floor, next to the dog's body, when the officers came up the stairs, guns drawn.

"Look," I said. "The dog. The dog was going too—the dog— damn dog saved my life—"

And then, I'm not ashamed to say, I started blubbering like a baby.

And then somebody let Larry come up, and he cradled me for a while, and then helped me put on my shoes, and I leaned on him all the way down the stairs to the street.

70

They arrested fourteen at the scene, then picked up the fifteenth, my buddy Jeremy, two days later, after he'd used my credit card at various establishments around the city. He was holding his black Baby Phat baseball cap in his hands when I identified him in the lineup. Not the sharpest pin in the pin cushion, ol' Jeremy.

Also at the scene, four thousand dollars in cash. Six illegal firearms. Several dime bags of pot. Crack cocaine, street value, $3000.00.

71

The Town insisted I take the week off.

I wasn't really happy about that. I would have preferred to work.

I was kind of at loose ends.

I drove out to Lollypop to see the dogs that had been confiscated.

There were eight of them. Six recovered at the scene. The other two were picked up the day after the raid, wandering loose around the neighborhood.

The dogs were being held as evidence. After which, they would be euthanized.

I called Trish when I got home. Tor was doing great. I told her the city had broken up a pretty big dog fight that was taking place right where I'd bought Tor.

But I didn't tell her any of the details. I didn't want to talk about it yet.

"He's going great," she says. "For a dog with his history, he's amazing."

Right after I finished talking to her, my cell rang. Gil.

I didn't pick up.

I didn't want to talk to him right that minute.

I didn't really want to talk to anyone.

72

Char moved in with me. "Just for a few days," she said, and went around daubing aromatic oils on my light bulbs.

"Char?" I said, following her.

"Mmmmm?"

"You know those two people, who were fighting over that cat. They got together."

She nodded. "You know as well as I do. It's never just about the animals."

She daubed another light bulb. Whatever she was using smelled like pine needles or something.

And I thought to myself about how she was right. About how it wasn't ever just about the animals.

About how it's Nature, but there's something else, too. Or maybe Nature is more than just birthing and breeding and death.

"He looked just like Tor," I said to her again.

She knew what I meant. She knew I was still off-kilter, and not only from the shock of nearly getting myself killed.

"What are the odds that the dog that saved my life was a brindle pittie, just like Tor?"

Char screwed the top back on the little jar of oil.

"Still think it's all just luck, Paige?" she said.

◊ ◊ ◊ ◊ ◊

I had to go to the arraignment, of course.

Char offered to drive, but then an hour before we left the doorbell rang, and it was Larry.

"You're the strongest woman I know, Paige," he said. "But this has attracted some attention. There may be press."

And so he took me, instead.

Then, outside the courthouse afterwards, he told the reporters he was my attorney, which he kind of was, and it shielded me from having to talk to them.

It would still be weeks before the investigation got anywhere near Kyle "Peter" Warren, since he hadn't been at the scene. And he never did get convicted of involvement in the fighting. They seized the houses, of course, for having been used to commit a crime. But Larry didn't care, because it was now a matter of public record that Kyle also owned the P. Warren properties. It gave Larry extra leverage in the fight over the Parsons building deal, and Kyle ended up paying Larry's client over twice as much as he would have otherwise.

73

Char went out for bagels, and when she got back she set the bag on the kitchen table and handed me the *Democrat and Chronicle*.

"You made the front page," she said.

I stared. I knew they'd been snapping shots of me and Larry outside the courthouse. But they hadn't used any of those pictures. Instead, somebody had apparently followed us when Larry walked me to his car. And had photographed us there, Larry holding me and stroking my hair.

"For crying out loud," I muttered. "What is this? Great Britain?"

I looked at Char. She shrugged. "Maybe the boring pictures didn't come out as good."

"Look at the caption," I said. "They're calling Larry my 'attorney and confidante.'"

"Well, he is, isn't he?" she said. "And they were bound to play that up, considering that he saved your life."

"A pit bull saved my life," I muttered.

"That was life number two. Larry saved your first life."

"Oh, so I'm a cat, now? Seven more to go?"

"Here," she said. "Eat."

I took a bite of bagel while I skimmed the article.

"Speaking of phone calls," I said, "am I still getting eight thousand interview requests a minute?"

"Mmmmm, no, it's tapered off to about seven thousand, five hundred a minute."

We'd turned the ringer off after it started getting crazy. I wasn't even checking voice mail at that point. Char was screening all the incoming calls.

"Well, that's something."

"You're lucky the national media isn't camped out in your yard."

"Aw, Char, it isn't that big a story."

"That producer won't give up, though."

"The made-for-T.V. movie guy?"

"Yeah."

I rolled my eyes. I suppose some people would have jumped at the chance to "sell their life story." But all I wanted was for my life to get back to normal. The thought of dragging out my little bout with celebrity one second longer than I absolutely had to was unbearable.

"One other thing," Char said slowly. "Gil called again, too."

I put my bagel down.

"Tell him 'hi' for me," I said after a minute.

"He wants to stop by."

"No."

She stood up and brushed the sesame seeds from her bagel into the bag. "Too late," she said. "He'll be here any second."

"Oh, Char." My eyes were brimming. "I can't do this. Not now."

She looked at me, a firm expression in her eyes. "You have to deal with it sooner or later."

I looked at her, then nodded slowly.

She was right, of course.

I wiped my eyes and put the rest of my bagel away. "I'll be right down," I said, and I went upstairs and to my bedroom, and I opened my jewelry box.

I picked up the gold fill chain.

And I unfastened the clasp, and drew the ring off the chain, and slipped it into the pocket of my jeans.

74

Gil ambled into the kitchen with that lanky, cowboy walk and yeah, like I said. I was overly emotional about everything.

My belly flip flopped when I saw him.

Char had let him in. Now she mumbled something about needing gas in her car.

A whirl of purple and brown India print and she was gone.

Gil stood for a minute, looking around—looking at me.

"Coffee?" I asked.

"Sure."

I emptied the grounds from the coffee machine and took a new filter from the box over the sink and measured out some new grounds.

"So, how are you doing?" he asked.

I sat down at the table and he sat across from me.

"I'm okay," I said.

"You had quite an adventure."

"Yeah."

His eyes had strayed to the newspaper on the table.

The picture of Larry, his arms wrapped protectively around me, was in plain view.

Gil must have caught my expression. "Relax, Paige," he said. "It's not a big deal. He's your lawyer. Right? I'm cool with that."

I stood up turned my back to him and took another mug down from the cupboard.

And then I heard him push his chair away from the table and stand up, and then his hands were on my shoulders and he turned me around to face him.

He leaned in to press his mouth to mine.

But then he stopped.

I'd stiffened.

The way a dog stiffens when he doesn't want to be petted.

He looked at me.

"Oh," he said.

"I'm sorry," I whispered. "I'm just—I'm all mixed up."

He shrugged.

"Whatever," he said. "You rest, then. Give me a call when you feel better."

"No," I said. "No. What I mean is—it's not working for me, Gil. We have to break up."

I realized later I still had the ring in my pocket.

It almost made me laugh, when I noticed it. The ring that didn't mean anything—that meant nothing at all.

Of course he never gave me a chance to give it back . . .

75

Pick up.
Pick up.
Pick UP.
He picked up.
"Larry," I said.
"Hey, gorgeous."
"I . . . I . . ."
"What is it, Paige? Everything okay?"
"I don't know."
Good grief. Could I be any more emotional?
"I'll be right over," he said.
"No. No. It's okay. I was just wondering."
He waited.
"You know Tor. The pit bull—"
"Well sure, Paige."
"I've been thinking I want to go back and get him. Bring him back to Rochester."
"Oh?"
I drew in a breath. "Because, you see, I realized that he's more than . . . he's more than just a dog."
"Sometimes they are."
"I realized that I feel a real connection to him . . . and Larry . . . when you have that sort of connection you need to treat it differently. You need to care for it."
The tears had started again. The tears were streaming down my face.
"He's in Ohio, right, Paige?"

I managed to get the answer out. "Yes."

"Well, how about this. How about we go together—how about I drive."

"You'd do that?"

"Of course I'd do that, Paige," he said. "As a matter of fact, I'm free this afternoon."

"Larry," I said.

"It's okay, gorgeous. Just say when."

"When," I said. "Larry. When."

- END –

ABOUT THE AUTHOR

Novelist Kirsten Mortensen loves to hear from her readers. You can find her on her website, www.kirstenmortensen.com, or on Twitter @Kirstenwriter.

And please look for Mortensen's other fiction and non-fiction titles, including:

Can Job

A crack team of marketers is launching a product that will save
their company.
At the biggest trade show in the universe.
Their careers are at stake.
Heck, the future of the entire CITY is at stake.
Then they discover that the product doesn't actually exist . . .
Can Job. Like your job. Only funny.

When Libby Met the Fairies

Libby Samson has figured out the perfect way to rebuild her
life after her divorce: invest her settlement in a 10-acre piece of
property and start an organic vegetable farm.

But then, as she's walking across one of her fields one evening,
a two-foot tall man stands up out of the shadows and greets her by
name.

It's hard enough for Libby to come to terms with the fact that
"little folk" exist, that she's able to communicate with them, and
that they're giving the advice she needs to make her farm a
success.

Then word of Libby's experience leaks onto the Internet, and
things get crazy. Her property soon swarms with strangers hoping
for a glimpse of fairies. Her sister thinks she should turn the farm
into a New Age retreat ("It'll be bigger than Deepak!") The media
show up. And hiding all this from her boyfriend backfires, as
well—he never liked the farm idea anyway, and he's under a lot of
stress since the biomedical research firm where he works was
acquired by Dormet Vous Luster, late night television's purveyor
of "Tight by Tomorrow" anti-aging cream.

Libby finds one person she can confide in: her next-door
neighbor. Granted, Dean Milbrant's a bit odd: withdrawn and
taciturn. But her attraction to him is powerful—and he seems to
feel it too.

Until Libby discovers that trusting Dean was a huge mistake...

A NOTE ON BOOK REVIEWS

Authors live and die on reader feedback. Literally!

DID YOU KNOW: If a book averages less than 3-3.5 stars, retailers will not display the book as highly in search results?

DID YOU KNOW: If a book averages 4 stars or higher, retailers make sure more people will find and read the book—helping to ensure the author gets paid?

Your rating makes a HUGE difference.

If a book is "not for you," please consider explaining that in your review, instead of giving the book fewer stars.

Thank you so much for your readership and support.

www.ingramcontent.com/pod-product-compliance
Lightning Source LLC
Chambersburg PA
CBHW071132170626
46809CB00002B/592